SUNSET *for* PEARL

BOOK ONE OF THE LAFORTUNE FAMILY CHRONICLES

SUNSET

for

PEARL

ELIZABETH SABIN

ARTIST: STEPHEN ADAMS

AuthorHouse™ LLC
1663 Liberty Drive
Bloomington, IN 47403
www.authorhouse.com
Phone: 1-800-839-8640

Published by AuthorHouse 07/11/2014

ISBN: 978-1-4969-2540-4 (sc)
ISBN: 978-1-4969-2539-8 (e)

FOR SISTERS

Between sisters, often, the child's cry
never dies down, "Never Leave Me,"
it says; "do not abandon me"

Louise Bernikow

LaFortune Family Tree

HAROLD GENE LAFORTUNE
(THIS MAN AND SPOUSE ARE GREAT GRANDPARENTS)
SPOUSE
HORTENCE MARIE LADUKE

SON
MARK LOUIE LAFORTUNE
SPOUSE
MATILDA JEAN ARNAUD
(THIS SON AND SPOUSE ARE GRANDPARENTS)

SON
HAROLD MARK LAFORTUNE
SPOUSE
LENORA ANN LAFAYETTE
(THIS SON AND SPOUSE ARE PARENTS
TO MINERVA AND PEARL)

DAUGHTER
MINERVA ANN
MARRIED
CHARLES GRAHAM BONET
(NO CHILDREN)

DAUGHTER
PEARL FRANCOISE
MARRIED
GREGORY ALLEN VANDECOURTE III

DAUGHTER
MATILDA ANN
MARRIED
BLAINE THOMPSON

DAUGHTER
MAGNOLIA LEE
(NOT MARRIED IN BOOK ONE)

MINNIE

———⟫●⟪———

My name is Minerva Ann Lafortune-Bonet. To me it reads like a hyphenated hot mess. I was born in New Orleans, Louisiana and raised there and on our mother's family homestead on the Choctawhatchee Bay in the Florida panhandle, the Gulf Coast, to be specific.

I come from a long line of moonshine swilling, gun slinging, scoundrels that go back three generations. I am 65 years old now and I would tell you that I don't look so bad, for an old bird. Sure, I could nip, tuck, lift and lipo everything smooth again if I wanted to, but I've never been vain. I regard my wrinkles as testimony to a life of drinking, smoking, and too much sun and wind in my face. I have deep laugh lines and crow's feet from squinting into the sun and holding genuine laughter for a minute too long.

I've always been thin and still am. I look damn good for the most part. At my age it's easy to feel dumpy, a little too thick here and there, and I could care less about that. I will gladly tell anyone who asks, my exact age. I find being shy about the topic as nonsense. You have to be comfortable in your own skin, whether it's young and taunt or old and slack. I've let my hair go grey, although we natural blondes end up looking like a salt and pepper schnauzer without regular salon visits. I keep my hair cut short and feathered, it's much easier to maintain and I spend a lot less time fussing over it. I dress simply, always preferring cotton. My best features are still my legs and blue eyes. You would see that my eyes still hold the sparkle that's always been there, a quality I hope to keep, even if the rest of me goes to hell in a hand basket.

As of a couple of years ago, I have added widow on any forms I fill out. I've been called "colorful," which I suppose is just a nicer way to say crazy. I blame that entirely on the genetic cesspool that is our family. Truthfully, some of them put the "fun" in dysfunction, but that is another story entirely.

My friends call me Minnie. If you happened to be a male in the South, then it would be "Miss Minnie." My nieces have always called me Mimi. Most of us Southerners have old fashioned names that end up being passed down from one generation to the next, often times a hideous burden. That's why, as children, nicknames saved us from many an ass kicking at recess. But we grow into our names, as easily as hand me down clothes.

All my family is gone now, except for my younger sister Pearl and her daughters. She's 63 years old, two years younger than me. She has two daughters, Magnolia Lee who's 26 and Matilda Ann who's 24. So far, they're not hyphenated. The three of them are my life and I love them more than words could say. I feel sad for Pearl; she is a widow now also. After marriage she became Pearl Francoise Lafortune-VanDeCourte. When she got engaged, the two of us had gotten drunk and had literally fallen out of our chairs laughing at the absurdity of what would become her new title.

We had cut our first teeth on seafood and fresh vegetables from the garden. The first music I ever remember hearing was Zydeco and Dixie Land Jazz. Our grandparents and parents were strict and never hesitated to bust our asses if we didn't toe the line. When we were very young, we were poor by most standards. We didn't really know that as we were never hungry and always had a roof over our heads. Our clothes were home made, but always clean and ironed, even if they were faded and threadbare. We'd always been told that cleanliness was next to Godliness, which meant you were expected to crawl into the large, galvanized tub each night before bed, and we never went to bed dirty or without saying our prayers.

Pearl and I have always been close. At times growing up we were mistaken for twins. The elders always referred to us as "two peas in a pod" or "frik and frak" and when we were naughty we were "thick as thieves." We are still inseparable and share everything about our lives with each other. As older women, we've found ourselves to be filthy rich. We hadn't set out to marry into wealth; it just turned out that way. My late husband Graham got tangled up in off-shore oil before I met him and Pearl's husband Gregory had been an extremely successful architect, who was born to "old money."

In the South, the older the money is, the higher your status becomes. I found this ridiculous, as far as I was concerned, you either had money or you didn't. What did it matter if it was old or new? I could care less about being on any "A" list and did not move in high society circles.

I am embarrassed to admit that I was guilty of taking my fortune for granted at times. I hadn't allowed it to change me so much, and I gave away large amounts as fast as I could. Pearl had used a huge portion of hers to set up trusts for her daughters. Between the two of us adding to their portfolios, they are by default, filthy rich as well.

We tell each other everything, and have always tried to be honest with the girls. For their protection, they really have no clue as to how wealthy they are. When they are older and more mature we will lay the fortune at their feet.

I've decided to make immediate and un-expected changes to my life. I've decided to leave the beautiful, log home my husband Graham built for me here on Bear Creek in Montana. I am ready to be done grieving and move forward. I worry that my grief will keep him earthbound somehow, when he should be rejoicing with the angels.

I've begun a journal for the girls also. Just glimpses of our lives, some of our history and a lot of our adventures. I hope that at some point they will read it and find humor in the insanity. Pearl and I attempted to create a family tree at one time, only to hit a brick wall at every turn. Our relatives, as each one passed away, took the family secrets to their graves. Maybe that is for the best, and at some point the girls will want to fill in the blanks.

But just now, I am packing up, leaving my wonderful ranch. It doesn't have the same light and air as when Graham was here. I'm going home, back to the Gulf Coast, and that's where my story really begins, even if later on my sister has to finish it for me.

Special Thanks

I begin with my husband Michael. Thanks for your patience with late dinners, ignored chores and 40 of the best years of my life. Jil Schmidt for being the first one to muddle through a stack of ratty, handwritten notebook papers, all the way to the end. Marlene Sabin, Janet Maples, and Sarah Soran, for taking your time and giving me advice, support and encouragement and Stephanie Martin. We are putting your degree to good use. Thank you all.

And a grateful shout out to the professionals at Author House for providing the services to make it a reality.

And to the reader, I hope you enjoy my story and thank you. Stay tuned for Book two in the Lafortune Family Chronicles, Matilda's Shining Boy.

Chapter 1

LEAVING MONTANA

Springtime in the Montana foothills was a sight to behold. As the snow melted and the ice receded, the grasses and wildflowers pushed to the surface and the warming sun. The trees were all covered in tiny leaf buds and some of the shrubbery by our house was already getting sprays of new needles at the tip of each branch. Dew covered and silvery in the morning sun they appeared vivid and alive. Each small needle contrasted the rich, deep green of the mature branches. The property on Bear Creek, outside of Missoula, had several large copses of aspens and we also had pines and other indigenous softwoods. After choosing this place, we had been determined to leave as much of the land, as possible, in a natural state.

It had been a mild winter last year. Now with the beautiful, sunny weather the hundreds of flower bulbs that Graham and I had planted were very near blooming. The protective layer of hay, dried matter, and old growth had been removed from every flower bed. It would be just a week or so, and then there would be an explosion of vibrant color.

Gazing out across the terraced front yard, I remembered one particular winter evening, our first year here. We had lounged on huge pillows in front of the fireplace with a bottle of wine and stacks of catalogs of bulbs. We had ordered some of every type and that following spring, we had spent an entire week, on our hands and knees, digging little holes, carefully planting each and every one.

When they bloomed it looked like a carpet of confetti. Now all those flowers are breathtaking and beautiful, and it had most certainly, been worth the effort. This amazing dance of nature took place each year whether we were here or not. We had spent a lot of time deciding which trees, shrubs and flowers to add to the landscape, knowing that they would have to withstand the elevation and climate. We'd had great success as none had died and nearly all the plants we'd chosen would bloom at different times of the spring and summer, some lasting through the fall, when sadly everything would succumb to the first frost of a new winter.

We had even put in a small apple orchard in one section and each of the twenty years we'd been here, every spring the sweet, delicate fragrance of the apple blossoms was heavenly. It was a lovely spot for a picnic with all the velvety, white petals spread all around us. I didn't particularly like the taste of the fruit, but they were best used for cooking and canning. We wanted to add more fruit trees but sadly, we had spent a large majority of our time detailing the house and had put that task on the "to do" list.

It had always been a special time for us whenever we had worked together outdoors, and that was one of the things I missed the most. It was becoming harder to be alone here, especially in the spring. It was a season that did not last long but had always been spectacular. Lately I realized that I was spending more time looking back at my life here with Graham than looking ahead to my future without him. Maybe my family was right; a change would do me good. It wasn't normal for me to mope and I always craved for any new adventure. My grieving had been long and painful and it was time to let go of my sorrow.

I had taken my coffee out to the front deck this morning to watch the sunrise and once I was cozy in my swing, rocking slowly, I was thinking about all the hard work and time we had invested in this place. There was a soft, cool breeze, causing the tallest tree branches to gently sway, the sun was rising, the mourning doves were cooing, and it was going to be a picture perfect day.

The other things that had held me here after losing my husband were my garden, greenhouse and what we had named, The Springs. The garden was too large for two people and part of the satisfaction of all the work that was involved, was taking the vegetables we couldn't use, and donating them to the local food pantry. The growing season in this zone and region was short and you couldn't grow much without giving the plants a head start in the greenhouse. I'd spent many enjoyable and contented hours out there fussing with all the sprouting vegetables and flowers. Always oblivious to the cold, snowy, winter winds raging just outside, while in there it was warm and had a tropical feel.

The springs were about two miles back of the main house and the other buildings. Graham had scraped out a one lane road, laid gravel and with a four wheel drive vehicle, it could be accessed most of the year. Our property had rolling hills and dipping valleys, and this amazing natural spring was in a small, rocky area, at the base of a hill. It was protected from the wind for the most part, and the view was unbelievable. The simple fact that we had a natural water source on the property made it even more valuable and desirable. The first time he had taken me to see it, I was surprised at how fresh and clean the water tasted. He had explained that it came from deep in the earth and flowed over rock, and nothing had contaminated it for who knows how many hundreds of years. We ended up making this our special place and spent time there whenever he was home. Over the years we had added beautiful river rock below the spout of water, forming a small pool, just big enough for the two of us. He made sure that there was a place for run off and it stayed clean and pretty much maintenance free. It had to be extremely hot weather before I could muster the courage to slip into the frigid pool, being slightly drunk helped also, and I always got out with chattering teeth and numb toes and fingers. It was refreshing and wonderful and the temperature of the water never changed all year.

Then there was my pride and joy, my orchid collection. Growing and nurturing them had been more of a challenge than I expected. The temperature had to be closely controlled, fans set to run when needed, and advice from the local horticulturalist as to which pesticides were safest and most effective. I had ended up with quite a variety and each one was a botanical work of art.

Sometimes the thought of leaving all this gave me a knot in my gut and a lump in my throat. But it was too late to turn back now. It was for sale, the whole kit and caboodle. I had discussed the matter with Jim, our dear friend and family attorney and he had recommended that I sell the entire property "as is." It would prove to be much easier than trying to sell all the toys and equipment we had accumulated, piece by piece.

Whoever purchased the place would get a spectacular, two story log home. We had dealt with local merchants for the logs and Montana was well known for their log home industry. It just felt better to serve the local economy whenever possible.

The house had five bedrooms, two upstairs, two on the main floor and one in the finished basement. The master suite upstairs was spacious enough to have a king sized bed and sitting area. The master bath was enormous and was done in some beautiful tiles we'd found in Italy. There were French doors leading out to a large covered deck, one of our favorite spots to relax. One end of this upper deck had a set of wicker furniture and a table and chairs for four. The opposite end had a hot tub on a raised base, so that the view would not be impaired by the railing. There were two ceiling fans which came in handy on hot afternoons.

One of the bedrooms on the main floor had been our office; we had shared the space and had put a desk on either side of the room. The larger bedroom down here had a king bed and my nieces always favored this room when they visited. There was a great room, spacious and full of light with ceiling to floor windows, the kitchen was large and outfitted for the most discerning chef. On one end there was a good sized pantry and beside that a wine cooler, filled with varieties that had come from domestic and foreign vineyards.

There was covered decking that wrapped around the entire house on the main floor. There were ceiling fans and of course my swing. I had convinced Graham that no respectable southern woman could live without one.

He had locked himself in his workshop and had built me one that was perfect. It was the only large outdoor item that would go with me to wherever my new home ended up being.

The spread consisted of roughly 2,560 acres or four sections. The house sat on a piece of high ground that sloped gently down to the other buildings. There was a four car garage that had a two bedroom apartment upstairs and on either side covered parking for, in this case, Graham's speed boat on one side and a barely used Airstream travel trailer on the other. There were his and hers' four wheelers, bicycles, kayaks, and a two man canoe. One stall of the garage held the ranch Jeep Wrangler, and another stall on one side had been converted to a man cave workshop with every conceivable tool you could want or need.

There was a corral and barn with twelve stalls, and attached to that was a large storage area for feed, tack and whatever else you needed to put there. The plan had been to purchase horses as Graham had ridden all his life and was always trying to teach me. He had surprised me on more than one occasion, working in excursions that included riding. He had wanted to raise, breed and sell thoroughbreds. Unfortunately he did not live long enough to see it all happen.

The last building which stood alone was for all the smaller equipment like my tiller, a riding lawnmower, weed eater and leaf blower. One side was also my potting shed and greenhouse where I kept all my tools and gardening supplies.

Once I decided I needed a change and couldn't bear to be here any longer, Jim had set me up with one of the local realtors and they assigned an agent named Wanda

Reynolds to handle the proceedings. The first trip she had made out here was to photograph every square inch of the place, and fill in the spec sheets and post the listing on their website. She took care of the documentation as I had offered to pay her extra to keep me from having to deal with that. She was, at my instruction, obligated to keep Jim abreast of her actions and nothing would happen without his scrutiny and approval. I had made it very clear that I wanted no interaction with new owners. I just couldn't bear to have a personal connection with strangers who would take ownership of my home.

There had been a new survey and appraisal and the septic tank had been emptied. The well had been inspected and passed with no problems. Any offerings on or around Bear Creek were worth a small fortune, especially if you owned the mineral rights and we did. She'd informed me that she didn't think it would take long to find a buyer and close the deal, even in a less than favorable economy.

Wanda felt confident that firstly, anyone who would take interest in this property would have the finances, and secondly, it was a rare opportunity to have all the extras that would be included in the sale. I figured she was mostly aware of what her commission would be and that was ok too.

She was a whirling dervish and I suppose that type of energy was required in her line of work. She had told me all about the software they used to produce "virtual tours" of their listings. She assured me that our ranch had photographed beautifully and encouraged me to go online and check it out. I had not done that because I lived here and knew every inch of the place.

The sun was up now and stretching I headed upstairs for a shower. I drove into Missoula where I had an appointment with Wanda to give her a set of house keys so she could show the property. She'd greeted me with enthusiasm and promised to have my listing online sometime today. Thanking her I left and decided to walk the three blocks to the market. Crossing the street I headed toward the small café, next to another realtor's office, Wanda's competition.

The sun was shining directly on a metal stand filled with rows and rows of brochures. I wasn't sure why, but I was drawn to the rack and pulled out a very colorful and tastefully done booklet advertising a gated retirement community in Beaumont, Texas. The photo showed large gates with the name Lancaster Estates on top, in scrolled metal. I grabbed three of the brochures and shoved them into my bag.

The café wasn't as crowded on the sidewalk so I chose a table outside and had some lunch so I wouldn't be going to the market on an empty stomach where I would end up with junk food and sweets. I was thinking of Jim and Pearl and would call them today. This town was getting crowded; the usual lunch crowd combined with all of the tourists that were beginning to arrive was my cue to get back to the ranch.

Now that things were in motion in Wanda's world, it made me realize I desperately needed a break from packing and pacing. It seemed like going to New Orleans and hanging out in our apartment sounded invigorating and I would get to spend some time with Jim. Maybe I could convince my sister to join us. I was feeling excited and it had been a while since I looked forward to a trip this much. There was a definite spring in my step heading back to the car and I hardly noticed I had bought too many things at the market and now had to carry it all three blocks.

I was home and barely got the front door open and realized the land line was ringing off the hook. I set down my bags in the living room and sprinted to the kitchen. The call was going to the message machine so grabbing the phone I answered quickly.

"Hello? Don't hang up, just a second. Sorry, hello?"

"Mrs. Bonet, its Wanda. I have the most astounding news for you, are you sitting?" She was bordering on being giddy and I could tell she was about to implode with excitement.

"What's up Wanda?"

"Well, in all my years in real estate this is a first. Barely five minutes after listing your property, there was a call from a couple in Texas who want to fly in tomorrow to see the place. I mean if that will work for you?"

I sat down at the kitchen bar, and was surprised things were moving along so quickly.

"Sorry, I was thinking that tomorrow is Wednesday and I have business out of town, so tell them to come on. They will probably run shrieking when they see the mess and boxes stacked everywhere." Wanda sighed.

"I'm so sorry for the short notice, but he was ok with your price, didn't even flinch, another first for me. I just can't believe this, so, may I ask what time you will be leaving in the morning?"

"I'm an early riser and let's say any time after 8:00 am and it's all yours. Thank you Wanda, this is incredible and if you have any questions or problems please call Jim, he will know how to reach me. So good luck and I'll see you in a week."

"Thanks Mrs. Bonet, I have a good feeling about this, have a safe trip, bye bye."

I gathered my groceries and bag and went into the kitchen to put on the tea kettle. I decided to add a shot of brandy to the steaming cup of chamomile, it couldn't hurt and it had to be five o'clock somewhere. I grabbed one of the retirement community brochures out of my bag and carried that and my tea out to the deck off the kitchen to watch the sunset.

This time the ringing was my cell phone, so I ran back into the house and scrambled to dig it out of my bag. Checking the name I smiled to see it was Pearl. Laughing I took the call.

"You have an uncanny ability to call me when I am thinking of calling you; I swear I was going to ring you after this cup of tea."

We both laughed happily, always delighted to hear each other's voice.

"How are you doing dear?"

"I have the most unbelievable news Minnie, but I can't possibly tell you unless it's in person. How would you feel about a long weekend on the beach in Seaside, Florida? I've booked a cute cottage near the point on highway 30. It's getting crowded and the tourists are piling in again, in droves. We have it from Wednesday thru Monday. What do you think?"

I could barely contain myself and almost squealing with joy I said, "That is about the most exciting thing I've heard in a while, so yes, I'm in! I have big news too. The sale of the ranch went on the web today. Before I could even get back home someone had called to look at the place. I was about to call Jim to see if I could get our plane to Missoula. I wanted to fly into New Orleans and hang out in our apartment for a week or so. But being with you sounds like a lot more fun. I'll keep you abreast of my plans and I'll be there on Thursday and I cannot wait to see you, we'll have so much fun!"

"I have plenty to do until you join me. I'm going to try to sneak away without having to explain myself to Clarissa, no easy task, as you well know. Something has to give Minnie, she is driving me batshit crazy and getting away will do you and me a world of good. So just travel safely and it will be amazing. Goodnight love, see you soon."

"You be safe also, goodnight."

I laid my phone down and went inside for another cup of tea with yet another shot of brandy. This called for a celebration. The best I could do tonight was to spike my tea and watch the sun slide behind the hills. I felt bad for Pearl, living in Savannah, Georgia all those years under her mother-in-law's nose. If anyone needed a change it was her and I had begged her to come live with me on the ranch. She always declined saying it would get too cold. I could relate and it just meant more fun road trips during the years we lived so far apart.

I read the brochure front to back several times and realized I should get to bed if I was packing and leaving early the next morning. I would give one of the three booklets I had to Jim and get him to do his investigative magic. Maybe it was a place I could consider as a new home. I got into my pajamas, settled into my bed and called Jim. I brought him up to speed on mine and Pearl's plans. He said all he had to do was make a phone call to have the plane waiting for me at the Missoula airport in the morning and couldn't wait to see me. I felt happy and hopeful and as soon as I laid my head down I was out.

I dreamed of two blonde headed little girls, one five and one three, running and leaping on the beach. They were squealing with joy trying to catch the sand pipers.

Chapter 2

NEW ORLEANS, LOUISIANA

⟫━●━⟪

I awoke feeling rested and renewed. The weather forecast was for clear skies all the way to the east coast, but I would be in New Orleans in a couple of hours. I packed one bag with casual, cool clothing, some sandals and a couple of sundresses. The only other bag I would take was my beach bag and camera. I loaded the car and grabbing my coffee, I did a quick check of all the windows and doors. I set the alarm and headed to the Missoula airport.

Our Gulfstream jet was sitting ready when I got through security and finally, out onto the tarmac. It shone beautifully in the morning sun and I couldn't wait to be aboard again. One of the pilots helped me get situated then went back to the cockpit to prepare for takeoff. I chose to sit in the middle this time, it always seemed odd being the only passenger as the cabin would hold 13 people. We had filled it to capacity many times over the years, mostly with our family and friends. The interior was so comfortable, with all the bells and whistles of first class. It was one investment we had chosen carefully and it had cost us an enormous amount of money.

I tightened my belt and gazed out the window as we taxied down the runway. I remembered when we had all joked about having our own jet and how much money we could save in the long run. To our dismay and only a couple of weeks later, Jim had arranged for us to meet with the owner and look it over. It still looked brand new to me. After all the oohing and ahhing, we decided that if the three of us put in as co-owners, it was doable. So Pearl, Jim and myself had each written a hefty check and Jim had sealed the deal.

We kept a hangar in New Orleans, had a coop of six pilots on payroll and standby, plus a full time mechanic, on call 24/7. The fuel prices went up and down, but it was one indulgence that we enjoyed beyond measure.

Once we were underway, I took out the book I was reading and my notebook where I kept my most current lists of things to do. I hadn't had time to see my Dr. in Missoula so I phoned ahead to see if I could get an appointment in New Orleans. They told me one of the doctors on staff today had a cancellation and would work me in at 11:30. That would give me plenty of time to drop off my things at our apartment, see the Dr. and then meet Jim for a late lunch. I just wanted to get my annual checkup out of the way and that would be one less worry in Montana.

There was hardly any turbulence and we landed right on schedule. The moment I stepped out of the plane, I felt the humidity in the air. My skin felt softer immediately, drinking in the moisture. It felt wonderful compared to the dry western climate that I was now used to. I could smell the river and a hint of salt on the breeze. It wasn't terribly hot yet and I took a moment to just breathe it in. It smelled like home. I loved this city, my birthplace. It could be many things to many people. It could lift you up and fill your heart with an unforgettable exhilaration or it might show you the dark underbelly, exposing an evil temptress to be wary of. I always encouraged people who asked, that the big easy was like any new adventure, everybody should visit at least once and take from it what you will. First time visitors were kindly reminded that after sunset, they needed to be aware of their surroundings. People came from all over the world to be here and for all kinds of reasons.

The limo service was waiting for me outside the terminal doors and they whisked me off to the French Quarter and Bourbon Street. Our building was on the east end and always referred to as the last house on the left. It wasn't quite as loud and rowdy here but this was an unspoken "turn around" point for wandering tourists. Anyone venturing any further into the residential areas of the French Quarter may not be so warmly received.

The car pulled up to the rear entrance of our apartment. I tipped the driver and he waited to make sure I got into the courtyard before pulling away. I stood there with the gate to my back and stared at how magnificent it looked. The blooming plants took my breath away and it was obvious that Ima and Bo had been here. Everything was trimmed, cleaned and welcoming. It always surprised me that places seemed to have personalities, each one unique and special, and I had never tired of being here.

I don't know what we would have done without Ima and Frank "Bo" Boudreaux. They had been close friends of our grandparents and we thought of them as family. They lived on the edge of town and we paid them well to keep an eye on the place. Ima was always excited to hear someone would be arriving and she spoiled us as best she could. She always dusted, cleaned and opened the rooms. She cooked meals, made tea and left the fridge full. And my favorite welcome site was the bouquets that she always left in each room. Bo took care of maintenance and the courtyard. He swept and hosed off the beautiful tile flooring. He kept all the plants fed, trimmed and watered and took care of the family car that all of us used when we were here. I thought they did too much as they were getting up there in years and becoming a bit frail.

I wandered around once, just admiring it all and feeling slightly intoxicated by the soft, exotic aroma from the blooms. I breathed in the jasmine and wished that exact smell could be captured in a bottle. The back wall was covered in red and purple bouganvillas, they were so bloom laden, they fell in clumps and long, slender limbs from the top of the brick wall all the way to the floor. The wall sconce planters were bursting with color and beautiful hanging vines. The huge palm trees in the back corners were healthy and thriving. And the wrought iron furniture had a fresh coat of shiny, black paint. I smiled at how magical and inviting it was.

We were so lucky to still have our apartment. We were the third generation to own it. It was upstairs and the only entrance that wasn't walled off was in the courtyard. The stairwell was original to the old building and very narrow. We had always rented the downstairs portion to small business owners and they sold everything from Mardi gras beads to tobacco pipes. They only had access to the street and could not get into our courtyard. The rental income had always paid the taxes and except for maintenance and upkeep, nothing much changed. The downstairs had been one flimsy business venture after another, and the whole family had considered trying some kind of business that wasn't a bar or kootchie joint. I had always thought that a coffee house might work, since a lot of people were quite often drunk if they were on Bourbon Street and how handy to grab a nice espresso to sober up with. So far it had just been fun to talk about and none of us had moved forward with any concrete ideas or plans.

I finally got upstairs and I dumped everything into the larger bedroom. I picked up an old photo that was sitting on the bed side table. It was an image of our father and his father, standing on the balcony of what was now their property. Back when grandpa had this place, he swore it was a whore house right before he'd purchased it. Our father had told us it was more than that and a great amount of illicit hooch had moved in and out of here. The women of the family were disgusted by the stories and history but managed to make it their own over the years.

The walls were thin in the bedrooms and once in a while rowdy visitors next door could be heard until all hours of the morning. Also there had been strange things that happened in the smallest bedroom to unsuspecting guests. Nothing more than flickering lights, the bathroom tap being turned on and doors that wouldn't stay shut. But a couple of times, people had been spooked enough to end up sleeping on the living room couch. We all figured that it was the spirit of someone from years ago that couldn't bear to leave.

This was, after all, a magnificent, mysterious city and those types of activities were pretty normal, no matter where you went. Some places had a lot more energy than others and there were still places I went out of my way to avoid.

After I had wandered from room to room and out onto the balcony, I knew I needed to get ready. This early in the day the smells lifting and falling on the soft breeze were all the restaurants gearing up for the lunch crowds. I realized that I was starving but had to hurry now to make my appointment. Grabbing one of my sundresses and some nice sandals, I freshened up and got dressed. Bo had left the family car out back for me and I headed to the medical center.

On the way there I couldn't help notice areas of the city that were still suffering from the last hurricane that had tried to drown every last drop of life from this whole place. There were entire sections that would never be the same, much less recover. But the strength that people are capable of exhibiting in times of crisis is enormous and the work was ongoing.

My visit with the young doctor was routine and thankfully I didn't even have much of a wait. My vital signs were good, after surrendering three vials of blood; I paid my copay and was done, that quickly. It was a great feeling to have that behind me. The receptionist assured me they would let me know when my blood work results came back in a few days.

Now I was headed to Brennan's to meet Jim for lunch. They served a breakfast to die for and that's what I always got. I spotted him right away at a corner table. He stood and we embraced, me close to tears and him beaming. As was his custom, and for my whole life, he placed his hands on either side of my face and kissed my forehead.

"You look wonderful dear; let's have something to eat, shall we?"

Laughing and moving into the chair he held for me, I said, "So do you! And I have to say that I have missed you terribly!"

Two waiters approached our table and we had our drinks and orders placed in a matter of minutes. I unfolded my napkin and smiling asked Jim, "Can you believe how quickly we're showing the ranch?"

Sipping his coffee, he sat his cup down and put his hands together, "It did surprise me Minnie, and it's a comfort to know, for your benefit, there are still individuals that can afford what you're asking for the place. But I have to agree with you, I would not have expected any response to the listing yet."

They brought our food and we chatted and laughed for the next hour, about the ranch, the girls, Blaine and Pearl. He was excited that I was meeting her for fun on the beach. We agreed to meet again on my return to New Orleans and after hugging and kissing him good bye, I headed back to the apartment. I wanted to shop for gifts for Pearl, Ima and the kids. I had planned on the River Marketplace and the French Market. I would grab delicious coffees and breads and of course some treats for the beach cottage.

By the time I got home it was late afternoon. The sounds and smells were ramping up and it could literally make your mouth water to smell all the different foods cooking all around you. The music came from so many different places at once, it could be a weird cacophony or all blend somehow, making you want to dance around or at least hum to the tune. Pretty soon the neon would come to life from one end of this street to the other.

I grabbed the food out of the fridge. Ima had fried fish, crab cakes, shrimp and fried green tomatoes. There was a big tossed salad, her delicious homemade tartar sauce and iced tea. I was in heaven. I ate until I could not hold another bite. I got the kitchen cleaned up and decided to turn in early so that I could get up, pack and get to the airport before 9:o'clock. I decided it would be better to fly to Florida and that would give me more time with my sister.

It had been such a good day. I hadn't been this contented and happy in a while. I snuggled in bed, read until my eyelids got heavy and I was out. I seemed to be tossing and turning.

I dreamed that I was in a strange room, lying on a steel table with metal rails on both sides. I was looking to my right at five people lined up, all staring at me. At the foot of the bed was a woman holding a huge syringe with both hands, next to her was a Dr. in scrubs and mask, next to him, a male nurse holding a document and ink pen, next to him was a man in a lab coat holding a magnifying glass, and standing closest to me was a priest. I felt panicked and terrified; turning quickly to the left, there was Graham. He looked young and handsome and he reached for my hand. I smiled at knowing I was safe and slept.

Chapter 3

JAMES McGREGOR

——⟫●⟪——

It was 6:30 am on Thursday morning. Jim was already locking his front door, heading to work. He always walked south on Iberville two blocks to his office. Going in the back door, he went to the kitchen and made coffee. Soon the aroma of the dark French roast beans would fill the rooms. The receptionist would unlock the front and turn on all the lights, but not until eight o'clock.

He sat behind the large, old, cherry wood desk in his favorite leather chair. The armrests were softened and slightly worn from his hours of sitting here with his head down over one file or another. A large Tiffany lamp sat on a corner of the desk and threw just enough light to read by. There were heavy drapes over a large, three panel window that went from ceiling to floor. The border around the antique water glass panes was very old stained glass that had somehow survived the ravages of time and storms. The drapes reminded Pearl of something from Tara, but he loved the rich, velvety texture and their ability to block out light and noise. He rarely ever opened

20

them. There was a small ornate lamp on a side table and the dim, colorful light it gave off softened the whole side of the room it shared.

A massive book case covered the wall behind his chair. It was full of his prized collections of books on law and history. In front of the desk were two overstuffed, leather chairs. Both were well worn and comfortable. One wall was old sliding wood doors and the entrance to the conference room. It was decorated in dark woods and leather with an enormous, imported Aubusson rug in the center. The table was long and oval and would seat twelve.

The door in the corner of this room led to the kitchenette and gave access to the small bedroom and full bath. From the bedroom there were French doors that opened to a covered porch out back. Pearl had found a beautiful set of wicker furniture for this space and it was another place to entertain clients or just enjoy a glass of iced tea with friends.

The entire building was Jim's. It was three stories and he occupied all of the ground floor. When you entered the front door you were greeted by a receptionist. It was never the same girl behind the front desk for very long. Jim worked with several groups that found work for women leaving shelters, or trying to get back on their feet, single mothers and troubled teens. The temp agency screened and interviewed them and they were each and every one paid well and treated with love and respect. It was a perfect platform to re-enter the work force and gain invaluable knowledge of the workings of a law office. So far it proved to be a win, win situation.

The waiting room had four chairs and was pleasant and comfortable. Pearl had assisted with the interior decorating and it was done in soft pastels with plants in every open space. The ceiling to floor windows had no drapes so the room was usually bright and cheerful. Jim's office was directly behind the receptionist's desk and a set of heavy, wooden doors.

The part of this building that drew renters was the elevator that went in where an old spiral staircase had been. The installation had taken up nearly half of the room. No one was interested in climbing three flights of stairs, and a lot of the older buildings still required customers to hike straight up.

After he had gutted the place and remodeled, he had listed the rentals and had waiting lists for every single space. There were four offices on each of the upper two stories, rented to a mix of people. There were no vacancies right now, the tenants paid their rent on time and it would take eviction or dynamite to remove any of them. They all liked it here. The rental income covered his expenses plus a tidy amount he banked every month. The last few years the maintenance had been minimal.

After the waters had receded from the last hurricane, the previous owner had taken his insurance money and unloaded the entire property for a song and dance. It proved to be such a favorable location, Jim had set to work immediately with the restoration. The building sat on a quiet street, on the western edge of the French Quarter. Anything you might need or want was within walking distance. It was easy to find and offered parking. The exterior was impeccably landscaped and this time of the year, in full bloom.

This wasn't the only piece of property he had acquired after hurricane Katrina. The one bedroom house where he lived now had been his second purchase. He had rebuilt the lovely old home, from the basement to the roof. He had also purchased two apartment complexes, each bordering the French Quarter on the east end. All four properties had taken over a year to repair. There was no scrimping after a flood. If you left even one soaked portion, mold and decay would rapidly take the rest. He felt like he was helping repair the city by obtaining these properties and bringing them back to life as fast as he could.

Sipping his coffee, he leaned back into his chair and sighed. He was thinking of the two stacks of folders on his desk. They sat where he'd left them last evening. One file was for the ranch at Bear Creek, and a file had been started for Pearl's new undertaking. He and Blaine were assisting with permits, survey and whatever else she needed as the project began to progress.

He thought about his young apprentice. Blaine had done so well on his bar exams that Jim felt guilty at times that his talents were being wasted in the type of law they dealt with. He was still deciding when to add Thompson to the sign out front. His best friend Aaron had come by one evening and they had sat out back, enjoying a snifter of brandy. He had been slightly embarrassed to ask Jim to hire his kid, but he was terrified his only son might leave the area, that would have devastated him and his wife Janette. Blaine was barely 20 years old at that time.

They were all born and raised here and it hadn't taken Jim long at all to see the advantages of having a young blood in the firm to help with the large estates and all the overflow cases they got. He had taken Blaine under his wing and for almost a decade he had groomed him to be one of the best Estate Planning and Management lawyers in New Orleans. The kid was brilliant and always well groomed. He thought before he spoke and that was a rare quality in youth. He was impressive and Jim knew he was blessed to have him.

Smiling, Jim thought about Blaine having gone to New York City just to hand deliver some contracts that required Matilda's signature. It could have been done by express delivery, but it was becoming more and more obvious that there was a romance brewing between those two. It would be interesting to hear what Pearl thought of her daughter having a relationship with her lawyer. The words conflict of interest rang in his head, but it was far too soon to get excited. He had always loved Blaine, and was considering leaving him the law firm in his will. He thought of him as a son and their relationship had become even closer over the years. The kid had already lost his parents within five years of each other and it had devastated him and Jim. It was something he thought of more often now that he was approaching his 85th birthday.

Even though he was mostly retired, he still had the final say on anything that went in and out of this office. And he would have to know he was near death before he would hand over the girls' estates, even to Blaine. They had amassed fortunes that had to have daily attention and their portfolios continued to grow. Jim had sworn to Lenora and Harold Lefortune that he would take care of their daughters. Magnolia and Matilda already had massive amounts of money and businesses to manage and it was enough to do at his age. It kept his mind busy but he still desperately needed Blaine's help.

There was a tap on his office door. Glancing at the clock on the desk, he was surprised to see it was already time for the day's business to begin. Blaine poked his head into the office. Jim looked up and thought about how handsome this kid was. He towered over Jim at 6'3" and had jet black hair and those devilish green eyes demanded your attention. His skin was the color of mocha and he was fit and then some. It was easy to see why Matilda was head over heels for him and they would make a handsome couple.

Blaine came into the room shutting the door behind him, "Morning, Boss."

"Come in Blaine, come in, the coffee is on, help yourself."

Blaine came back from the kitchen with a steaming and fragrant cup of coffee, sitting in front of the desk, he said, "So, it seems as though we are going to be very busy this week."

Reaching into his briefcase he pulled out a file folder and slid it across the desk to Jim.

"Here are Matilda's and Magnolia's other paperwork that I grabbed last week."

Jim peered over his glasses and asked, "And how are my girls faring in the big city?"

"You wouldn't believe what they've done with that loft of theirs. They couldn't have been smarter picking the spot they did. It would be a lot harder on them if they were not in the fashion district, and really, they're close to everything they need. I have a feeling they will be making some very big decisions soon. They are seriously considering launching both their lines in their own boutiques, so that was the topic while I was there, did I miss anything here? Has there been any activity with Minerva's ranch?"

"Just a call from Wanda, she will be showing the place today. Minerva is taking the jet to Seaside sometime this morning. She and Pearl are staying in a cottage on the beach. Frankly, I am so glad she is moving forward and not so blue over Graham anymore. I think that Pearl is going to surprise her with the new project and we will have our hands full once again. Regardless, being together for the next few days will do them both good."

"Well, I have some chores to finish and I need to get into the courthouse records early so call me if anything comes up."

Blaine took his cup to the kitchen, rinsed it out and called over his shoulder, "Have a good day, Boss."

He left through the back door where he'd left his car. They all parked back here in the shaded parking lot, leaving all the front spots for customers.

Jim could hear activity in the front of the office and the laughter of two females. He was about to get up when Minnie opened the door.

"Good morning Jim, I need to give you something I had meant to bring to lunch yesterday."

She walked in and he stood. They kissed each other on the cheek and Jim returned to his chair.

"You look lovely today my dear, are you excited to see Pearl?"

Minnie had flopped down into one of the chairs in front of the desk.

"I can hardly wait to get my arms around her, it's been too long and the beach is calling my name. Laughing she bent down and pulled one of the brochures out of her bag.

"I have a favor to ask of you and Blaine."

She handed the thick booklet across the desk to Jim. He raised his eyebrows in question. She hurried to add, "I need you to check this place out for me while I'm in Florida. I am seriously considering moving to Beaumont, Texas."

Jim kept a poker face, showing no reaction.

"I'd be happy to investigate this for you Minerva, and don't worry about a thing, just have a wonderful, long weekend. Hopefully I will have all the information you need by the time you return. Do you need a ride to the airport or do you have your car out back?"

Minnie thought for a moment and said, "Maybe I should leave the car here, its eight o'clock now and I'm supposed to fly out at nine. That gives me plenty of time. Let's call the car service."

The limo pulled up out front before Minnie could finish hugging Jim goodbye. She stopped with one hand on his office door and looking back she said, "Call me if anything happens, will you? And I'll be in touch."

"You will be the first to know when I get any word on the ranch, have fun and be safe."

He leaned back in his chair and heard the car roll over the gravel in the parking lot.

He couldn't imagine how his life would have turned out without these kids. They kept him going, gave him a reason to get up every morning and always included him in anything the family did. He loved them a great deal and would give them the moon and stars if he could. He felt blessed to have been with the family all these years. He'd watched Minnie and Pearl grow up and then Pearl's daughters. He hoped he'd get to see at least a couple of grandchildren. He peeked into the reception area and smiled to see Janet Parker was back. She was a single mother of four. Her husband had drowned during the Katrina flood and Jim had a soft spot for her and her children. He had housed them in one of his apartments as soon as they had become habitable. And she had worked her butt off to make it on her own.

He walked in and gave her a hug. "Good morning Janet and welcome back."

"Good morning Mr. McGregor, did I see Minerva leaving?"

"Yes, you did, how do my appointments look for today?"

She flipped through the large binder and smiled. "It appears you have an open day and Blaine is doing all the legwork. Is there anything else you need?"

"Thank you, nothing at the moment. I have to work on something for Minerva, and that should prove to keep me busy most of the day. There's coffee in the kitchen, help yourself."

"Thanks, don't mind if I do."

She took her cup and headed to the kitchen for a refill.

Jim sat reading the brochure for the retirement community. He tried to imagine Minnie living in Texas and picked up the phone to make the first call. It would prove to be a very busy day after all.

Chapter 4

THE ELDERS

———⟫●⟪———

It was going to be a hot and very humid day and Jim woke more tired than he had felt in a while. He had been thinking about the old Lafortune family files and what he wanted to do with them. They went back two generations and they held secrets. In fact, they were some of his first responsibilities as an Estate lawyer and they had helped launch his career in New Orleans. Minerva and Pearl's parents and grandparents had been among his very first clients. The paperwork filled two, tall cabinets and spanned an entire financial lifetime of these people.

As he slowly walked to his office he caught the familiar scent of gardenias. There was a very old, large and bloom laden plant spilling over the fence into the sidewalk. He took out his pocket knife and gently cut a handful of the fragrant blooms for his desk. It was a heavenly smell and would perfume his office for days.

At the time he had first met the Lafortunes and the Boudreauxs he had been young and full of dreams. He thought about these people he missed as he walked. He was considering Pearl's wishes to have everyone with her at the plantation when it was completed. It was sounding better every day and he felt like he was ready to make up his mind about accepting her offer. They hadn't even discussed anything in depth yet, but the idea kept rolling around in his mind. He would leave the firm to the youngsters and retire. He would never relinquish complete control of the accounts belonging to the immediate family. The older files would stay wherever he was at all costs. He had promised never to divulge their contents to the girls, no matter what. Today seemed like as good a time as any to get started boxing them up. It would also free up space and the boys could do as they wished once he was gone.

Putting on a pot of coffee he decided to stack the boxes of files in the conference room so no one would trip over them. He figured he would complete this task before heading up the coast to be with the family. He chose one of the many vases below the kitchenette sink and placed the flowers in water. With this and his coffee in hand he got comfortable and set to work. Blaine and Joshua had come and gone, busy with a day that would be spent in the courthouse, he was alone and got done packing the paperwork before lunch. He sat back in his chair thinking about the boys and the future of the law office.

Joshua was Blaine's childhood, best friend. He was an only son as well and had lost his parents at an early age to a terrible auto accident in foggy weather. The boy was brilliant and after passing his bar exams had come to Blaine looking for a job. He fit in perfectly and enjoyed managing other people's estates. He was born in New Orleans and raised by his mother's sister Carol. He was a good looking man at age 26 with a muscular build that suited his 5'8" frame. He had eyes that looked like sky blue pools. His hair was jet black and cut short. His skin had the lite brown shade common of a creole Cajun mix. He was always impeccably dressed and well groomed. Women were drawn to him and he dated but always put work first and had not committed to any serious relationship as of yet. Jim felt confident that these two young men could run the business without him, probably sooner than they expected.

Glancing at the clock on his desk, Jim was surprised to see it was lunch time. He wasn't hungry but did feel like a nap. With a clear schedule for the day he moved to the single bed off the kitchen and lay down. He was out in minutes and dreamed of how he had come to know Minerva and Pearl's parents, grandparents and friends.

He was 21 again, out with his friends and looking for fun. He ran with a fast crowd that enjoyed the occasional mason jar of moonshine and the always eager girls of ill repute on Bourbon Street. The man to see for both was Big Daddy LeBon. He and his friends ended up there one evening, at the last house on the left, and walked into the dimly lit store front that was supposed to be just a smoke shop. There were Cuban cigars and imported tobaccos from all over the world. You could buy hand carved pipes of all sizes, shapes and materials. However, this was the only license that had been issued to the establishment. The other two money makers were behind closed doors and quite illegal.

Big Daddy had been run out of his first place of business and home town in northern Louisiana and ended up where he knew his efforts would be more appreciated and lucrative. He had become wealthy almost over-night once he'd met the men who made the hooch. Finding a staff of eager working girls was the easiest part. Most were young, homeless and helpless and he lured them in with open arms and the promise of wealth. There were a couple of the women that were older for the men asking for more mature companions, they dressed more conservatively and always in feathers. The younger girls were normally dressed very scantily and hung out on the upstairs balcony hawking and flaunting their bodies for men in the street, twenty four hours a day. There were two bedrooms downstairs and at that time there was a door that led to the stairs and the four bedrooms on the upper floor. Business was booming the night Jim and his friends entered LeBon's Smoke Shop.

They were taken to the back where they each purchased a mason jar of freshly brewed moonshine then escorted up the narrow staircase. The Madam, Sissy, met them at the door and let them wonder among the girls. After a half hour of pleasure, Jim had ended up in the parlor where he joined two other men for a drink. They were feeling no pain and introduced themselves as Mark and Louie Lafortune, father and son. Another man joined them while they were enjoying their third drink. He was acquainted with Mark and Louie and was introduced as Frank "Bo" Boudreaux. There was mention of a poker game, held weekly, for clientele only and the men laughed, saying that Big Daddy always joined in and always lost when he got too drunk. Jim left with a promise to attend the next game, a week from this night.

Many of Jim's college friends had lost their virginity to the ladies of the evening. During these years in the Crescent City, prostitution and illegal liquor made many wealthy. It was common to see the half-naked women hanging over every balcony up and down Bourbon Street barking in customers. The difference today was they were fewer, there was a heavy and obvious police presence and the few that had stayed in this line of work had quietly and discretely moved behind closed doors.

One week later Jim went back to the smoke shop to join the poker game. He was pleased to find Louie, Mark and Bo there. The room was tightly packed with a round table filled with close to a dozen men. The ceiling fan barely made a breeze in the thick cigar and cigarette smoke. It was obvious these guys were serious, so drinking too much would not be an option until Jim felt relaxed and confident. As the evening drew to an end, Big Daddy could barely sit up. He was losing and had been all night. On the last hand of cards he produced and threw in a deed to this very property when the call was made. The other men around the table eyed one another warily, not sure how to proceed. Louie won the pot including the deed. Big Daddy turned white and being a man of his word, he reached out his hand and shook on the deal. He didn't say a word, just clumsily stood and stumbled out of the room. A little while later they could hear the loud, drunken yelling in one of the upstairs bedrooms. It was obvious who was paying for the result of his bad judgment. They recognized the low, pleading voice as that of Sissy, trying to calm the large, furious man.

Out on the sidewalk Jim, Louie, Frank and Bo were involved in a conversation. They explained that they had thrown in on a business investment that was guaranteed to make them rich men, and wondered if Jim wanted a piece of the pie. He declined, explaining that he was about to open a law office specializing in Estate Planning and Management. Had he known then what he knew now, he would have felt stupid for not getting involved. The men met several more times and friendships were cemented. They approached Jim with a request and he gladly accepted. Managing their family fortunes would launch his career and the rest was history. There was only one stipulation. He was sworn to secrecy concerning the amount of their wealth to anyone, even their immediate family members.

Big Daddy had been given a ninety day grace period to vacate the premises once Louie and he signed the deed. The place was remodeled by Mark's new, beautiful wife Lenora Ann Lafayette and Louie's wife Matilda Jean Arnaud. Together they made it comfortable and closed the access to the downstairs so that part could be rented to other businesses. This proved to be a wise move as the income paid the taxes with money left over. They would all share the apartment, gathering there for special occasions or events in the city and decided it would remain in the family being passed down from one generation to the next.

Jim had become so close with all of these people that he considered them family and was there when Minerva was born then two years later came Pearl. Sadly, Lenora would bear no more children. He was and forever would be Uncle Jim to them and Pearl's daughters. Bo had continued his shrimping business and kept everyone supplied with fresh seafood. He and Ima hid their new found wealth as well. Matilda Jean was Bo's wife's first cousin. Ima and Bo were always around and you couldn't ask for a better group of people.

Everyone was afraid of Matilda Jean and when Jim questioned Bo one day while aboard the shrimp boat, it was explained that rumor had it she was a voodoo queen who had put a love hex on Louie. They both had a good laugh at this, but Bo reminded him to be very respectful and cautious around Matilda, just in case. All the women crossed themselves when she was around. Jim would have to remember to never offend her. As Minerva grew, she and her grandmother were inseparable. No one understood or questioned their bond, and she was the only one who could console Minerva when she had bad dreams. Even as a tiny thing, Minerva called the woman G-ma, as she couldn't wrap her tongue around the letter "R". Pearl's second baby was G-ma's namesake. She adored and doted on the children at every opportunity.

Over the years, Mark continued to work the large farm of his wife's family on Choctawhatchee Bay, never discussing his incredible wealth. The business deal they all had invested in was with a regular that frequented the smoke shop. He had brought them in on one of the first and most lucrative oil strikes in the region. The money just kept coming and only Jim and the men knew anything about it. Mark never changed how he ran the household or farm in Florida. Later in life Jim wondered that neither Minerva nor Pearl questioned where their father came up with the money for their educations. All the evidence was now tucked away in the boxes piled up in the conference room.

Jim awoke to a loud noise in the back parking lot and the smell of hot, fragrant food. He slowly rose and freshened up in the bathroom before going back to his office. He was feeling lonesome for all the people that had left too soon and decided a late lunch might cheer him up. He donned his coat, went out to tell the receptionist he was leaving and greeted the boys coming in as he left.

He sat eating his lunch and decided it was a good choice to retire and move to Florida. He would leave everything he owned in Louisiana to Blaine and the girls.

Elizabeth Sabin

It would make the rest of his years less complicated and he looked forward to relaxing. It was a good plan. He would tell Pearl soon. He decided he would not betray the confidences of the elders; the secrets would go to the grave with him. If the girls or their children discovered the truth after he was gone, then so be it, at least he would die with a clear conscience.

Chapter 5

SEASIDE, FLORIDA

———⇒●⇐———

I made it to the airport in plenty of time. One of the pilots helped me with the bags of delicacies that I had purchased yesterday. I helped him stow my things this time. I hated to be a burden to these guys. They had more important things to worry about than my French Market croissants. I sat in the rear of the jet, near the kitchen. I got my belt tight and watched out the window. Just a couple more hours and I'd be with Pearl. I was grinning at the thought.

We had to sit on the runway for about ten minutes waiting for clearance to take off. We were flying into Panama City, Florida. I hadn't checked the weather on my way out so I took notice of the black clouds that were beginning to surround us. This was common springtime weather for New Orleans and most of the panhandle of the gulf coast.

After we got underway, the turbulence seemed to be fighting the jet as we kept rising. It must have smoothed out for a while because I had fallen asleep reading and was awakened by a sharp crack of thunder and the jet lurching to one side. I had a feeling the pilots were very focused up front. The cabin alarm pinged and the red light outside the cockpit was blinking. Captain Taylor spoke to me calmly on the intercom.

"Sorry for the rough ride Mrs. Bonet. We are about to get you out of this storm. Going around it will add ten minutes to our approach to Panama City. Please tighten your seatbelt and we should arrive in approximately one half hour."

I leaned my head back in the seat as the plane seemed to go straight up and banked to the left. They would just fly up and around the thunderheads and avoid the beating. I wasn't worried, they were all top notch pilots and what could I do anyway?

I was thinking of Jim and how much he had aged in such a short time. It saddened me and made my heart ache to even imagine not having him in our lives. I loved him like a father and wanted him to be young and capable forever. He had been very handsome as a young man. He was 5'7", had broad shoulders and angular facial features. He wore his hair shorter now and it was completely white. The sharp lines of his jaw had softened considerably and I noticed a slight stoop in his posture. He was tanned and the wrinkles around his eyes and mouth had gotten more noticeable. He seemed to be wearing his glasses constantly and still strained to see at times. He wasn't fat so much as he was getting paunchy from drinking. His soft brown eyes still had a loving and patient glow and his cheeks were rosy. I would have to remind Pearl that we needed to pay closer attention to his health and be there for him more than we had been.

Even as excited as I was, I felt tired this morning. It had to be all the running around I had done yesterday. I wasn't getting any younger; my brain just wanted me to be. I was a little perturbed with myself for forgetting to give Jim the brochure at lunch yesterday. That wasn't like me, I was an excellent organizer and it was on a list.

I laughed to myself, I could hear Pearl now, telling me to chill and not worry about it. My lists irritated her but she was a thousand times worse than I was. And God forbid if things did not fall into the order of her schedule. To be fair, that was usually her work mode, when she was out for fun, nothing else mattered. She was always up for activity, and usually the spark of the party.

She still looked so beautiful, at 6'3", with an hour glass body. We always joked that she got the boob genes and her daughters were no different. They all had a rack. She stayed slim and had just enough weight to cover her long frame. Her legs went on forever and her green eyes were a shade I had trouble describing. She had long blonde hair and always wore it up in a loose knot. You would be hard pressed to guess she was in her mid-60s'. She was one of those women who absolutely did not know how beautiful she was.

The intercom pinged; we were making the approach to Panama City. I couldn't stop grinning and I was getting anxious to be off the plane. I knew that Pearl wouldn't have to drive more than twenty or so miles to pick me up. Even though we both had enough food for an army, I was hoping she would be game for lunch. I hadn't had breakfast and I seemed to be on the fringes of a headache. I dug some pills and a bottle of water out of my bag and was determined to not let anything spoil our reunion.

It was sprinkling lightly when I and the pilot dragged my bags across the tarmac and into the hangar. Pearl was there jumping up and down and laughing. I ran to her and we embraced like we'd been apart for ages. I held her back and said, "You look great! I am so happy."

I hugged her again, tearing up like we always did. She followed suite and we both wiped our eyes and noses. She looped her arm through mine and we almost skipped to the car, the guys already had it loaded. Kissing my cheek she said, "Minnie, I can't believe you're here. And I can't wait to show you my surprise."

We were both grinning like Cheshire cats. She got the air blasting, put on some music and we were on our way.

"Are you hungry Min, maybe we should grab some lunch? It just so happens that while procuring my morning paper, a young couple engaged me in conversation about where to eat in Seaside. The kid's wife had a drawl that dripped, but she was raving about this old place between here and the beaches. They said it was called "Bubba's Shrimp Shak.""

We both laughed and snorted.

"Well, if it's good enough for the locals, why not. I have been thinking about a shrimp po'boy since I got off the plane."

I reached over and turned up the radio. We both danced in our seats to some grunge tune, watching closely for the sign on the side of the road where we needed to turn off for this restaurant.

The landscape had been mostly sand and sea grass with dunes and dirt. The further we drove away from the city our surroundings changed quickly. The foliage was getting denser and there were a lot more trees. I could see water and asked Pearl about it.

"What body of water is this, are we following a river?" She thought about it for a moment and decided,

"I think it's the backwaters of the State Park. There's been a lot of rain and look its right up to the road in places."

Soon we spotted a small, crooked sign on the side of a short drive that went back into a parking lot. It was just as the girl described and in bright red letters read, "Bubba's Shrimp Shak," the line under that read, "best shrimp on the gulf."

Pearl turned left into the narrow lane. Laughing I said, "They're certainly confident, so how bad can it be; besides I'm starved."

Pearl drove slowly, the bushes and weeds lightly scraped the sides of the car. The crushed shell parking lot crackled under the tires and it was beginning to look spooky back here. I grabbed my camera and got out of the car. I got several good shots of the front of the dilapidated building. The vines and weeds were doing their best to choke the life from the old wood structure. The roof, in the spots that were still visible, was rusty and bent. There were several huge oak trees that had so much Spanish moss in them; I couldn't believe they could breath.

Pearl waited for me to take the pictures and just said, "Wow!"

The smell that hit us now had us drooling. The old screen door was hanging crooked in the frame and whined on the hinges as we entered. It took a few minutes for our eyes to adjust. We could hear noise back in the kitchen but we seemed to be the only patrons at the moment.

The inside wasn't much better off than the outside. The wood was showing its age and the results of standing against salt air and high humidity for too many decades. The ceiling fans were softly whirring and looking around we'd noticed there were tables in the front room and the back portion of the place was a room with screens half way up to the roof. I smelled brackish water and mold. There were six or more picnic tables in rows back there.

We entered the room through a screen door and sat where we wanted. We glanced around waiting for a waitress. There was a lot of noise outside the screened area. I could hear cicadas, fish flopping out on the water, birds and frogs. I saw that there was a screen door leading outside to a narrow walkway with a flimsy railing. It seemed to go around the whole porch. We could hear the water lapping at the boards beneath our feet. So this whole part of the building was stilted out over the swamp.

A tall pretty, black girl came shuffling into the room to take our order. She was extremely shy and would barely look at us. Her hair was platted in about twenty small pony tails and she had a wounded look on her face. I had an urge to hug her but didn't. She was back in moments with our glasses and a large pitcher of iced tea. It had at least a half of a lemon sliced and floating on top. We were situated at the table nearest the back screen door. She came back with our shrimp po'boys and potato salad pretty fast and the only words she uttered on her way back to the kitchen were, "Yes, Mam."

We chatted away, trying to talk over each other, catching up on the months we'd been apart. The food was excellent and we plowed through it. We were done eating for the most part when all hell broke loose.

Pearl was telling me about Magnolia when a huge lizard with an extremely long, blue tail had apparently lost his grip on the rafter above our heads and fell onto the table with a loud plop. He landed right smack in the middle of our lunch mess. We simultaneously shrieked and it was on to see which of us could leave the table the quickest.

"Jesus!" I yelled.

Pearl tried to stand quickly and her long legs got hooked on the table. Before I could try to stand the whole thing was on top of me. I threw my hands up shrieking when I realized the damn lizard was in my lap, sitting atop what was left of my potato salad. Pearl was in a panic to get untangled and get it off me. At all the yelling, the young girl came running from the kitchen to our aid. She ran up to me, seeing the table on top of me and had no idea why we were even freaking out. As she bent down to help me that lizard looked up and launched itself onto her head and sunk his front claws into her hair for a better grip. She stood up and being unsure about what was attacking her, she began to scream like a scalded banshee. This brought the cook running out from the kitchen wielding a butcher knife. He looked around to see what the hell was happening and saw the reptile on the girls head. He laid the knife down and took two steps, grabbing the lizard, he clawed the thing out of her hair and opening the back screen door, he flung it out into the swampy water.

We looked at each other and the mess. We laughed until we were doubled over. The cook apologized and offered to comp our lunch. We paid him happily, tipping the wide eyed girl extra for all her trauma. When we got back in the car Pearl took a good look at me, with food and lizard cooties all over my clothes. We lost it again and must have sat there for a good ten minutes; about to pee ourselves, there was no way in hell I would ask to use their facilities. No way. I dug around in one of my bags and changed into a fresh top and shorts, right there in the parking lot.

Pearl finally caught her breath and asked, "Can you believe that shit just happened?"

I was wiping my eyes and using a wet wipe to get the crap off my hands,

"No, I cannot and that poor guy is probably wondering why two grown women are so afraid of a lizard."

We would rather have died than let them know we were sissy southerners. Both of us had always been terrified of reptiles.

Pearl headed back out to the blacktop and we were about ten minutes from the beach. She laughed again.

"So much for refined, lady like behavior. And didn't Grandpa tell us the ones with the blue tails were poisonous?"

I pulled down the visor and checked my face and hair in the small mirror,

"Hell Pearl, we were fed so much bullshit growing up, there's no telling what the truth was. Most of it was old wives tales and drunken lore."

She laughed loud again and said, "Well we're off to a good start, surely there is more trouble we can get into, and it certainly always seems to find us."

The sun was high and brilliant reflecting off the white sugar sand. Pearl parked in a small driveway in front of the single level house. It was sitting right in the middle of what looked to be about two acres of sand and sea grass. They had given up long ago on growing a lawn from the looks of it. The quaint old house had a screened in front porch and I could see a swing and one wicker chair. The exterior looked whitewashed and there were chunks of peeling paint in places. The wood was dry and splintered on the side that caught the most wind. I noticed the white lace curtains in the windows.

Pear got the front door open and we checked out the interior before we began hauling in my things. It was one of the older cottages and it had a lot of charm. There was simple but comfortable furniture in the living room and bedrooms. The bathroom had been remodeled recently and it was the most modern portion of the house. There were fresh cut flowers in all the rooms and a fruit basket with a bottle of good champagne in the middle of the kitchen counter.

We got the car unloaded and decided we had to be on the beach. Pearl showed me my room and I drug all my stuff in. There in the middle of the pillows was a beautiful gift bag, with bows and tissue poking from the top. A card was leaned against it. I smiled and was almost weepy again; this had been something we always did for each other after being apart. I decided to save it to open after a long walk. I got my swimsuit on and grabbed a towel. I tied a colorful sarong around my waist and with my flip flops in hand, I was ready.

We went out through the back of the place and as I passed the large dining room table, all the blueprints and maps caught my eye. I started to go look at them when Pearl sidestepped, grabbed my arm and said, "That is what I have been so busy with lately and I swear I'll show and tell as soon as we get back."

Laughing I reminded her that we didn't have anything to put shells in. She ran to the kitchen and got a sandwich bag and we headed out to the surf. I threw my head back and soaked in the sun. From the looks of the sky, the sunshine would be short lived. It was humid today and trying to rain, but even with clouds moving in, the sun could cook you like a lobster.

We walked right at the water's edge and talked. Neither of us actually swam out past the breakers anymore. The threat of sharks kept us at about knee deep and no more.

The wind off the water was heavenly. It felt heavy and moisture laden. None of the natural smells were ever overwhelming as long as the wind was blowing. We walked for miles, laughing, talking and gathering shells. With the sudden threat of lightening looming we decided to turn back toward the cottage. It was beginning to rain and we squealed at how cold the huge rain drops felt.

At some point during our walk back to the house, it was as if someone flipped a switch on the weather. The wind we had been enjoying had blown in a hefty little storm and the clouds got black. By the time we were running to the back door, we were thoroughly soaked. We started in the kitchen and ran from room to room, shutting all the windows. I went back with a towel and dried everything off. The storm was right over us now and the thunder was booming through the house. The lightning was fierce and made the hair on my arms stand up. I walked over to the edge of the closest window and peeked outside. I looked at Pearl and told her, "I'm going to change and then I want to hear everything."

Pearl laughed and agreed. We met back in the dining room. Pearl pulled out chairs and we sat facing each other. Taking my hand she said, "Do you remember what Gregory gave me for my 50th birthday?"

I had to think about that for a minute,

"I won't lie, I haven't a clue." Pearl was beaming.

"The old plantation estate Minnie, remember? It's always been called The Oaks."

I did remember now. Pearl's husband Gregory been excited when he'd purchased the estate. His mother, Clarissa had a huge snit fit. She was insulted that her son owned a broken down, forlorn mansion, with hundreds of acres of ignored land. Gregory has seen the potential in the beautiful property. He was thinking ahead to when Pearl would obtain her degrees in Drafting and Design and Interior Design. He was proud of her and knew she would see it as a project, a challenge. He had gotten sick and died. Eventually everyone had forgotten about it.

"Yes, now I remember, so what are your plans?"

Pearl reached across the table and placed the old blueprints in front of us.

"Here is the original floor plan."

She shuffled papers and showed me another smaller map with wiring and pipes.

"It's taken me weeks to find these documents. There's even a book on the founding family. I haven't read much of that yet, but at one time the place was a working, producing farm and the house was spectacular. Anyway, here's the deal. I plan to move a trailer out there. I'll have to have utilities, but I plan to live on site while I have professionals rebuild the house and outbuildings. I want to put in a pool too. Minnie, I'm so excited! I have been dreaming of this and I feel like I'm supposed to be there, with all my family around me. I know that's weird, right?"

"I am the last person on earth who would think any of that was weird. Make it happen and I will be there for you from start to finish."

I leaned over and gave her a big hug.

"I love you sis and I'm excited for you, it's just like us to go big."

"Well, I want us to go out there tomorrow. I have never set foot on the place. I want to see what I will be up against, and I would appreciate it if you would take pictures for me?"

"Absolutely, this is going to be good. Just don't be disappointed if the place has rotted down to a heap."

We both started howling with laughter. We joined arms and went to fix dinner. The storm was raging and we were hungry. I was right; my sister had laid in enough provisions for a scout troop. We took our plates into the living room and ate.

After cleaning the kitchen I got the gift bag off my bed and went back into the living room, Pearl must have been in her room. I gently lifted the top piece of tissue. Peering into the bag I held my breath. There was a small white box. That usually meant jewelry. I opened it and saw the delicate chain, then the silver charm that was a replica of The Oaks. But this one was different. Pearl had changed the name to Live Oaks and the O held a diamond. She walked back in as I was trying to put it around my neck. She got it clasped for me and I hugged and thanked her.

"As always Pearl; this is a brilliant gift. You have always had a knack for making it perfect. And I love the name change."

"Glad you love it, I have one just like it. It's to remind me to stay grounded while I tackle my first big endeavor. I have one more surprise before we turn in."

She reached in her hoodie pocket and pulled out a joint. We both howled and got to work smoking it. We talked and laughed until our stomachs hurt. In the wee hours of the morning, the storm had moved north and we dragged ourselves to bed.

I collapsed and was out like a rock. I dreamed that Pearl and I were standing on the front porch of an enormous, old house. It smelled bad and had been overrun with thick menacing vines. It vibrated and hummed and tendrils of the vines were snaking around our ankles. We were being strung up, and I couldn't breathe to scream. The house was now emitting a low growl and I was sure I would die.

I woke up suddenly, sitting up in the strange bed. I was covered in sweat and my head hurt. I got up for some water and lay back down. I was almost out when I could have sworn someone gently brushed my cheek. I tried to ignore that and the very faint, far away singing.

Chapter 6

THE OAKS PLANTATION

———⊰●⊱———

I woke up to the sound of Pearl, padding around in the kitchen. She was trying to be quiet as she made some coffee. It had taken me a moment to realize where I was. Soon the whole place smelled like dark roast, Sumatra. Glancing out the window, I could see it was still dark. I could hear the soft slapping sound the waves made this time of the morning. The breeze ruffled the curtains and the salt air wafted over me. I stretched and turned on the bed side lamp.

Pearl leaned into my room; she had two large, steamy mugs. Smiling she came in and sat next to me on the edge of the bed by the window. She handed me the coffee and said, "Good morning, I hope you slept ok. I thought I heard you stirring last night."

I had sat up and leaned back against the headboard. I blew on my coffee before sipping it and thought about the horrible dream that had awakened me. I decided not to share this with Pearl. She always got uncomfortable and frightened about that sort of thing.

"Yes, I got up, sorry if I woke you; I had a headache and went for water."

Pearl drank her coffee and stared at the small window. I knew she was thinking about The Oaks.

"Why don't we grab a couple of blankets and a thermos of this coffee and go watch the sunrise. By then we'll be starving and after breakfast we could head out."

"That sounds perfect, and thanks for making the coffee, I can't ever seem to get going without it."

We both laughed and she left to get dressed. I just threw on some light sweats, a hoodie and grabbed the blanket off the foot of my bed. I met Pearl in the kitchen; she had a tote with the thermos, some cream, a little tub of sugar and a small blanket over her shoulder. I found some plastic spoons and threw them in the tote.

We didn't walk too far; we hadn't even brushed our hair. We spread out one blanket to sit on and put the other one around both our shoulders. Pearl fixed us each a new cup of brew and we just sat quietly, shoulder to shoulder and watched the glorious sunrise. The colors were spectacular and I loved watching the way it lit up the gulf out over the horizon.

The birds were swooping in and out of the water fishing, and the dolphins were feeding out past the sand bar. They leapt and dived, swimming back and forth on a mission. The little sand pipers were fussing and chattering as they ran right up to the wave that was going out then ran back squawking as the next wave came in. The tiny sand crabs were starting to peak out of their holes and were scurrying about. Pearl leaned her head on my shoulder for a moment.

"This is where I want to be Min; I can't live in Savannah any longer. I want you to be here too. I want us all together again."

I kissed the top of her head and laughed.

"That applies to both of us. While we have breakfast I will show you where I might live in Beaumont. Jim is checking it out for me." She moaned.

"Oh Min. Why Texas? What about New Orleans? Why not stay with us?"

"Well you are going to be living in a trailer, remember? I like to think of the apartment as a safe haven right now. Besides the girls have their loft in New York and Beaumont was always a fun place. The whole family went there a lot. We'll have to wait and see what happens. Maybe we can do something different by the time you finish the plantation." She sighed.

"I intend to work very diligently until it's done. I am asking for two year bids from contractors now. I have to be confident that I am at least close on all the costs. I left a lot of wiggle room and they don't need to know I have all the money I need to make it happen. There's one particular contractor that has my interest. I'll show you that stuff tonight. I know I will be starting at the bottom of the place and working my way up." Capping the thermos she said, "We should go back and get something to eat. I think the drive out there will be close to two hours. I'm anxious to see if my calculations are even close."

We got up and folded the blankets. We had a lovely breakfast of sweet breads, fruit and yogurt. I had iced tea but Pearl always drank juice. I had given her the brochure on Lancaster Estates and she thumbed through it while we ate. She said,

"I'm going to want to look at this more closely this evening Min, the place has potential." Laughing, I agreed. "That's exactly what I've been thinking."

We showered, dressed and all I took was my camera. Pearl had everything she needed for today's excursion stowed in the trunk.

She put the address in her car's GPS and we headed out. It was supposed to be partly cloudy today but right now it was bright and cheerful. It was a beautiful drive. There were many kinds of cranes out in the cypress marshes. I'd noticed the alligators too. We had music on and both of us were tapping our feet lost in thought as we drove.

I had an overwhelming sense that our great grandmother was with me. I'd been thinking about her since last night and that horrid dream. We called her G-Ma because I couldn't say grand when I began talking. The name stuck. No-one in the family liked Matilda Jean. My first memories of her were when I was around three.

For some reason Pearl and I was spending the night at her house. She put us in a small sewing room that was connected to her bedroom. There was a daybed that I used and an old, antique cradle for Pearl. The room was pleasant enough during the daytime. But at night the closet was my worst nightmare. I had awakened that night to chaos, voices, murmurs and unfriendly laughter. I couldn't breathe and hiding under the thick quilts did me no good. I slipped from the bed, checked on Pearl and ran on short, chubby legs to G-Ma's bedroom. It took all my strength to push the door open. Standing at the foot of her bed, I squeaked her name, on the verge of tears, with my hands in tiny fists, I wanted to scream. She rose up in the bed, saw me and said, "Child, what is the matter, it's late?"

She continued to get up and slowly stood then moved to the old, padded rocker next to her bed. She held her arms open to me and said, "Come here to G-Ma."

I ran to her, crawled into her ample lap and curled into a tight ball. She put her arms around me making shushing noises and rubbed my back. She looked down at my tear streaked face and said, "You need to tell me why you're frightened child, tell me everything, you're safe now."

Stuttering I could only say, "I'm scared, they won't let me sleep and there's a scary thing in your closet."

I was shivering. She reached behind us and grabbed a shawl off the back of the rocker. She draped it across us both and sighed.

"Minerva, I want to tell you something. You must pay attention and try to remember."

She rocked slowly, choosing her words carefully.

"You are a shining baby, you're light has been very bright since the day you were born. In fact you were brighter than any other baby I ever seen. That light is in you and all around you and there are dark things not of this earth that are afraid and jealous of it. But it also welcomes others that shine too. You must never be afraid, and when you are, just ask the Lord to light the way for you. You must pray for courage and then you will always be safe. You can think about me too, I'll always watch over you."

She hugged me just a little tighter. I wasn't sure what she wanted me to do. I was just hoping I didn't have to go back to that room. She stood with me in her arms and laid me in her huge feather bed. I was engulfed by the soft bedding and the smell of violets, her favorite fragrance. I'd fallen back to sleep, unafraid and somehow knew that thing in the closet was no match for G-Ma.

This childhood memory has been so strong and vivid, I find myself thinking of her whenever something un-natural frightens me. The elders always referred to her as the old voodoo queen. I didn't know what that meant as a child. I just knew that I loved her and no one else understood or made me feel safe. But they were sure enough scared of her. Several of the female relatives always crossed themselves whenever she came into a room. She just laughed at them in her low, gravely tone. She thought they were all spineless ninnies.

She had once told me that goose bumps and cold air were your first signal that someone from the other realm was with you. I couldn't get her off my mind this morning.

The GPS was telling us that we were getting close. I looked at Pearl and asked, "Have you been noticing all the oak trees on the left side of the road?"

"Yes, they seem to go on forever, I'm not sure I've ever seen this many in one place."

Pearl slowed and turned left as instructed by the navigation system. She drove over the cattle guard and stopped. We both got out. I was covered from head to toe in goose bumps. I grabbed my camera and she grabbed her clipboard. I couldn't help thinking that if G-Ma was here; she would have brought out her big guns. That included Holy water, her rosary and the family bible. All I had was a camera and a bad feeling.

We both looked around and Pearl started writing right away. I breathed deep and began my digital documentation of this day. I noticed that there wasn't a mailbox or drop box for packages. I leaned over Pearl's shoulder and her list already had my first observation, then the entrance archway, trim trees, clean orchard, and clean and wash the driveway. She was on a roll.

I was looking into the oaks and as far as I could see they had been planted with purpose, staggered, not in straight rows. They were overgrown, in desperate need of pruning and they were so thick, the only light getting through was dappled. There were a lot of long shadows. The trees looked like old, bearded giants. The lower limbs gave the impression that each one had joined hands with another. The thick, long Spanish moss was fluttering in the wind. I wasn't hearing a lot of birds or squirrels, which seemed strange.

I felt like the trees were sentries and they all had their eyes on us. I couldn't even see a house from here. The driveway seemed to go on forever. It was full of branches and limbs. Leaves were piled up here and there. Grass was struggling to grow, but only in tall, ugly patches. Everything else was sand.

Pearl was focused on the drive itself.

"You know, this crushed shell material is almost impossible to get any more. But this has so many layers and was done so well, that I believe we can salvage the whole thing, if the rest looks this good. If we blow it off and wash it with detergent, it might even be white again."

I didn't agree or disagree. "Well, let's go see this house, I've got all the shots I need of this view."

She drove slowly; the years of debris crunching under the tires, making it a bumpy ride. Looking up at the dangerously low limbs and with a sigh she said,

"I'm going to have to make pruning these trees the first priority, otherwise no trucks will be able to get in here, or a trailer either."

I was looking right, as far into the orchard as my sight allowed and the shadows were playing tricks with me. I could've sworn I could see a group of children, black and white. They looked to be from four or five years old to maybe nine or ten. They were laughing breathlessly and playing hide and seek. They darted in and out of the massive trunks.

"Minnie!" I looked at Pearl and she was shaking my arm and looking at me. "What is it? You're white as a sheet!"

I realized I was looking into the orchard, mouth agape with that faraway look in my eye. It was something I did unconsciously and it had terrified her since we were children.

I tried to laugh it off. "Sorry, I was thinking about more pictures of the trees." Actually I had sweat running down my sides and I was nauseated. I wished I had a bundle of sage and a large, white dove's feather.

We finally saw it. Pearl drove on the only even patch of pavers in the large, circular driveway and pulled right up near the front steps. We sat for a minute, trying to take it all in. The place was gigantic. It was also over run with thick foliage, lichens and mold. There were broken windows with boards hanging askew, one of the porch ceiling fans hung by a tattered chord. The old warped porch swings were sitting on the porch itself. The boards were sprung and stuck up here and there. Pearl reached in her pocket for the keys to the front door. Looking at the old broken door, barely hanging by the top hinge, we laughed long and hard, more out of nervous energy than humor. Leaning against the car, we looked up at the roof of this once majestic building. This was one tough old place. It had been skillfully built with no spare to detail. I could not believe so much of it was intact. Pearl had stars in her eyes, I had more goose bumps.

I turned on my camera and walked slowly from one side to the other. I didn't miss an inch as I clicked off photos of the front. I was dreading going inside. I looked around and tried to imagine the place as someone's home, new and whole. Alive and full of people, all busy and involved. Of course the original owners would have had a full staff of servants and slaves for the fields. That meant slaves quarters too. I couldn't imagine any of those buildings surviving this long.

Pearl started up the broad, concrete steps. "Wow Minnie, look at these old planters. I wonder if they're original, they seem to be." I laughed.

"We need to find as many original photos of this place as we can. It can only help you and there has to be some archived somewhere. And hopefully, we can find some aerial photography of the property."

"You're right, I've already found a few photos of poor quality but there has to be more."

Pearl remembered the two high powered flashlights in the trunk and ran to get them. We went up the steps arm in arm and pried the old front door open enough to squeeze in. It wasn't completely dark; there were a lot of broken windows so the sun spread rays through parts of the huge entry hall. Dust motes floated on an invisible air current and as our eyes adjusted, we noticed the leaves and trash in small piles here and there. It smelled moldy and dirty and there was a hint of something unpleasant that I couldn't put my finger on. We were standing frozen inside the front door, clinging to each other. I laughed and said, "Come on, let's use our flashlights and do this."

A door upstairs slammed and we both jumped a foot off the ground. A broken window rattled and we saw the breeze was gaining momentum and clouds were piling up.

"Jesus!" I muttered. I shone my flashlight into the darkest corners and reminded Pearl, "Just keep your eyes open for snakes and wasp or hornet nests. We could find anything. This place is so isolated that getting hurt would not be good. Watch your step."

We could smell ozone and knew a storm was blowing in and it was close. My head was hurting and I wanted to be outside. We got through the downstairs, and went back out to the car. I had a thought.

"Pearl, we don't have to see everything today. Let's wander the grounds before it rains, and come back tomorrow. I don't have the right kind of shoes anyway and I don't want to get snake bit."

She agreed with me and we strolled around the whole house and part of the back yard area. It was too grown up to go further.

Driving back I felt better with each mile away from there. I was exhausted and I hadn't done anything. It was as if the energy had been sucked out of me. Pearl looked tired and drawn too. I was thinking of G-Ma and knew I should do a cleansing of the place when we went back tomorrow. I would approach the subject tonight. If Pearl agreed, there was an old Native American Indian woman who had a bead and jewelry kiosk on one of the beach paths downtown. This woman also had bundles of sage, feathers and all sorts of interesting artifacts.

We got back into the cottage and grabbing drinks, collapsed in the living room with the air conditioner humming away. We heard a ringtone and Pearl jumped up, running to her bedroom, she came back with her cell phone. I was suddenly aware that I had ignored mine for going on two days now. I went to get mine and we both sat there checking messages. I was feeling bad about missing two calls from Jim and one from Blaine. There were also four calls from the New Orleans Medical Center. I didn't mention them or listen to them. That could wait. My phone rang, which made me jump and I saw it was Jim.

"Hello my dear, I was beginning to become concerned. Are you both well?"

I laughed and said, "I am so sorry Jim, I completely forgot my phone. How are you doing and what are we missing?"

He cleared his throat and said, "Put me on speaker, will you?"

I could've sworn I heard Blaine and Joshua in the background, excited about something.

"Ok, go ahead Jim; Pearl is right here next to me."

"Hello love, let me be the first to congratulate Mrs. Bonet on the sale of her fine ranch. You are officially a millionaire, again!" He chuckled, pleased with himself.

We both squealed and hugging each other, I said, "That's fabulous Jim, thank you for letting me know. I hope that doesn't mean I have to rush home."

"No, if anything becomes that urgent, we would use the jet and come join you. That doesn't sound like the worst idea either. How are the beaches?"

Pearl took over the conversation.

"As beautiful as you remember and you and the boys are welcome to join us any time you want, that sounds like fun. We have tons of food and can free up at least one bed. The couch folds out and we always seem to manage. Please, join us. We went to the plantation today and will go back tomorrow."

I could tell the guys were thinking about it. Jim spoke up.

"If we can clear our schedules, maybe we will fly in Monday or Tuesday with the contract you need to sign for the ranch Minerva. I have information about

Lancaster Estates as well. You are now the proud owner of a two bedroom house by the front entrance of said establishment and I have your keys and contract. We should seal that deal together at your convenience. Even your taxes are paid in full for one year."

We laughed like kids and agreed to see them next week.

Pearl ran in the kitchen to chill the champagne. We would celebrate later tonight. I couldn't believe my ranch belonged to someone else as soon as I signed the papers. I was also glad that I wouldn't have to leave yet, even though I had a new home waiting for me in Texas. What a day this turned out to be. I was so excited; I wanted to walk on the beach, grabbing Pearl, we headed out back.

We spent a few hours on the beach, had dinner and drank every last drop of the expensive champagne. We laughed and cried and hugged. Everything was falling into place for both of us and it was just so special to be together and share these events as they unfolded.

We discussed the need to cleanse and pray over the old house and property. Pearl agreed and said it couldn't hurt. Whatever I thought we needed to do was fine with her. I was relieved and hoped it would help. Something about that place gave me an overwhelming sense of danger and pain.

I took some pills in anticipation of a headache and went to bed. I dreamed G-Ma and Graham were sitting at a small table somewhere in the French quarter. I looked closer and there were all of my relatives seated around them. They were drinking and laughing and all turned to smile at me at the same time. I felt at peace and as I drifted off I wondered if Pearl had a radio on in her room. I could hear faint and faraway singing again.

Chapter 7

PEARL FRANCOISE LAFORTUNE-VANDECOURTE

───➤●◄───

I was the first one up this morning. After yesterday, I decided to let Minnie sleep. I needed to stretch so I decided to walk on the beach.

I thought we should not go back to The Oaks today. It might be better to wait until Monday when the guys got in. I wanted to call Magnolia and Matilda later so that both of us could talk to them. I eased out of the rickety screen door as quietly as I could.

Walking right at the edge of the water I let the cold sand ooze between my toes. It was one of those things that could take me back to my childhood in a flash. I was worried about my sister. How could a place make her that sick? She had one of those spells or whatever you want to call it. She had them a lot when we were kids. She would stare at nothing I could see, and her mouth was literally agape. Her eyes lost their sparkle and somehow I knew she wasn't really there anymore. It had scared me so bad a couple of times, I almost went screaming to mama. I actually slapped her on one occasion, trying to make her come back to me, and she'd had a hard time forgiving me. We were supposed to be able to count on each other no matter what, and I had let her down. It was because I had been the fearful child.

I am still a coward. I don't believe in any of those things and she is so headstrong about her faith. The first thing I wanted her to tell me was why wasn't I seeing or feeling what she did? We never could figure that out. The few times I had pressed her to reveal the details of what was happening, I'd had nightmares for weeks. I'm not as strong as Minnie. I panic sometimes because I don't know how to help her and I don't want to lose her. I've always looked up to her and counted on her to know what to do.

Today if she feels well enough, we will go shopping and get enough sage and feathers to cleanse the whole county. I'm going to trust her on this one. I would do anything to keep her from being ill. I plan to ask about the headaches too.

I smelled bacon frying as I got to the back door of the cottage. Minnie was up, happy and dancing around the kitchen to the music on TV. I was relieved to see she seemed to feel better and asked her, "Do you still have a headache Min? It sure smells good in here."

She danced over to me, drying her hands on the dishtowel and said, "I feel fantastic this morning, the pills I'm taking are great and besides, I don't normally have this many headaches. I'm blaming it on moving myself from almost four thousand feet above sea level to below sea level. Altitude sickness, I guess."

I thought about that for a moment and it made sense so I let it go for now. I hugged Minnnie, stole a piece of bacon and she smacked my ass with the twisted dish towel. We were both howling and chasing each other around the kitchen when my cell phone rang.

It was Magnolia and she was excited. "Hello, my darling, how are you doing?"

"Hello Mother, Tilly is here with me too. We just heard that Uncle Jim and Blaine are joining you at the beach! Are we invited?"

I waved at Minnie pointing to my phone; she joined me at the dining table to listen.

"We would love to have you if you can get away. The boys will probably be here Monday and we could send the jet. It all depends on your schedules darling." I heard her and Matilda discussing it.

"Matilda agrees that we are at a place with our fall line where we could get away. We'll just fly in and be there when they arrive. Is that ok? We're dying to see Mimi. It's been a while and we could use a break. Do we need to bring anything?"

I could tell Minnie was bursting so I gave her my phone.

"You girls get here whenever you want and I can't wait to see you. Bring your sleeping bags because you will be on the floor. Travel safe and we'll have a party! I love you both." She handed me my phone and went to finish cooking some eggs.

I told my children, "It will be a week to remember in Seaside. Fly into Panama City if at all possible, that's closest and me and Mimi will come to get you with bells on. We love you and travel safe."

I set the table and had a relaxing meal with Minnie. Her color was good and she seemed her usual happy self. I'd make sure we had a great, yet stress free day. I had enough balls in the air already for a brand new project. Everything depended on permits anyway. There was time to kill.

We talked about the gated community where she would soon be living and I told her that it might be fun and if not, well, there were always other options. We cleaned the cottage and decided to go shopping and stock the pantry with enough supplies for all the mouths we'd be feeding. We were both in an excellent mood and drove into town.

We hit all the little shops and open air kiosks first. We bought every last bundle of sage the Indian woman had and white feathers too. Just for fun we bought some incense and she had some exquisite jewelry. We grabbed gifts for the girls and found a fun party store where we purchased paper lanterns and table decorations. We bought out the local market and hit the florist shop last.

It took us a half an hour to lug all our booty back inside and put everything away. We both agreed we needed our daily dose of beach and throwing on our suits, ran out to the surf. I hugged my sister and said,

"I can't believe everyone will be here in two days. I'm so excited Minnie. Maybe this romance brewing with Matilda and Blaine will be out in the open too. Heaven knows why they think we would object. Sometimes I don't understand anything they do. I must be getting old."

Minnie laughed loudly. "Hell Pearl, we're both getting old and we just have to remember what it was like being their age. We sure as hell didn't tell our mama everything we'd done; otherwise she would have been grey in her thirties. And there is one small detail you're not considering. He is also your daughter's lawyer. That screams conflict of interest and scandal."

I agreed with her and said, "I never thought of that; let's talk to Jim about the situation over cocktails without the kids. And dammit, speaking of cocktails, I know what we forgot. We absolutely have to remember to get some more champagne and remind me to make a list. We have to set up a bar before they arrive." Minnie laughed and said, "God forbid this family gathered without a sufficient amount of hooch!"

I wanted to spend some time on the computer and when we got cleaned up from the salt and sand we settled in for the evening. I didn't mind that we didn't go out to the plantation today. There was a lot I could do from right here. I desperately needed a reputable tree service right away. That's what I worked on until dinnertime. I felt so content and happy. There weren't many of us left but we would all be together soon and that's what mattered. I've decided that life is too short to waste a single moment, and my babies were coming here. I opened a bottle of very good wine and Minnie and I relaxed until bedtime, life was good.

Chapter 8

THE LA FLEUR NEW YORK, NY

———⟫●⟪———

Magnolia and Matilda were drinking coffee and discussing their flight leaving LaGuardia Soon. It wouldn't be more than a two or three hour flight into Panama City, Florida. The trip was just what they needed to decompress. Right now they were frantically trying to get organized.

They both ended up back at the coffee table where they had left their cups. They had placed all the living room furniture they had in the exact middle of their loft apartment. It was a cozy and neutral spot where they relaxed together at some point in each day. Matilda sat her cup down and asked, "Mag, do you remember where we stored our camping gear? If we need to take sleeping bags, we might as well dig out our backpacks and pads also. We need to get busy. The car service is supposed to pick us up in an hour."

Laughing Magnolia threw one of the couch pillows at her sister and said, "Relax Tilly, I know right where they are and what do we need to pack besides our swimsuits and some shorts and tops? We're going to the beach, not a fashion review."

Magnolia snorted. "Well let's get moving. I want to take Mother and Mimi a sample of the bags that were chosen for the Fall line, I guess I can fit them in my pack. And are you taking some of your jewelry samples for them? I know Mimi will flip when she sees the orchid jewelry you created, that's her favorite flower."

Matilda got up and took their cups to the kitchen saying,

"Yes, I'm giving those to Mimi and I'm giving Mother the set that we presented to the buyers. I still say that's the most beautiful bag you've ever done. She will love both. Come on, let's get packed and going. You know what a pain in the ass that airport is."

Her sister got up and they scrambled to get ready, both so excited they were walking on air.

The doorman was buzzing their intercom letting them know the car had arrived, Matilda ran and hit the button,

"Be right down." She looked at Magnolia laughing and said, "Let's go! The traffic will be hideous, and these backpacks are too big for carry on so that means standing in line." She was furiously scribbling a note and had a hundred dollar bill in her hand.

Impatiently, Magnolia exclaimed, "What are you doing Tilly? You always drag your feet and honestly it makes me crazy, come on!"

Laughing she replied, "For your information I am leaving a note and tip for Juanita, in case you hadn't noticed what a slob you are, this place is a mess and the last thing we need is for our housekeeper to quit because we're pigs."

Magnolia stood with the door propped open and then they were sprinting for the limo.

They owned the entire top floor of the building. The elevator downstairs didn't have a button for the 18th floor, it had one separate from the others that said Roof Terrace and in red letters beneath that was the simple declaration, Private. The building was called The LA Fleur and while the new owner was in the process of a few small remodels in his lower apartments, the girl's realtor had a brainstorm. She had informed them that the minute he heard the name VanDeCourte, he had his ears up.

They had negotiated the purchase and remodel of the entire top floor with exclusivity to the roof deck and terrace. This was all done under their Uncle Jim's watchful eye and legal guidance.

The owner had lost a lot of tenants. A couple of them had died, but when he announced his most recent increase in rent and fees, several had told him no thanks, and had moved on. It was the age old cliché, they just happened to be looking at the right time. The remodel had opened up all of the eighteenth floor apartments into a huge loft. With their Mother's help they had designed a phenomenal living space that would resell for three times what they had paid.

Each girl had a whole side of the expansive loft to herself. The entire wall facing the street had windows from ceiling to floor and light filled every corner allowing them to enjoy all the plants they wanted. Each also had their own art studio and spent most of their time there, on the phone, or rushing to meetings. They rubbed shoulders with all the movers and shakers in one of the most cutthroat businesses they could have chosen. They were invited to all the best parties and engagements and knew all the people that counted. After their last presentation to various buyers, they were busy.

They'd gotten the best education that money could buy, including study abroad. They had spent several years traveling and researching every detail that would give them the edge on the best and most desirable product that they could produce. Matilda had even spent a year in China, studying and learning everything there was to know about porcelain. Magnolia was crazy for textiles, precious metals and stones, the finest quality of crystals and leather. Her handbags were individually a work of art and Matilda's porcelain and silver flower jewelry was already being sought after.

It was apparent someone had gotten excited and leaked a set of the sample jewelry and matching bag to a group of the beautiful people at a cocktail party. It was one of their launch sets and there was more calls and demands than they knew what to do with.

They were ready now to jump in with both feet. They needed Uncle Jim and Blaine's help. Even though they both had a degree in business management to go with their design degrees, they were stumped by the manufacturing and production aspect of business. It was time to figure it out and the deadlines were looming. It was now or never. They could not find a suitable situation that was cost effective in the USA. They were determined to not outsource unless it was the only recourse. Uncle Jim would know what to do. Their first run of samples had been made in China.

This wasn't the only reason they were so excited to get to Florida, Matilda wanted to see Blaine very badly. It had only been a few days since he was with her, here in the loft. But she was going to announce to the family how crazy mad in love she was. They were tired of hiding their relationship. She couldn't stop thinking about him, and they had so much fun together. He was a hottie and she was already imagining a home and gorgeous babies with him. Magnolia tolerated her sister's obsession, but didn't have a boyfriend herself right now. She dated but nothing serious had happened yet with any of her suitors. She had gone out with Joshua to have dinner and see a movie, but so far that had remained a plutonic relationship.

Matilda told her once that she needed to lower her standards, that Prince Charming had died slaying the last dragon and she was going to be waiting forever. She only had eyes for her work and designs for the bags she was creating right now. You had to be sharp, pay attention and create items that a fashion conscious and well, dressed woman could not live without. These two brilliant, young women were going places; they just had no idea yet how far that was going to be.

The limo pulled up to the airline gate they needed, they tipped the driver and ran to catch their flight. They hated flying out of LaGuardia. It was always crowded, loud and frantic. Once on board the huge jet, and comfortably snuggled into their first class seats, they relaxed. They both had a book but just like when they were small children, they used each other as pillows and were out cold.

The stewardess walked up and down the aisle checking seatbelts and she stopped to smile at the two beautiful, sleeping girls. She had daughters and suddenly she was lonesome for home. The plane was chilly now so she quietly and gently laid a blanket over them and would check on them later for food and drinks.

Matilda's strawberry blonde hair fell over part of her face. It was very long and curly. She had her mother's green eyes and her father's olive skin tone. She was 5'6" and had the body of a model. Her sister Magnolia towered over her. She'd gotten their mother's height and she was 6'2". She had dark brown hair, wore it in a pageboy cut and she had gotten her Aunt Mimi's blue eyes. Her skin tone was pale like Pearl, but she tanned very easily. Magnolia had modeled as a young child and teen and so had Matilda, but they had become bored with that profession fairly quickly.

They were stunning when they dressed in high fashion. Truth be told, they would rather wear halter tops and cutoff jeans. But they lived in Chelsea, a neighborhood of Manhattan in the fashion district. People rarely dressed down in this business. So what an unspeakable relief to leave this stress, pressure and all the demands people were making on them behind for a few days.

They wanted family opinions on the names they were considering for their boutiques. That would be an announcement as well. They planned on throwing out their ideas and taking a family vote. These girls were smart beyond their years. They had traveled all over the world and let's not forget they had been raised by three generations of strong, intelligent and loving southern women.

Their mother, Grandmother Clarissa and Aunt Mimi had thrown a fit when they decided to leave the VanDeCourte estate in Savannah, Georgia and move to New York. It wasn't that they were afraid for the girls, they had seen the mean streets of New York City all their lives. It was a matter of them respecting their surroundings and being street smart. They knew how to conduct themselves and they were inseparable anyway. Their mother had lamented once, concerning either of them finding a husband. What would they do then? The family was closer to finding out the answer to that than they imagined.

The plane hit turbulence and it woke the sleeping beauties. The stewardess brought them both a cocktail and snacks. Eating could wait until they got there. Soon the pilot was telling everyone that they were making their approach to Panama City. This was going to be fun and they couldn't wait to get off this plane. Giggling, they hugged and waited.

Laughing, they struggled not to run as they headed to the baggage claim and their Mother and Aunt.

Chapter 9

DESTIN, FLORIDA

———⟫●⟪———

With their loaded backpacks slung over their shoulders, Minnie would have sworn it looked like the day these girls had gotten off a flight from Istanbul. We were laughing, crying and trading hugs. Pearl took each of her daughters and lifting them off the ground twirled in a circle, happier than she'd been in months.

We all headed to the parking lot and car. When the trunk opened the girls saw all the hooch and Magnolia said, "Damn! Mother what have you and Mimi been doing? That's an awful load of alcohol!"

Pearl laughed with her head thrown back and told her, "Always prepared my darling, now who's starving? How about we find a nice place to eat and discuss our game plan. Today will be girl's day out. Frankly, once the guys fly in tomorrow, we won't get to talk at all. Where do you want to go?"

The four of us were thinking. It was a beautiful sunny day and Minnie had an idea. She was grinning from ear to ear and told them, "I think I know where we should go. Give me the keys Pearl, I'll drive while you three gab and you will know where we're having lunch when we get there. It's only an hour drive. So, is everybody up for a small road trip?"

Squealing and laughing, we all piled into the car and I headed to Destin. Once we were underway Pearl had given me a smile and a knowing look. We knew most of the beaches on the Gulf Coast like the back of our hands. Our favorites were Destin and Santa Rosa. Today we were going to the old Crab Shack on the beach in Destin.

All through our lives Pearl and I had a five word code that we had never shared with anyone else. "Meet me at the park," meant that one of us had a crisis and we would drive to our spot no matter how far away we happened to be at the time.

There was a small stretch of beach in Destin that was owned by the State. It had no buildings, just sand, dunes, sea grass and privacy. We would meet there and console each other. Many times it was just our secret place away from family. We had gone there often, together or alone.

The three of them were chattering non-stop until they discovered where we were. Shouts of approval rang out and we proceeded to stuff ourselves with seafood. We decided a long walk was in order so we left the car where it was and walked behind the restaurant to the beach.

The water was the most magnificent shade of emerald green today. The light reflecting off the bottom allowed you to see every creature in the water, until you went out too far. The sugar sand was so white it was blinding and squeaked under your bare feet, like snow sometimes does. There was a nice breeze blowing and it was perfect.

The seagulls were awful here, they were pretty but such a nuisance. They reminded me of starving, begging dogs, desperate for a bite of anything. A lot of people loved them, I thought of them as garbage birds. The pelicans were my favorite and you just couldn't help loving the sand pipers. They were always busy eluding waves.

We started walking, each of us arm in arm. The kids soon tired of our poking along, and ran ahead of us. They were loudly trying to wrestle each other into the water. Splashing and screaming they were already thoroughly soaked. I had grabbed my camera before we ate and I already had some beautiful images of everyone. I let the girls take pictures of us then a kind elderly woman got an image of the four of us.

Their antics reminded me of Pearl and me at that age. Soon we had to sit down. We'd already walked more than three miles, I was pooped. Magnolia ran back and sat down facing us. Matilda did the same and breathlessly told her Mother, "I want to tell you something Mother." She took the time to catch her breath, smoothed her hair back from her face and grabbing Pearl's hands said, "I am madly, completely head over hills in love with Blaine Thompson."

We sat there waiting to see how Pearl would respond; I was smiling and winked at Magnolia. Pearl reached up and put Matilda's stray hair behind one ear, with a sigh she caressed her baby's cheek, saying, "Whatever makes you happy darling. Are you sure? Does it feel right from head to toe?"

"Matilda laughed and leaning forward to hug her said, "Oh yes Mother, he makes my heart sing and is always on my mind. I'm breathless and clumsy when he's around and he is all I dream of. I'm praying that he wants to marry me, start a home and have babies. It's all I've ever wanted. I want yours, Mimi's and Uncle Jim's blessing I know Blaine loves me, I can tell. I'm not naïve."

Thinking about it Pearl knew she could never deny her daughter's anything. She felt excited at the thought of a big wedding. Where would they live? What about Blaine's career? Surely the kid remembered that she and her sister were about to mass produce and sell their art and that was going to take up most of their time. There were just so many things to consider. Pearl only said, "I'm happy, really. I'm thinking that if you two could handle a long engagement, we could have a party at the plantation when it's done and announce your wedding plans to the world. If you can wait two years, you could even get married there. Whatever you want is what we will make happen. I'm thrilled for you darling. There's nothing on earth quite as exquisite as your first true love."

We headed back to the car and set out for Seaside. Pearl was driving and lost in thought. I found a rock station and turned the radio up. We danced in our seats all the way there. The old song by the Dixie Cups came on and we sang along to "Going to the Chapel" and roared with laughter.

After unloading and getting the girls settled, we had a light dinner with a very good wine. They loved the cottage and were happy we were so far from the tourists. They might stroll by occasionally, but none came near the house. It was private even with all the visitors in the area.

We tidied up and decided the kids would take my bed tonight, I'd be on the couch and then it would all change tomorrow night with Jim, Blaine and Joshua here. Pearl came out of the bedroom with her hand behind her back. She looked at all three of us and said, "I'm going to share something with you and if you tell Uncle Jim, I'll never forgive you."

She raised the joint, lighting it and taking a deep hit, she then passed it to Matilda who did the same. The kids laughed and Matilda said, "Uh, I have a news flash for you Mother. We've always known you and Mimi smoke pot and we do too. The only person that doesn't is Uncle Jim."

We all laughed then coughed and laughed some more. We laid the joint in the ashtray, grabbed blankets and ran to the beach to catch the sunset. It was a breathtaking sight. We came back, washed our sandy feet at the spigot by the back door and finally got settled to go to sleep.

I was exhausted and the old, soft couch was large enough that I could stretch out. I fell asleep right away.

I dreamed that Matilda and Blaine were holding a beautiful shinning baby. I realized that I was looking down on them instead of being with them. It was a dark haired, smiling boy.

Chapter 10

REUNION AT SEASIDE, FLORIDA

———◄•►———

We got up early and were gathered around the dining room table eating breakfast and chatting when we heard a car pull into the driveway. Looking at each other, we ran to a window and the girls were at the front door and outside before Jim and Blaine had even killed the engine.

Blaine was the first one out and he scooped Matilda up, kissing and embracing her like they'd been apart for years. Laughing we helped Jim with the bags. At the last minute a frantic client had convinced Joshua to meet with him and once again he was the one left behind to hold down the fort at the law firm.

Once we were inside and the decibel level was such that we could hear ourselves, we insisted they have a bite to eat. We got them fed and everyone was trying to talk at once.

Jim spoke first saying, "This is a beautiful, old place. How did you ever get in at the height of tourist season?"

Pearl laughed and told him, "I think it's less desirable because it's so old and too far away from downtown for most vacationers. That is actually why I asked for this particular cottage, it has such charm and no one is on top of us."

I came out of the kitchen and added, "We were expecting you to call us from the airport, but I'm thrilled you're here so early. We have a lot of business to discuss with both of you and we'd like to make a run out to The Oaks, then we have a special evening planned."

Blaine was out back with the girls, checking out the rental property. He was smiling and had an arm around Matilda's shoulder. Magnolia was pointing at something further down the beach and they all were laughing loudly.

Jim sipped the coffee Pearl handed him and said, "Do you mind if I change into more comfortable clothing? I am overdressed for sand and salt and I would like a stroll on the beach. Let's leave the youngsters and take a walk shall we?"

Pearl and I went and changed in her room, throwing on our swim suits and sarongs. Jim came out of the other bedroom and we took one look at him and doubled over.

Pearl told him, "I'm wondering what your clients would think of your Hawaiian shirt and Bermuda shorts Jim, and I'm sure they have never seen you wearing flip flops."

He stood up perfectly straight with a hand over his heart and said, "When in Rome!"

Howling we all headed out back for a walk. It was a sunny, perfect morning and not a cloud in the sky. We walked for about a mile and sat to catch our breath.

He sat between us and said, "Well, I have a feeling that we are going to need the very detailed pre-nuptial agreement that I prepared some time ago and possibly very soon. Blaine has confided in me and I believe he has serious ideas about Matilda."

Pearl spoke up, "Yes, she informed us yesterday that she's head over heels in love. I think you're right. Minnie and I were worried about all the legal aspects involved if she were to marry him. It's not that we don't love and trust Blaine, but there's too much at stake if their relationship was ever compromised and we figured you would know what to do with all of that Jim."

He stared out at the water thinking and said, "It shouldn't be a problem. I plan to leave him everything in my estate; he will be set up for life even without Matilda's fortune. You two need to decide when we're going to sit these youngsters down and make them take a hard look at just how large their holdings are. I know we've been waiting but it needs to be done soon. None of us is getting any younger and well, what if something happened to one or all of us, we need to move forward."

We agreed with him and Pearl added,

"I was thinking last evening. If Matilda and Blaine decided to get married I would be thrilled to give them part of the plantation estate to build on. But they need to wait anyway. There's too much going on right now and they don't need to rush. I plan to have The Oaks remodeled in two years or less. We should probably let them tell us what they have planned and go from there."

Jim and I agreed. The kids walked up and sat around us on the sand. They had all gotten into their swimsuits and it was amazing to see how beautiful and voluptuous the girls were in bikinis. Blaine had large, low slung swim trunks on and he was tall, tanned and in very good shape. He and Matilda actually did make a gorgeous couple. I was proud of them all.

Everyone was laughing and talking, excited for the next part of today's adventures. I sat thinking, it was so typical of Jim to be planning ahead and I wasn't the least bit surprised that he already had a contract filed away for when either of the girls announced they were getting married. Nothing got by him, especially where business was involved.

Pearl spoke up, "Why don't we all get cleaned up, pack a picnic lunch and head out to The Oaks. Jim, I hope you and Blaine thought to bring boots if you plan to walk the property. It's terribly overgrown and all of us girls need to wear sneakers."

We all took turns in the shower and after a couple of hours we loaded the trunk with the gear the men would change into once we got there. We threw in a cooler filled with ice and drinks and an old, wicker picnic basket from the cottage. There was enough food for twice the head count. I loaded the bags of sage last and we were ready to go. The only other thing I took was my camera. Pearl was driving and the radio was turned low so we could talk. The adults took the front seat and the girls had Blaine between them in the back seat.

When we finally turned into the driveway of the old plantation, the tree service was already there and busy. We stopped and got out, stretching and looking around. There were four huge white trucks with green logos on the sides. They read Braxton Tree Farm. Below the companies name it said, Sales, Service and Maintenance Since 1943. I noticed a gentleman walking toward us with a clipboard in his hand. He introduced himself as Edward Braxton, owner of the family run business. We all shook hands and he and Pearl walked a few feet ahead.

He had four trucks lined up on the left side of the long driveway with the large baskets raised into the limbs. We heard the saws slicing through wood, and there were already heaps of branches and twigs piling up near each one. They had made a lot of progress on one side and Pearl asked if they minded if we drove around and up to the house. He informed us that they would be here and busy for at least two weeks just focusing on the driveway. He planned to work around the house next and then move back into the oak orchard.

His plan was to have as much cleaned up as he could before the different crews that Pearl would hire arrived. She was extremely pleased that she had made a wise choice in calling Edward. She had found the company online and had made all the arrangements with a phone call and hefty deposit. She had asked him to take the most minimal amount off the old trees and to leave as much Spanish moss as they could. That was an unusual request to him considering most people called him to remove the invasive plant.

She asked if he could check and treat them all for disease and decide if they needed tree food. Mr. Braxton had told her he knew the property and what a large undertaking it would be, but insisted they could handle it with no problems. He was thrilled that someone was finally going to bring the old place back to life and was glad she had called them. He had a radio clipped to his belt and spoke into it. They stopped working long enough for us to carefully and slowly drive around them and the piles of limbs.

The kids were speechless at the enormity of the old oak orchard, and commented on how spooky the Spanish moss made it look. I didn't say a word, Pearl was watching me. We would get the girls involved in the cleansing before we did anything else. Nothing that their mother or I did surprised them much anyway.

Pearl parked in the same spot as before and we all piled out.

Matilda spoke first saying, "Oh, my God, Mother! You sure have your work cut out for you. This place is huge and a mess."

Laughing Pearl told her, "There will be so many men working around here soon; it won't be long before the place will be alive with activity."

She turned to the left and pointed back the way we'd come in.

"I plan to put a two bedroom trailer somewhere over there and will be living here until every last detail is finished."

She hadn't told anyone those plans except for me and Jim and the kids mouths were on the ground in shock. Pearl just let them think about things and the guys went behind the car, gearing up to walk the property.

They had long sleeve shirts with elastic cuffs and loose pants with elastic around the ankles. This was to keep ticks from getting inside their clothing. Magnolia was spraying each of them from head to toe with insect repellent and they both had baseball caps on.

Pearl had given Jim a copy of an aerial map and she informed him that when the surveyors showed up they were going to mark the boundaries of the entire property with new stakes and flagging. Her intention was to put up some type of fencing around the entire estate and post new no trespassing signs She was waiting to decide on which contractor she would use and would discuss the fencing with him.

I went to where the guys were standing and told Blaine, "I'd feel a lot better if one of you had a handgun. Did you think to bring one Jim? I left mine at the apartment in New Orleans."

Blaine patted his chest and told her, "I have one right here. I'm sure I won't need it but better safe than sorry."

The men said they would be back for lunch and took off behind the house chatting and looking at the map. We women decided to take a closer look inside the house. That was when I spoke up and asked, "I brought some sage and white feathers. I want you two to help your mom and I cleanse the exterior of the house first then we can go in. Would you mind?"

Matilda said, "I've heard of that Mimi. It's supposed to bring peace and wellbeing to a place. I would love to join in the prayer. Here, let me help you get the sage lit."

When the four of us had our bundle of sage burning, the smell was pungent but extremely pleasant. We decided our prayer would be,

"In the name of the Father, the Son and the Holy Spirit, May Peace be with you."

We walked around the entire exterior of the house gently waving the heavy sage smoke away from us with the feather we each held, chanting our prayer. We went up on the porch and picked up the two large flashlights and squirmed through the door. Matilda was the only one who carried the sage indoors and she fanned the smoke as she followed behind us.

There was so much more we were noticing today. We told the girls there might be stinging bugs and snakes and told them to watch where they put their hands and feet. Pearl was noticing the beautiful wood moldings and trims everywhere. When we saw the huge fireplace and mantle we stopped to stare. It was a carved, marble masterpiece that had to have been imported. It was a work of art. We stayed together and made our way up the old, filthy staircase. It had been a beauty in its day and was the focal point of the massive entrance hall. None of the boards were missing but we still climbed slowly and carefully. The upstairs had about the same amount of funk as downstairs. I was very lightheaded and sweating, but tried to hide it. We just walked from room to room trying to memorize what we saw. Finally we headed back out front and Pearl grabbed her notebook and began jotting notes. When she wasn't sure about one room or the other, we tried to help her fill in the blanks. It was a relief to breath fresh air and my nausea wasn't as bad out here. I averted my gaze away from the orchard and could feel it pulling at us. I sensed that something did not want us here.

Blaine and Jim came around the corner and went to the car to change. We told them lunch was served and we gathered on the steps. Pearl was handing out paper plates, napkins and plastic forks. She sat out the sandwiches, potato salad, fruit salad, and napkins. We drank from cans and bottles. Nobody said much during lunch. Pearl was the first to comment saying,

"I'm anxious to find out how much of the interior can be salvaged. It amazes me that so much of the woodwork is intact."

Jim spoke up saying, "It will be a lot of work dear, but I can imagine the place rebuilt and full of life."

Magnolia and Matilda were wandering around, and I had been taking a lot of pictures.

Blaine cleaned up his lunch mess and said, "We only walked a couple of miles and it seems the place is on high enough ground. There was a creek and the only way to cover all the property would be on a four wheeler or find the original access roads. There were three graveyards and I think you should get someone to clear the entire place with a bush hog. Then you can safely walk about and see what's back there. We had to walk around a few spots that are so overgrown you'd need a machete to get through."

Jim agreed saying, "it's a magnificent spread Pearl and has so much potential. You could do whatever you want out here and your building permits should be in any day. Have you chosen a contractor yet?"

Pearl was putting everything back in the trunk and said, "I'm very close to making that decision. I was waiting on the permits. How about we head back to Seaside and have some fun while we're together. I have a better idea of what I will be up against now and the gnats are getting bad. I want to let you all know how much I appreciate you being here and I'm thrilled you get to be in on the project from the beginning."

We piled into the car and I turned to look back at the old, sad house. There was a small, black child in the upstairs window waving at me as we drove away. It looked like a little girl that was five or six years old. I smiled and turned my back on the place. I did not bother to ask if anyone else had seen her. We carefully drove past the Braxton men and machinery and headed back to Seaside.

Once we had showered and changed I wanted to decorate for the evening's festivities. Pearl volunteered to help me and we decided to string the paper lanterns first. I took the two poles attached to the tattered volley ball net out back and removed the dry, rotted strings. I walked ten or twelve feet out into the yard and planted them evenly forming a square off the back of the house. We put the strings of lights inside the colorful, paper lanterns and went all the way around the square. Pearl plugged it in and we were delighted with the results. Tonight the lanterns would throw multicolored, soft light around us and it would be beautiful.

Jim was checking the condition of the old grill. He told us it just needed a good cleaning. We found a rake in an outside shed and raked all the debris and sand spurs out of the lantern area. There was an old portable fire pit and we cleaned it, filled it with driftwood and put that in the middle. We scrounged all the chairs we could find and it was looking like a party. We accomplished all this without the kids knowing.

Pearl set up a fully stocked bar inside with fruit garnishes, and we had even gotten the little paper umbrellas just for fun. I had lost track of the kids, Pearl said they were still out swimming and collecting shells.

I went inside and fixed the three of us cocktails and brought them outside to Jim and Pearl. We took a break and sat watching the tourists strolling on the beach and sipped our drinks.

Jim said, "I propose a toast, here's to family, love and new beginnings."

We both touched our glasses to his and threw back our drinks. We were feeling very festive when the kids came back. In fact, we were on our third cocktail when they made their first ones. We cooked hot dogs and hamburgers. Jim was the grill master and the kids put on some fun music. It was perfect.

As soon as the sun had set Pearl and I sneaked in and plugged in the outdoor lights. The girls squealed with delight when they saw the paper lanterns light up. The evening breeze had them swaying gently. Before we knew it the music was louder and we were all dancing around the fire pit like a bunch of native savages. I was getting a lot of it on my camera. We laughed, danced and drank until we were exhausted. Jim bowed out first and we gave him his own room. I was staying with Pearl,

Magnolia was on the couch and Blaine put the sleeping bags together and made a pallet on the floor for him and Matilda.

I would give the girls their gifts in the morning and was hoping that no one had to rush away. It had been a perfect day with my family. I fell asleep as soon as my head hit the pillow.

I dreamed Blaine and Matilda were on the beach somewhere. He was down on one knee with a black velvet box in his right hand, looking up at her expectantly.

Chapter 11

MATILDA'S WISH COMES TRUE

Blaine couldn't sleep. He had big plans for this morning. No one was awake, it was still dark out. They had decided it was the last day they could spend in Florida. Everyone had to head back to their homes and business.

He lay on the floor next to Matilda, watching her sleep. He also had an eye on the clock above the TV stand. He reached over and gently shook her awake and before she could protest he motioned for her to be quiet. He whispered in her ear, "Get up and come with me, don't wake anyone up."

They both crept from the living room to the back door of the cottage and once outside she looked up at him sleepily. He leaned down and opened the cooler that he had cleaned out last night. Pulling a folded quilt out of it, he stood and draped it around Matilda's shoulders and taking her hand led her down the beach and away from the house.

It would be sunrise soon and the special place he'd found yesterday was about five minutes from here. He'd pretended to need a jog on the beach but was really looking for the perfect spot. He put an arm around her and said, "I want to show you something, it's not far, come on."

She laughed leaning into his warm body and they nearly ran until he stopped and said, "Its right over here."

He realized she hadn't grabbed her sandals so he scooped her up and carried her over a very large sand dune. Below them was a natural depression in the sand. It formed a deep bowl and was protected from the wind and passersby. No one could bother them unless from the air. He gently took the quilt from her shoulders and spread it out on the sand. She lay on the quilt in the semi darkness and smiled. She now noticed a small Styrofoam cooler and realized he had this planned.

He sank down on the quilt. He smoothed her hair from her face and said, "Matilda, I love you more than I can say. I'm not very good at romance but I'll try very hard to always please you. He rose up on one knee. She sat up also. He fumbled in his swim trunks pocket and pulled out a small, black velvet box.

The sun was just starting to peek over the horizon. Just as the first rays of light spread over them he said, "Matilda Ann, will you marry me?" He held his breath waiting for her response.

She already had tears streaming down her cheeks, reaching up and throwing her arms around his neck she said, "Yes, Blaine, I will marry you!"

He took the diamond and ruby ring from the box and slid it on her finger. It was a two karat diamond, cut square with beveled edges; on each side were graduated oblong ruby baguettes. The band was platinum gold.

She drew in her breath and told him, "Oh Blaine, it's the most beautiful ring I've ever had, thank you."

She pulled him down next to her on the quilt and they made love, slowly and more passionately than they ever had. While the waves crashed and the sea breezes cooled their sweat, they lay back and just held each other. Matilda was weeping again, but only because she was overcome with joy. After a few moments he sat up and they put their clothes back on. He lifted the cooler lid and brought out a small bottle of very expensive champagne, a bottle of orange juice and two glasses. He poured each of them a glass and they sat there and drank their mimosas watching the sunrise. He was ecstatic; it went just like he planned. He still had a couple of surprises for her their last day here with the family. They were beaming at each other.

Knowing that the others were early risers they decided to head back and announce their engagement. Matilda grabbed and folded the quilt and Blaine carried the cooler. They chatted as they walked, excited and full of hope and plans for their future. It would be good, Blaine had promised her.

Jim was up and sitting at the dining table. He had just put on the coffee and was organizing the papers that required attention and signatures. Everyone was beginning to stir and take turns in the bathroom getting ready for the day.

Matilda walked up to the table and hugging Jim's neck said, "Good morning Uncle Jim."

He looked up over his glasses at her and smiling said, "Good morning to you my dear, looks like you've already been on the beach."

Laughing she blushed and said, "We watched the sunrise; it's beautiful out early in the morning before it gets too hot."

She looked up at Blaine and shook her head. She had the ring spun to the inside of her palm, they would tell everyone at the same time. Right now Jim needed Blaine's attention with all the contracts and paperwork. Matilda was the first to fix three cups of coffee and giving the guys theirs, she went outside with her cup to sit in the sun.

I had gotten up still feeling a bit drunk and headed for the coffee where Pearl was pouring the last two cups and making another pot. She looked pretty hung over also. I knew what I needed and reached for the brandy. I added a splash to mine and Pearl's cup. We both went to join Matilda out back.

Magnolia was just getting up. Jim looked up as we passed and said, "I need for everyone to stay close to the house for the next couple of hours and be available as I call you. When we're done with business I suggest we go into town where I would like to buy everyone breakfast."

We agreed and left him to his work. Matilda was careful to keep her left hand tight around her coffee mug. We chatted and waited for Jim to call us. The breeze was heavenly and it was supposed to get pretty warm today. I was happy that none of us had to cook breakfast and clean the kitchen. I didn't even want to think about everybody leaving tomorrow. But Wednesday was the latest anyone but Pearl could be here. She was lucky there were no new reservations on the cottage until Friday. I would need to go back to New Orleans with Jim and Blaine. Magnolia and Matilda were going back to New York and had their hands full.

Magnolia joined us girls outside. She looked very hung over and said, "Mimi, Uncle Jim needs you."

Thanking her I went in and sat next to Jim and the folder with the ranch papers waiting for my signature.

When I was done he put them in his briefcase and said that we would run into the Missoula courthouse and get everything updated there. I winced slightly, having forgotten I had to be at the ranch one last time. He asked me to send in Magnolia and Matilda and I went back outside with a freshly spiked coffee. The girls went inside and sat with him, discussing their manufacturing options.

He looked at them both and said, "Blaine and I have crunched your numbers every way conceivable. I am not seeing where it would benefit either of you to do business with anyone other than the company that took care of your prototypes. It won't be cost effective otherwise and your price point would be too high. Meaning, they did a beautiful job based on the samples you have and your product is pricy to begin with. If you attempt to produce and manufacture in the USA, you will have to charge entirely too much per piece. You will also be missing out on a vast market. I will make sure Blaine files your copyrights and I need a name you intend to use for the business and boutiques. What have you decided for that?"

The girls looked at each other and Matilda said, "We think we've decided to open two accessory boutiques and showcase each of our products. We were thinking we should have one in New York and need to decide on an exact location on the west coast. The name we want is Maggie & Tillie."

Jim thought about it and said, "I've been looking over these business plans you worked up with Blaine. I'm going to go with equal partnership and ownership. If at any time one or both of you want to go it alone, we can restructure the entire plan. It won't be a problem. Blaine and Joshua will handle all the books for both stores. You will give them every receipt, and nothing will transpire without them or me approving it. You should get with your mother and get an idea of how you want the store to look and what other vendors you will bring in. We're going to be very busy for the next several months and you two need to stay focused. Don't fret, we won't let you stumble. We are a phone call away. I feel very confident that you are going to be extremely successful."

Magnolia hugged his neck and said, "Thanks Uncle Jim. We already have lists of products we want to bring in and the vendors are waiting on us to order. The only thing we haven't done is decide on the two pieces of real estate we'll need and the location. We're brainstorming it right now."

Smiling Jim said, "Very well, send your mother in will you, I'm starving and I know everyone needs some food. We're almost done here."

They got fresh coffee, went outside and told Pearl she was wanted in the dining room. She pulled out a chair next to Jim and he slid papers in front of her asking, "Now, what name will you call your business Pearl, we need to get you squared away and where do you want to set up your accounts?"

Pearl had already decided and said, "My business name will be VanDeCourte Designs and I will operate out of the plantation. I already have plans for an office separate from the main house. And I believe it would be most beneficial to a local banker in Seaside if I keep the money here."

She smiled and signed the papers then moved to the kitchen for more coffee. Jim closed his briefcase and was relieved to have these details out of the way. They were going to be buried in paperwork soon. He knew each of them would need to hire assistants and office staff. But it was enough for now.

He went out back and said, "Who's hungry?"

Everybody was finally feeling better and starved. They gathered in the house finding their shoes and combed their hair to go out to eat. Matilda cleared her throat and grabbing Blaine's hand asked for everyone's attention. She was trying not to blubber and holding out her left hand to show the beautiful ring said, "This morning Blaine asked me to marry him and I said yes!"

The room erupted. Pearl put both hands over her mouth and then started crying. I was tearing up myself and after lots of hugs and congratulations we finally got loaded into the car and headed for food. We chose a place that had outside seating and once we got our orders in we grabbed Matilda's hand and drooled over the beautiful ring.

Pearl asked Blaine, "How did you know she's always wanted a ruby ring?"

Blaine blushed and said, "I overheard her talking about one to Magnolia. I had been looking for the perfect design since."

I laughed and said, "You did good Blaine. A man needs to have good taste to keep a woman happy. Just remember to keep it simple. Those are often the most appreciated gestures. I want to congratulate you both and hope you're always happy. Take care of each other and be patient and kind. The smallest things mean the most."

Jim stood with his water glass and said, "A toast to Blaine and Matilda, may they live long and prosper, and a few babies wouldn't hurt our feelings either!"

We laughed, touched our glasses and yelled, "Here, here!"

It was a relaxing day and we wandered around shopping and talking. Blaine was acting nervous and kept looking at his watch. He looked up at the sound of an advertisement plane out over the beach and hurriedly stated, "I'd like to be the grill master today and I'm cooking at 1:45 this afternoon, be there or be square."

Magnolia punched him in the arm and told him not to be so corny. We grabbed cool drinks and drove back to the cottage. Jim took a nap and I went in Pearl's room to get the gifts I had wrapped for the girls last night. Handing them each a bag, Pearl and I sat with our drinks waiting for their reaction to the southwestern jewelry. They loved it and after hugging us they proceeded to each wear the whole set.

Matilda said they had something for us too and went to her backpack in the corner of the living room. She came back with a large, flat jewel case and handed it to me. It was embossed leather and the gold lettering said Maggie & Tillie. I opened the silver clasp and was speechless. The set of jewelry was done in silver and lightweight porcelain with very thin silver wire. The flowers were orchids and it was a work of art. I felt like I was holding live, miniature orchids in my hand. I thanked Matilda with a hug and Magnolia handed me a bag with the same color scheme. It was amazing. It was a very small, dressy clutch with sterling silver chain and hardware on top. It was encrusted with crystals and the pattern was the orchid. I couldn't believe how well they had done. I told them both how proud I was and was near tears.

Pearl's set was very delicate gardenias. They were so lifelike we expected them to smell. The matching bag was unbelievable. I took loads of photos and promised to be a walking testimonial for both of them.

The day was slipping away from us. We were relaxing in the living room, chatting and passing the beautiful gifts around when Blaine yelled from out back, "Can a guy get a little help out here?"

We laughed and headed out back. Jim was up from his nap and joined us. We saw that the grill was on fire and not much else. Just as we started to question him we heard the plane. He started out by grinning and was now laughing hard. He faced us and threw his arms up to the sky.

We looked up at the small plane. It was towing a very long banner that was straining in the wind. In bold, block letters it read, "Matilda said yes! We're officially engaged."

We laughed and clapped, hooting and hollering. It was the sweetest thing I'd seen in a long while. Matilda was beside herself and beaming with pride. He went back in and started working on the burgers. Jim and he had their heads together so I knew something else was up.

I fixed each of us cocktails and we gathered under the paper lanterns for our last evening together. After dinner, us girls went inside and put on light sweats and grabbed light jackets, it was cool this evening. We'd been instructed not to come out until we were called.

We sat chatting and about a half an hour later the sun had finally set. Blaine and Jim called us to come outside and asked us to be seated. They had long sticks that were burning on the end; they took a flashlight and ran toward the edge of the yard.

The fireworks started exploding with huge bursts of color and it was so spectacular and loud, tourists from a mile away had walked closer and sat watching. The kid had sneaked away today and bought a trunk load of fireworks and cannons. The grand finale even had a rocket that exploded in red hearts. I looked over at Matilda; she had a smile I would never forget.

We drank, laughed, and danced under the Florida moon. The whole week had been perfect and my heart was full.

I went in early and took pills for a pounding headache. I feel asleep right away.

I dreamed the plantation was completed and we were all soaking up the sun in a huge, blue swimming pool. There was faint singing and whoever it was seemed to be very happy too.

Chapter 12

New Orleans, Louisiana

Pearl managed to get us herded into the car and our bags loaded. We arrived at the Panama City airport with time to spare. Matilda and Magnolia had to catch a flight back to LaGuardia and our jet was waiting for me, Jim and Blaine.

After tearful hugs and promises to call soon, we got situated in the jet and prepared for takeoff. I sat in the back and the guys were in the middle with their heads down working. Once the pilots said we could leave our seats, I put on coffee. I tapped on the cockpit door and both men welcomed the brew. I settled back into my seat and checked my cell phone. I was irritated that the New Orleans medical center kept leaving urgent messages. I finally decided to hear one, and then deleted the rest. It was from the Dr. I'd seen before we left.

"Mrs. Bonet, this is Dr. McCleary. It is urgent that you contact our office at your earliest convenience. Thank you."

I couldn't help wonder why. I must have really high cholesterol or something. I decided to shut them up by calling from the plane and scheduling an appointment at 10:30 this morning. My car was at the office so it wouldn't take long to go straight there when we got in. I leaned my head back and napped the rest of the short flight.

The limo was waiting for us at our hangar and we headed to Jim's office. I told him I'd call later to see if he was interested in dinner and left for my appointment.

I was having a really good day until the Dr. came back into the small examination room and told me I was going to die.

Well, not in those words exactly. I was aware of him speaking for at least another half hour. I could see his lips moving, but it all just sounded like white noise. There were a couple of comments that got through, "Sorry, there's nothing we can do." And "You could have one to five years, with symptoms worsening toward the end."

I remember stopping at the desk, paying the bill, and the nurse handing me a thick envelope. The next thing I knew I was sitting in my car, in the medical center parking lot, which was blissfully shaded, here under the huge oak tree.

This was the most favored and rarely available parking spot. I looked around and saw no one else outside at the moment, the birds were singing, squirrels were chattering and the insects were droning away. Normal is all I could think. Except that now I wasn't sure anything in my life would ever be normal again.

As soon as I felt able to drive, I headed back to the apartment and made a cup of tea. The large envelope sat on my dining table right in front of me, but I left it there. I needed to think about things before I opened it. My first very clear thought was how could I possibly tell my sister and nieces? It seemed like all we had done for the last ten years was bury our families. I realized that I had a splitting headache and got up for some pills. Should I even tell anyone? And what about all the plans I had made? I still had so many places to go, and always, people to see. Everything I did was spontaneous, spur of the moment. Unless others needed to know in advance for travel or scheduled events, it had always seemed more exciting that way. I knew I wouldn't live forever, but five years wasn't much.

The strangest part of this was how I felt physically, which was fine. I stayed in shape by swimming and walking and had not felt anything other than tired and headaches once in a while. Finishing my tea, I realized the pills had kicked in and being aggravated, I decided to just go to bed. I needed a nap anyway and my head was buzzing. I was in disbelief.

I woke up hours later. Looking at the bedside clock it was already 4:30 in the afternoon. I got up, washed my face and called Jim.

"Hello dear, are you feeling rested and ready to grab some dinner? We've been working steady and I am ready for a break."

I tried to keep my voice neutral and said, "Would you mind terribly if I made us dinner here at the apartment Jim? I have something urgent I need to discuss."

He didn't hesitate to reply, "That sounds wonderful. Are you alright? You sound very distressed."

I assured him it could wait until dinner. We agreed on six this evening and I got dressed and walked to the French Market to get something to prepare. There were loads of fresh shrimp and I grabbed enough for us and would leave a large package for Ima and Bo. I grabbed some interesting bread and ingredients for a salad and walked back to the apartment.

I preheated the deep fryer and threw together the rest of the meal. Everything was almost ready when I heard the courtyard gate click shut. The intercom buzzed and Jim announced he was coming up. I heard him slowly climbing the narrow stairs. It was hard on old legs and it was the only part of this place that none of us liked. He came in and I was trying very hard to keep my shit together.

He raised his nose in the kitchen and said, "I smell fried shrimp! How lovely, I'm famished and feel like I need a vacation after our time with the gang. It's getting harder for me to keep up with all of you and to be honest I am exhausted."

I hugged him and told him we were ready to eat. I pulled the toasted bread from the oven and sat across from him and told him, "I don't know how to begin. I've been given the most horrible news today."

He laid his napkin on his lap and looked at me. "Tell me Minerva, take your time."

He could see I was tearing up and struggling to find the words. I wiped my face with my napkin and continued, "It seems I am going to die. I've been informed that they found a microscopic parasite in my blood and it's killing me. This thing is extremely rare and deadly. They gave me a bottle of pills on my last visit. Apparently they were so excited that I wasn't dead already, they've added two more pills. They were convinced that they might have made a breakthrough in their research. I am one of two people who haven't died within two weeks of discovering this thing in our blood and the survival rate up until now has been a whopping one percent. It's all there in the envelope. I haven't read it."

I couldn't be strong any longer. I began to sob and Jim got up and walked over laying his arm around my shoulder. He said with a shaky voice, "There has to be something we can do Minerva, we'll do whatever we have to and see you through this, maybe they've made a mistake"

"I don't think so. There was a parasitology expert, a research scientist from the CDC and the local team that gathered them together when they found this in my blood samples. I only agreed to leave more blood and to take their pills. They insisted on a follow up in a week. They sat right there and told me they couldn't believe I was alive." I saw the look of horror on Jim's tired face and wished I hadn't told him.

"Jim you have to promise me you won't breathe a word of this to the family. I need time to think and if the doctors are right, I have five years left at best. The last victim was on these same drugs and lived that long. Most people who get this damn thing die in seven to fourteen days. I have already decided that I will not agree to be their lab monkey. I don't want to tell Pearl and the kids. It would literally change their lives along with mine. I'm not telling anyone else until I can't hide it any longer."

Jim thought about that. He wiped tears from his eyes and said, "Well if that isn't a son of a bitch, nothing is. I am sorry dear. What can I do? Just tell me, and I'll do anything you want. We can travel abroad and try to find a cure elsewhere."

I thanked him and mentioned that he would see the folly in that after reading the two inches of data the Centers for Disease Control had sent home with me.

We took our iced tea and moved out onto the balcony. It was a hot, humid evening with just the slightest breeze. I smelled the stench of the night life on Bourbon Street. It was overpowering for a few moments. The mix of aromas was turning my stomach and I grimaced. There were throngs of rowdy tourists, partying and drunk.

Some asshole looked up and seeing me yelled, "Show us your tits!"

In one swift motion, Jim being totally disgusted proceeded to lean out over the balcony railing and dumped his tumbler of iced tea on the guy's head. He took my elbow and led me back inside while the drunk man screamed loudly in protest.

Once back inside and seated in the living room he asked, "Did the doctors have information concerning how you contracted this parasite?"

I sighed, "They know that much about it. Seems it lives in water. Mainly things like poorly maintained pools and a whole list of other scenarios all involving water. They asked me where I'd traveled. I laughed and told them the better question was where I had not traveled."

We both sat there thinking about the enormity of my announcement. Jim rose and told me, "If you wish, I could speak to the research team on your behalf and get some direction on what they have in mind regarding treatments and testing. Would that make you feel any better? I'm not sure I am willing to take this at face value."

I agreed with him. "I know Jim, I feel the same way, and I don't want to believe any of it. Thank you for joining me for dinner and I hope you will forgive me for laying this on you. I just had to tell someone and it really is hard to believe."

He walked over to me, hugged me and rubbing my back, he let me cry.

"You call me the minute you need me, I'll be here for you. Why don't we take a day to rest before we head to Montana, I think we both need it. The oil baron can wait a couple more days to get into the ranch. Does that sound agreeable dear?"

I agreed and walked him downstairs. I had gone in the bedroom before we headed down. I had a joint in my pants pocket and as soon as he pulled away, I sat in the courtyard and smoked every last bit of it. I sat there thinking and wondered how this could be happening to me.

Later after I'd taken the pills, I dragged myself to bed and passed out.

I dreamed it was an abnormally bright day. There were so many cars at the cemetery; they lined the street on both sides. There were hundreds of people gathered around a gravesite. They were all looking at me, lying in a beautiful coffin of white satin. There were mountains of flowers and I floated above it all. The singing was a little louder and I still didn't know where that was coming from.

Chapter 13

BEAUMONT, TEXAS

———⇒✦⇐———

Jim was in his office early today because he had spent the night in the small, back bedroom. As soon as Mrs. Parker got settled in the front he leaned in and instructed her to clear his schedule for at least three days. He intended to escort Minnie back to Montana where they would file the documents for the ranch in the Missoula courthouse. They would meet with Wanda and give her the contract and all the copies of the updated deeds. He would then take Minnie out to the ranch, pick up her few bags the moving company had left there and fly to Beaumont, Texas to get her settled into her new home at Lancaster Estates.

He had taken the heavy manila envelope from the medical center with him last evening. He locked himself in his office reading every word. He had gone online and done more research, hoping for a better understanding of this microscopic monster named Primary Amoebic Meningoencephalitis. He had ended up in the small bathroom where he had dry heaves. He washed his face and had sat there crying. He felt his age and realized he was helpless to save his precious Minnie. She had been right, no one survived this parasite. He drank several shots of brandy then curled up in the single bed. He was exhausted and passed out immediately.

As soon as he realized the sun was up, he grabbed his briefcase and went home. He wanted to shower and rest before their trip. He was picking Minnie up at 11:30 this morning. He needed to be strong for her, but he felt weak and beaten. He lay on the couch and drifted off remembering all the exotic trips they'd been on and wondered why she was the only one who had come in contact with this invasive, amoebic killer.

Minnie was packed and ready to go. She left a beautiful package and card on the dining table for Ima. She took her coffee out to the apartment balcony. It was early enough to be relatively quiet and there was a strong breeze ruffling the palm fronds behind her. There was a faint scent of the courtyard blooms and she breathed it in. She wondered how much time she actually had. So far the medication had not had any side effects that she'd noticed. The headaches disappeared within moments of swallowing the three large pills. That was a relief. What would come next? She hoped she would not end up being a helpless, sick burden on her family.

The one thing she was very sure of was that she would savor every second of the life she had left. Matilda was engaged and she prayed she would be able to see the kids married. She had been asked to be a bridesmaid and had accepted. Pearl would be the maid of honor and Jim would give Matilda's hand to Blaine. Joshua would be the best man.

It took all her strength to not be furious. She knew this wasn't something she would blame on God. Her faith would get her through this nightmare and besides these pills, it was all she had. She was tormented by her decision to not tell Pearl. She could only pray that at some point she would be forgiven and that the family would understand her reasons for keeping it secret.

She had an hour before Jim would be here so she got busy making sure the apartment was spotless. She didn't want to leave Ima with any chores; just a pretty, cheerful gift, the card and the shrimp in the freezer. She made up her mind to not shed another tear as she rammed the vacuum into the corner of the couch; no water bug was going to rule her actions. She would be as strong as she could, stay positive and try to be happy. She had a whole new chapter in her life about to unfold and she fully intended to meet it head on with her eyes wide open. The lights in the smaller bedroom began flickering as she entered. Turning off the noisy, antique vacuum, she spoke to the empty room angrily, "You just mind your own business, I'm not afraid of you and besides don't you need to move on? After all, you are the one that's dead!"

She turned her back on the room and headed down the hall. The door behind her suddenly slammed shut with such force a photo fell off the wall. She just laughed and kept walking.

Jim buzzed the intercom and I told him I'd be right there and to not climb the stairs. We got through the lunch hour traffic and were finally settled on the plane. We sat closer together this trip and Jim was quieter than usual, both of us read and napped the entire flight.

It was a sunny, blue sky day in Montana. We took a taxi to town and the courthouse. Wanda insisted on having a late lunch so we met her at the café across the street from her office. She was on cloud nine and Jim gave her all the documents and copies. Both of them continued to talk but I couldn't have told you a single word they'd said. I knew that Wanda's life had changed overnight with the commission she'd take from the sale. Finally Jim laid his hand over mine and explained to the realtor that we needed to grab the remaining personal articles from the cabin then had a flight to catch.

The driver left us at the front steps of the log house. I stood looking around at the place, feeling sentimental about being here again, I told Jim, "There are only two totes I need to grab and then we can go."

We let ourselves in and I could see that not only had the moving company been here but the cleaning crew had polished each and every log. The house literally glowed in the afternoon light. I smiled and thought of my darling husband. When I was a child G-Ma had told me that earthly matters didn't concern those that had departed, but I wanted to think Graham thought I was making a good decision. We walked through the entire house and ended up outside on the front deck. We sat on the top stoop waiting for the taxi.

Jim took my hand and said, "We'll arrive in Beaumont late. I have us booked at the Hilton for this evening. I wanted you to be able to see the place during the day. It really is quite beautiful and meticulously landscaped. I think you will be pleased, I hope you are anyway. If for one solitary instant you become unhappy, we will of course move to plan B."

Laughing I told him, "I'm not sure what plan B is but I'm sure it will be ok there. Beaumont is a pretty cool place with a lot of amazing sights and activities. Think of the photographic possibilities alone. Remind me to call Pearl would you? I'm anxious to see how things are progressing with her trailer."

Jim agreed and the taxi pulled up. As we drove away I never looked back. We went to the airport and headed for Texas.

Jim had a limo take us to the Hilton and after a wonderful dinner, we headed to our rooms for the night.

He kissed my cheek and said, "Goodnight love, do not forget to call your sister. I will meet you downstairs in the morning and we'll find some breakfast."

I gave him a long, tight hug and kissing his cheek told him goodnight.

I called Pearl and she answered on the first ring.

"How are you Minnie? You're going to think I've lost my mind, but I own the cottage here on the beach now. I got so frustrated with the property manager, I asked for the owner information and they were happy to sell. I only did it so that I wouldn't have to go back to Savannah and everyone is welcome to use it of course."

I laughed saying, "Pearl, nothing you do surprises me. What did Jim say about that?"

She laughed and said, "He put Blaine in charge. Jim seemed extremely distracted when we spoke."

I quickly changed the subject and asked, "I wondered how long it would take to get your trailer out there. How is that going anyway?"

"Well, they poured the concrete two days ago. The contractor and I decided to lay a nice foundation, better for insurance purposes and he had a brilliant idea. It's more of a small prefab home than it is a trailer. He mentioned that if we put it in the most suitable location, it could be used for guests, clients and him once I have moved into the main house. He asked if I would rent to him so he'd be closer to the project."

I laughed and said, "It sounds to me like he wants to be closer all right. And who is this mystery contractor anyway?"

She laughed and said, "The Company is McCord & Sons Construction. They operate out of Pensacola. The owner now is Jarrod. He's the third generation to head the outfit and Blaine and I investigated them until we were blue in the face. They are squeaky clean, never a lawsuit, rave reviews and I'm very pleased. We clicked and he's not the least bit intimidated by a woman with blue prints. He's not half bad to look at either, wait until you see him and his two sons."

Laughing I said, "I'm sorry to miss all of this, let me get situated in the new house, get my bearings and I'll come back and resume the photos of your progress. I especially want to see this Jarrod character. What did he think of the old mansion anyway?"

"He is extremely focused and wants to jack up the whole house to repair and rebuild the basement. He found a lot of rotten concrete and says we have to start there. Right now they are focused on the manufactured home for me and getting the septic tank in, they're drilling for water and running new electric. I've added a row of portable bathrooms and picnic tables for the workers and they are crawling all over the place."

I yawned and looked at the clock and told her, "Well, I'm happy for you and I'll be back as soon as I can. We're going to my new place first thing in the morning so I should let you go and get some sleep. Good talking to you and it was a special week in Seaside for sure, I love you, keep in touch." She said goodnight and we hung up.

I put my pajamas on and called room service for a bottle of champagne and some snacks. It was only ten o'clock and the bubbly would help me sleep. I turned off the lights and took a glass and plate out onto the small private balcony of this room. The view was gorgeous, the town was lit up and I could hear the night life of Beaumont in full swing. The breeze was heavenly considering the humidity was so bad this late. I let it blow my hair around and sat there getting deliciously drunk all by myself.

I could smell the river below me and thought I detected salt in the air. I did not believe in living with regret or guilt. So I finished off the bottle and tried not to fall off the balcony on my way back into the room. When I finally crawled into the luxurious king sized bed, I fell asleep with a goofy grin on my face.

I dreamed I was sitting in a small fishing boat with an outboard motor. I was slowly navigating an overgrown bayou and it was teaming with huge alligators.

Chapter 14

JARROD WILLIAM McCORD

———◆———

It was 4:30 in the morning. I was already showered, dressed and bent over my drafting table in the office. I stared out the window toward the dark gulf, sipping my coffee, and wondered about the green eyed beauty that was now my boss. She had presented me with the largest job we'd taken on in the last few years.

My property here was an inheritance from my father. The beautiful, three story home sat right on the gulf in a large, quite cove. The front of the house faced the green, thick lawn that extended right down to the water. There was a two stall boathouse, pier and dock. I owned several hundred acres of prime coastal real estate. The land was covered in long needle pines, magnolias and live oaks. It was secluded and private and you had to drive a mile off the blacktop to see the house. I had a massive shop and storage area to one side. There were neatly arranged rows of trucks, several flatbed trailers and smaller equipment. They sat on pavement and all were spotlessly clean. I had my own sunken gas supply and truck wash. The business operated from here and I had no plans to change the set up. My two sons had families and homes in Pensacola. I was a few miles out of town and preferred it that way.

I looked down at the photographs of the old Beauford plantation and couldn't believe how fortunate I was to get this bid. I worried my figures were high and this woman had laughed and said our estimate came in well under what she was expecting the costs to be. She had been very close with the time range as well. It might take two, hard years to accomplish the renovation. I remembered she mentioned having a couple of degrees, but I should have paid closer attention. She had done her homework. She was adamant about what she wanted. And she was incredibly smart.

Beside the fact that she was drop dead gorgeous, she had a patient and friendly disposition. She was extremely easy to get along with and all the research and planning she had already done would make our job easier. This place would be a masterpiece when completed and could only do great things for both our future business endeavors.

I had done some checking on her background and frankly, I needed reassurance she actually had the financial chops to pull this off. She wasn't concerned with any of the expenditures as I was presenting them. She had excitedly informed me that she had supplies being delivered from all over the world. There would be shipments of priceless stained glass and French doors arriving soon. She had commissioned an artist in Europe. She told me she had semi loads of imported tile on the way. She had already purchased four 10' X 14' sheds that we delivered for her. These were for the supplies that would start arriving and piling up. She was organized to a fault and knew exactly what she wanted. I loved a woman with a plan.

Her young lawyer was a different matter. What was his name? Had it been Blake or Brian? I reached beneath the aerial map and pulled out one of the forms the young man had given me. There was a business card stapled to the corner. It read Jim McGregor and Blaine Thompson. The kid was all business, came back and forth in a jet they owned. I think she had introduced him as one of her attorneys and future son in law. It made me feel better to know these people had money and there shouldn't be any delays waiting on funding.

The one bit of information that kept rolling around in my head was her being a widow. I was three years into my divorced life. My marriage had been a miserable failure, except for our two awesome sons. Belinda had taken her whoring and drinking to a new level and I couldn't take it anymore. She was a dick tease to me, her husband, but I was the only one in the county she didn't screw. The kids were grown and I deserved better.

I had served her the divorce papers while she was in the county jail for disorderly conduct and assault on an officer. She'd gotten shitfaced drunk and was doing a striptease in one of the seedy beer joints that she frequented. The bartender called the cops. She had attacked him and the young officer with one of her spike heeled, whore shoes. That's what I called them anyway. Once she slipped those on her feet, she only had one thing in mind. I had shoved the papers at her through the bars of the jail; she shrieked and screamed like I had shot her in the head. The sheriff ran back and I walked out.

I haven't talked to her since and I feel like I am a new man. Her scandalous behavior had not hurt our family run business. Truth be told, everyone felt sorry for me and my boys; they knew my wife was a tramp and headed for a bad end. I was determined to remove the sympathy from the equation; I needed their business not their opinions of a drunken floosy.

I was sitting here watching the sun come up and thinking about driving back and forth. It was already taking almost three workable hours out of my day. This morning I made the decision to put my largest camper on one of the company trucks and stay out on the site for a few days at a time. I would make sure Mrs. VanDeCourte didn't mind. I hoped she wouldn't. I needed every hour to bring this job in on schedule.

Today Adam, my oldest was already headed out there with one of our flatbeds. He had loaded two bush hogs and a garden tiller. Mrs. VanDeCourte was ready to landscape around the prefab. He and his brother Phillip would begin clearing the property. Adam had strolled part of the land while I was busy with blue prints. He came back telling us he had discovered a huge pecan orchard. The owner had been thrilled and decided to go ahead with the clearing since we were waiting on the concrete trucks. The first load had gone in the foundation for the prefab. There were going to be trucks in and out for several days while we got the huge basement in order.

There was a second contract already. This woman had purchased one of the oldest beach cottages in Seaside. She had asked me if I would bring it back to life and I couldn't refuse. I was picturing a nice stay on the beach while we took care of that place. Just my luck it would happen in December. I didn't need to get ahead of where my focus needed to be anyway.

I was amazed that the majority of termite damage was in the exterior walls of the old mansion. These tenacious bugs had been gnawing the wood around here for decades. Maybe they had devoured the outbuildings first. Whatever the reason, the interior had huge amounts of salvageable wood. I was excited for this whole project. The Mrs. was open to suggestions and improvements. I had studied her blue prints and saw the beauty in the changes she'd planned.

I was driving among the hung over and brain dead tourists, headed out to the site and reached to turn on the radio. I needed a distraction. People drove like idiots here. All of us locals blamed the tourists, but any one of us could drive just as poorly. It was a challenge during the three worst parts of the day, morning, lunch and dinner rush hours added with confused outsiders made for white knuckle driving at times.

I pulled into the long, tree lined driveway and was impressed by how much the tree service had done. It already looked manicured and all our vehicles, so far, had gotten through with room to spare. There was still too much Spanish moss everywhere. When I had questioned the Braxton fellow, he told me the boss lady wanted it left on all the trees, I thought the stuff was a nuisance and there was quite a market for the moss. It was one thing besides whippoorwills that I thought was creepy.

It was time to get busy and there she was, standing with papers in her hand, showing the truck driver where to put the first load of tiles. Of course they were to be separated by type, color and count. I wasn't going to get involved in that but I would ask if she had any coffee.

Chapter 15

LANCASTER ESTATES

———❖———

I found Jim in the lobby, seated and reading the morning paper. I walked up and was relieved to see that he looked rested and refreshed. He smiled when he saw me.

"Good morning Minerva. I hope you slept well, Are you ready to eat?"

I hugged his neck telling him, "I slept like a rock and I'm starved." I was happy he couldn't see how hung over I actually was. We headed into the café and had a filling breakfast.

He sat back, sipping his coffee and asked me, "Well, are you ready to see your new home?"

I laughed and told him, "Yes, in fact I woke up feeling so good that I'm excited. This town sure has grown up. I hardly recognize the place any longer."

He sat his cup down, motioning to the waiter for a check and said, "Your sister purchased the beach house we stayed in did she tell you?"

I shook my head and put my napkin across my plate. "Yes, she couldn't bear going back to Savannah right now.

It is inevitable and she needs to make amends with Clarissa. She's getting on in years and there isn't a sole left to take care of her. I'm going to try to convince Pearl to go back and talk to her mother-in-law. She deserves the respect of having the truth and Pearl told me she is signing her home there on the estate back over to her, she doesn't want it and has never felt it was hers to begin with. I know why Clarissa is so pissed about the plantation. You know as well as I that Gregory left several million dollars with the deed to help cover the renovation. That's the stick up Clarissa's ass."

Jim sat thinking about this for a moment and said, "Well, I do agree that Pearl should be forthright with the woman. Otherwise it isn't fair to let her mother-in-law sit and wonder about her wellbeing. She is probably beside herself with worry and deserves the truth. I know that at times she can be difficult, but there are so few family members left. Shall we go dear?"

We left the café and went outside where it was dreadfully humid and hot. We took a limo from the Hilton and the driver turned on a side street past the center of town. We were heading east now and the sign said Magnolia Street. I noticed a super grocery mart where we turned, maybe that would be close to me. After several miles I saw a reddish, wooden, security fence along the left side of the road. There were magnolia trees lining this entire stretch all the way to the gate we approached. Some were still blooming and piles of spent blossoms littered the ground. The car slowly rolled up to a five foot block with a small roof. This contained a numbered key pad with a card slide and beside that was a phone.

Jim lowered his window, picked up the phone and simply stated, "Jim McGregor here, escorting Mrs. Minerva Bonet."

The huge, iron gates swung inward. Jim pointed to a small house to our left and said, "There is your new place dear, near the front and no neighbors on one side, as per your request."

I laughed and said, "I don't know how you do it Jim. We would be absolutely lost without you. Thank you for all of this."

He just patted my hand and said, "Sometimes I think I don't do enough Minerva. I want to help all of you for as long as I am able. It gives me a reason to always be right in the middle of everything. What would my life be without you?"

I looped my arm through his as we drove around the circular driveway and pulled up right in front of the main building.

He was correct; the place was clean as a pin and beautiful. There were so many blooming trees, shrubs and flowers, I could get lost in these gardens. We climbed the stairs and the covered porch was nicely decorated with sets of wicker furniture. They had lovely, plush, floral cushions. There were bent cane rockers placed here and there and the ceiling fans whirred above us moving the humid air around. There were window boxes full of flowers and large colorful planters in between the pillars.

Jim held my elbow as we entered the large double doors. This whole building was huge. The reception area was a place where residents could relax. There were ceiling to floor, flat fountains on two of the walls that sounded like waterfalls. The decorators had filled every corner with palms and overflowing planters that were bursting with color. There were several groups of people seated at small tables placed here and there around the room, playing cards and quietly chatting and laughing. They looked to be anywhere from their mid-fifties to seventy something. There were at least two that looked older than dirt. They didn't pay much attention to us as we walked past them.

I noticed the large desk toward the back of the room. It had been placed in front of a wide hall that had rooms on either side all the way back to two doors that reminded me of a school house gym. I was looking around as Jim began to introduce me to the pretty, black woman that manned the desk.

"Minerva, this is Miss Evelyn Pepper."

She looked us over and said, "Welcome and I am pleased to meet you Mrs. Bonet. I hope you will be comfortable and happy here. You have free run of the place and this information here will give you all the other details you need. Your extra house and car keys are in there too. I'm always available if you need anything." She then reached forward with a large manila envelope which I took and handed to Jim.

She had shoulder length, styled hair and reading glasses on the tip of her nose. She looked to be in her late fifties or early sixties and was dressed to the nines. Her dress was pink and could barely contain her ample boobs. The belt at the waist was straining but the full skirt below took your eye away from that detail. She was about 5'6" or so and when she smiled one gold capped tooth in front shone brightly. I had a hard time trying not to stare.

We turned and went out the way we had come in, no one was on the porch, and it really was too hot. We got back in the limo and drove to my new house. We dug the keys for the front door out of the envelope and Jim let us in. The driver brought my bags and went back to the limo to wait.

The little house was nice, it had a good sized, covered front porch and there, already hanging, was my porch swing. I knew at a glance that I would be planting flowers to cheer up the front. Jim got the door open and I took one step inside and stopped. I was fighting tears and said, "Oh Jim, it's lovely with my things here and perfect."

He smiled and we walked from room to room. There were boxes of my personal items stacked in each one. I was happy to have the extra bedroom for guests. I went into the kitchen and was thrilled to have a huge pantry. All the appliances were modern and new.

The living room was very spacious and had a wide bay window with all of my beautiful orchids. Someone had watered them with ice cubes just like I'd asked and they seemed as happy as plants could be, soaking up the morning sun. My huge couch was here and the other pieces I'd brought from the ranch. I hugged Jim thanking him again.

He put the envelope on the dining table and said, "I have kept my room at the Hilton for one more evening. I'm going to get some rest and wanted to be close your first night here. Call me if you need me, otherwise I will see you in the morning before I fly back to New Orleans. I'll let you absorb your new surroundings and you may want to explore. It's a lovely place dear; you've made a good choice."

I walked him back outside and there was my Toyota from the ranch sitting outside the garage. Hugging and kissing him goodbye, I watched him drive away. For a few moments I felt a little disoriented. I went inside and to the sliding glass doors off the dining room to look out back.

There was a spacious and tiled area that was covered and had an overhead fan. The houses sat close to each other but the back areas were separated by a tall security fence. I looked around the corner and there was a ten to fifteen foot space between mine and the next place. The ground here was covered with small, round rocks and I guessed it was to keep the ground from getting muddy when it rained and water poured off the roofs.

There were no neighbors on one side, just lawn, flower beds and flowering shrubs all the way to the property security fence and those majestic, old magnolia trees. I walked over and couldn't resist reaching up and plucking off a fairly fresh bloom. The smell was wonderful and familiar. I took it inside with the intention of placing it in a shallow container of water and would let it perfume the dining area.

I wandered around and went in the bedroom where I found the several boxes of photos I'd packed. The movers had put my birds' eye maple furniture in the largest bedroom. I went back into the living room and saw the large, framed pictures leaning against one wall.

I didn't know where to start or what to do with myself. I went in the kitchen and began unpacking and organizing in here first. I found my tea kettle and made tea. I was sitting at the dining table where I dumped the contents of the envelope. There was too much to read at once but sorting through it I found the information on the golf carts and laid that aside.

This place had spectacular amenities. There was a nine hole golf course, tennis courts, bocce ball and shuffle board courts, and horseshoe pits in a large sandy area that shared half with a volley ball set up.

In the main building where I had checked in, one side was a recreation room then a large cafeteria. The other side of the hall had a pharmacy with a gift shop and the rest of that room was a well-stocked convenience store. At the end of the wide hallway and through the metal doors was an Olympic sized swimming pool with several hot tubs on one side. The pool area had glass walls and looked like a tropical paradise in the brochures. It was stunning and beautiful and I wanted to see if it lived up to the pictures.

I was excited to see they rented and sold the golf carts to residents. It would prove to be the easiest way to navigate the expansive grounds and they had wide, paved paths all over the place for this reason. I finished my tea and went in search of the pro shop to buy one. I walked slowly admiring all the landscaping and stopped to really look at the fountain in the circular driveway. It was dolphins caught in mid leap and one had water spouting from its mouth. I noticed the bottom of the fountain was lined in coins. I wondered how many of those wishes had ever come true.

I followed a path around the main building and saw an herb garden thriving outside a screen door, which I thought had to be the kitchen. It smelled like lunchtime and I was getting hungry. There was another ornate fountain in back of the building and it was much more detailed. It was an underwater scene and the water trickled from several fish mouths over coral and seaweed. It was beautiful and I wondered where they'd gotten it.

Finally I saw a lot of activity about a block from the main headquarters. A young man approached me asking if I needed any assistance. Looking at his name tag I saw he was Brent. I told him what I wanted and we chose a brand new, red cart. It had a top, a large basket behind the seat and the heavy duty extension cord was included. I was tickled to death and went for a spin. This could prove to be fun and I hoped I wouldn't get fat and lazy using it.

It was shocking how far and wide the grounds went. I hadn't noticed where the brochures said how many acres there was but you could spend all day just navigating the paths. I went all the way to the back boundary and parked at the edge of the manicured lawn. It was densely wooded and full of undergrowth and vines. This area went straight back as far as I could see and I could smell decay, and a swamp or something. That would be the first place I would explore. I could see footpaths, so it might be worth a walk to get some excellent photographs.

Right now I needed to get something to eat. I parked behind the main building, pocketed my cart keys and went in through the pool area. It was even more beautiful than the picture. It was so inviting I felt like diving in right away. There were several residents being assisted in the hot tubs. It seemed some of the people lad their nurses or aids living with them. I went past them and through the metal doors.

The cafeteria had glass walls here in the hallway and inside it was bright and cheerful. The smells of simmering food had me drooling and I looked around. Inside the door were two coolers. The shelves of one were full of pitchers and bottled drinks. It looked like assorted juices with the fruit sliced and floating on top to indicate the flavor. The other cooler was nothing but deserts. There were cakes, pies and small bowls of puddings and Jell-O in every color of the rainbow. I looked down and there was a chalkboard listing the lunch fare. You could have fish, shrimp or crab cakes and the side dishes were collard greens, squash casserole or sweet potato fries. I filled my plate and went back to the area with fountain drinks and thankfully an iced tea dispenser. I went to turn around to find a booth and almost dropped my food.

There in front of me was a tiny, old woman dressed oddly. She was barely five feet tall and had on a blonde wig that sat a little crookedly and loosely on her small head. Her blouse was too small and her skirt too long. She looked up at me with pale blue eyes and smiled like an angel. There seemed to be a bright light all around her and I wondered if I was the only one that could see this.

She spoke in a soft, quiet voice and said, "You're new here, they call me Maddy." She seemed unusually pleased with herself, as if it was an accomplishment to remember her own name.

I thought she was precious and said, "Hello, I am new here. Moved in today, my friends call me Minnie, and I'm pleased to meet you."

She wondered out of the cafeteria and I sat down facing the back windows so that I could look outside while I ate. I wondered what was wrong with the woman and why someone would let her leave her home dressed that way. I heard other voices and activities behind me but chose to ignore them.

I was watching a young man outside with a weed eater. He was carefully going around the flower beds and he was almost too pretty to be a man. He happened to glance over at the window and I just smiled. Maybe he was one of the resident gardeners.

I cleared my table and went out back to my new golf cart. I parked it behind my car and would have to remember to plug it in after each use as instructed. I went inside and sat on my familiar couch.

The weather was changing and fast. Now that I lived on the gulf coast again I would have to get back in the habit of watching the forecast. It was hurricane season and it paid to keep an eye on things. I turned on the television and stretched out on the couch.

I woke up hours later and the thunder and lightning was fierce. Soon it would be pouring buckets and the wind was whipping the trees every which way. I got up and turned on some lights. I didn't feel up to any unpacking so I took my pills, got into my pajamas and smoked a joint I had in my bag. I was feeling slightly overwhelmed and had enough for one day.

I didn't feel like making the bed so I went back to the couch with my favorite pillow and a comfy throw. I fell asleep again.

I dreamed there was a class five hurricane moving in. Everything was floating on the rising tide. My couch swirled and bobbed on the current. I was being pulled out to sea and no one could hear my pleas for help.

Chapter 16

GETTING SETTLED IN TEXAS

My phone woke me up and I wasn't sure where the hell I was for several seconds. It was Jim, he was on his way over here to say goodbye. The storm from last night had moved out of the area and it was sunny, extremely humid and hot. I knew we were roughly thirty miles from the gulf, but there was plenty of water nearby. I would have to get acclimated again; it had been a while since I lived with high humidity.

I put some coffee on and heard a faint tapping on the patio slider. Without even thinking of how I must look, I went to the door and there was the young man I'd seen yesterday with the weed eater. I opened the door and invited him in.

He was holding a very large, hanging basket of flowers that he sat down before he came in. The first thing I noticed about him was his eyes. They were a shade of translucent emerald. They reminded me of tropical lagoons I'd seen. He looked to be about Magnolia's height. He was thin but very muscular. His hair was so dark and shiny, it reminded me of a raven's wing when the sun hits it just right. His skin was the color of milk chocolate and he was dressed in an aqua tank top and tan Capri, cargo pants. He wore a silver St. Christopher medal around his neck.

I ran a hand through my bed head and asked, "I have fresh coffee. Can I get you some?" He smiled shyly and nodded yes. I fixed us both a cup and served him. He added cream and sipped daintily.

So he was shy and I tried to wake up and engage him in conversation. I asked, "What's your name? Are you the gardener here?"

He sat his cup down and looking around my place said, "My name is Pepe' and yes, I am the head gardener. You are Mrs. Bonet, correct?"

I wondered how he knew this already. I supposed that on a slow day a new arrival was big news. I smiled and said, "Please call me Minnie. I might need your advice on where the closest nursery is; I want to get some plants and gardening supplies."

He smiled and said, "There is one outside of town about three miles. I could go with you to help if you wish. We can use the truck."

I thought he was being very generous but appreciated it. He was a soft spoken young man with an accent I couldn't place There was a knock at my front door and I excused myself.

"Come in Jim, I'd like you to meet Pepe', our head gardener."

Jim smiled and walking over to shake his hand said, "Yes, we've met. How are you doing today young man?"

The kid sipped his coffee and putting the cup down, he stood, shook Jim's hand and moved to the back door.

He looked at us both and said, "I am very well sir, I brought Miss Minnie a basket for her front porch. I'll get back to work and leave you two. Have a good day." He left through the sliding door and was taking the basket of flowers around front.

I fixed Jim some coffee the way he liked it and said, "Hmm, he's a friendly kid, cute too." I looked at Jim's face and he looked like he had slept well. I was still feeling bad about dropping my bombshell on him. He drank half of the coffee, took his cup to the kitchen and came to hug me.

"I have to get back dear, are you going to be ok?"

I hugged him and walked him out front to the waiting car and said, "Yes, I will be fine and if anything comes up, I'll call you."

He stood thinking for a moment then said, "There was one thing in the information from your doctor that I think we need to address. It's a questionnaire done on a weekly basis. It charts changes in how you feel on the medication they gave you. If doing this small thing can improve your chances, I want you to fill it out then email it to me and I will take it to the medical center. Will you do this for me?"

I didn't think twice just told him, "Yes, that's easy enough. If it doesn't help me maybe the next person will benefit. Have a nice flight home and give everyone there my love. I'll let you know the moment I am on the move again. I want to go back to the plantation and might spend a week or so with Pearl. Have the girls chosen the locations of their boutiques yet?"

He smiled and said, "I gave them a deadline; they're scrambling right now to make a decision. I'll keep you posted. Good bye Dear."

He kissed my forehead and hugged me. I always hated when people I love left me. I felt selfish and needy. That's what Clarissa always said also, but no one ever cried when she left.

I organized the bathroom, linen closet, made my bed and took a shower. By noon I had everything unpacked but the living room. I was getting hungry and realized I had to go shopping. I grabbed my keys and went to the market on the corner. It took me three trips to lug it all back inside and finally I got everything put away.

I wanted to hang the pictures today and grabbed the large, old family portrait I intended to put over the big couch. I slowly wiped it with Windex remembering the day the picture was taken.

The photographer was from DeFuniak Springs. He was short and fat and had only sprigs of hair left on an almost bald head. It was hot as hell that day on Choctawhatchee Bay. There were five generations of us on the porch of our parent's old homestead. He tried in vain to bring order to the rowdy group and kept nervously mopping his brow with a white hankie. G-Ma was laughing in her low, gravelly voice and refused to relinquish the corncob pipe she always smoked. Great grandpa had a well-worn, silver flask full of moonshine that he kept sneaking out. Mama and Daddy were fussing at everyone and Pearl was trying to soothe two hot babies. One was only a year old and the other was two. They were miserable and Grandpa kept yelling, asking who had shit their pants. Great grandma kept telling him to quit cussing. Our great-great grandparents sat stoically, not really sure of what was happening. Matilda had a full diaper adding to her discontent. Gregory tried to help with the babies but mostly looked mortified to be a part of this family. It was a circus and Graham and I were laughing and stoned to the bone. Just as the photographer said smile, someone would stand, bend to cough or the babies were squirming. His tripod was trying to sink into the sand and I feared he would have a nervous breakdown. The photo in my hand was the one successful proof he'd presented the family. The next time one of the relatives had called him, he had refused the job. Pearl and I have told this story so many times, it always makes us hysterical. The portrait is one of my prized possessions. I hung it over the couch and it is comforting to see all their faces there.

I decided to go for a swim. I rode over in my cart and went in the back door. No one was in the pool area so I took off my outer clothing, adjusted my swimsuit and slid into the pool. It was heated but not excessively. It was heaven right here in Texas. I swam laps until I was beat. I got dressed in the shower room and went into the cafeteria to see what was on the menu today. The chalk board listed; fried chicken, fried chicken livers, and the side dishes were mashed potatoes and gravy, field peas with speckled butterbeans and the squash casserole from yesterday. I wondered if the cooks here read minds. They prepared all my favorite southern dishes.

Today there was activity at the grill. A very tall and wide black man stood there. He had on a chef's hat and white apron. He looked like a body builder and he was extremely handsome. When I looked up and noticed him, he looked down very quickly. I continued down the line of hot, aromatic food, filling my plate. Today I sat facing the glass windows, looking out into the hall. Mostly so I wouldn't have to look at the guy at the grill. I could feel his eyes on my back but resisted the urge to turn around.

Just as I was getting done I heard an awful racket coming toward the cafeteria. It sounded like a huge metallic rattle and clunk. There in the doorway was an extremely tall, older man. He had ear buds with wires dangling into a small, square box that was in his top shirt pocket.

I looked up and he noticed me sitting there and he yelled, "Hello there! I'm William Everly Stamford the Third!" He went to move his outrageously tall walker forward and farted long and loudly. His walker seemed to have risers on the top to accommodate his height. He was yelling at the top of his lungs.

"Jesus," was all I muttered.

He rattled and clanked over to the food and I made a very hasty exit. So far I had met a tiny, crazy woman, a deaf, farting giant and the beautiful gardener. I wasn't going to stay through dinner to see who else may come in.

When I got back to the house my phone was ringing. It was my sister. "Hello Pearl, how is the old house coming along?"

"You won't believe it, but today when they started jacking the house up off the foundation the wood seemed to be screaming. I mean, it sounded like nails on a blackboard or worse and all of us had to cover our ears. It was really strange!"

I didn't laugh at all, but said, "Well, I hope you want some company. I plan to come back very soon. I want you and the kids to come here too. It's a pretty cool place so far. Magnolia needs to meet the gardener, the kid is gorgeous."

Pearl laughed and we talked for another hour. There was a lot going on and it was good to hear her voice. I promised to see her soon and hung up.

I thought I'd go find Pepe' and see if he could get away and take me to the nursery. I found him in his tool shed eating lunch. I knocked on the doorjamb and said, "Anybody home?"

He told me to come in and was excited to go. We took the truck and headed to the nursery.

I filled the bed of the pick-up with gardenias, bougainvilleas, a strawberry pot and colorful flowers for that. I found lattice and had them cut a large enough piece for the privacy wall out back. I grabbed three different colored trumpet flowers and potting soil. It was a good start. We headed back and Pepe' helped me unload everything. We left the larger plants near each spot where I'd plant them tomorrow. I tried to tip the kid and he looked hurt.

Looking down he said, "This made me happy Miss Minnie. I will come tomorrow and help with the planting."

With that said he disappeared around the house. I liked the kid, there was something about him. I finished hanging all the framed pictures, put all the photo discs in shelves and was done unpacking. It was a lot of fun to sit and look at slide shows of the pictures I'd taken and much less bulky than the piles of photo albums I'd already filled over the years. My other belongings had gone into storage in Montana. At some point I'd have to move it all again, but to where, I wasn't sure.

Looking at the clock, I had plenty of time for a nature hike at the back of the property. I changed into long pants and tucked them into the tall, leather boots I always wore if there might be snakes. They were men's shoes and looked like army boots. I only cared that a snake's sharp fangs couldn't pierce the thick, tough leather. I hosed myself down with insect repellent, took the cart and headed out back.

I had my favorite pocket knife and cut a fat limb off the closest low hanging tree. I realized my handgun was at home and I hoped I wouldn't need it. I took off on the visible path. My footfalls were muffled by the leaves on top of the sand. I almost ran into a huge spider web across the path. I took several photos of this and some blooming vines close to the trail. I used the stick to clear the web and continued on.

It was terribly overgrown back here but I kept going. The funky smell was more pronounced now; I was getting close to the source of the dank odor. The trail opened up and the light was dappled through the thick canopy of trees and vines. I followed the narrow path all the way back to where there was an old, rickety fence with a gate. I was trying to be very quiet, there was a sand hill crane standing on one leg preening its feathers and I captured some amazing shots of the tall bird.

Just beyond the gate there was an old, rotten and moss covered pier. Beside it was a small fishing boat with an outboard motor. I had a moment of incredibly strong deja'vu, but let that go. I wondered if that chef came back here to get the fish on his menu. This was a bayou and to the left of the far bank, I saw a very large alligator sunning himself. I held my breath and zoomed in to get some great shots. It was the largest reptile I'd ever seen that wasn't in a cage. He rolled his thick eyelids back and looked at me like I would be very tasty. I stayed behind the fence. The water was dark and ominous and I wondered where it went.

Just as I turned around to go back I ran face first into a man walking toward me. I gasped loudly and stopped. He was my height and not bad looking. He had short, greying hair under the fabric hat he wore. It had fishing lures attached and he wore a creel around his neck and over one shoulder. The basket hung to one side and he held his fishing pole in his right hand.

I waited for him to speak and he just stared at me, which made me nervous. I spoke first wanting to get away as quickly as possible. "Sorry about that, I need to look where I'm going, excuse me."

He didn't budge and now I was feeling bullied. He finally spoke in a low and flat tone, "Guess we both do, I'm Alex Jackson and I live here. I don't recall seeing you around."

I tried to keep the fear out of my voice and said, "I just moved here and I like to explore with my camera. Nice to meet you, name's Minerva."

He looked around but only with his eyes and said, "You want to be careful back here, never know what you'll run into."

I took offense at this remark and could see he was now looking at my attire and trying not to smile. I smoothed my hair back and said, "I'll keep that in mind." I moved around him on the path and tried not to sprint back the way I'd come.

Once I was back in my house and changed I wondered what Mr. Jackson's story was. I couldn't decide which of us had been more surprised. He seemed to be around my age or younger. I thought he had acted strange but busied myself looking at the pictures I'd taken, trying to calm my nerves.

It was dinner time and I ate at home. I took some cold tea out back to watch the sunset and noticed humming birds flitting around, chasing bugs that I couldn't see. There was so much moisture in the evening air; it felt like you could cut it with a knife. The lightning bugs were everywhere blinking and moving about. They had to be my favorite insect. Their soft, green glow dotted the whole area and I'd never seen so many. It was getting late and after a shower, I got into my pajamas and turned on the television. Stretching out on the couch I thought about the kids. They would love a visit here and there were lots of things to do. I was getting drowsy and moved to my wonderful bed. It didn't take long for me to pass out and I'd fallen asleep to the soft whirring sound of the ceiling fan and air conditioning humming in the background.

I dreamed about Pearl and the old plantation. I had a feeling in the pit of my stomach. All I could think was impending doom. All hell was about to break loose and I feared Pearl was in trouble. I knew the spiritual natives were not only restless, they were pissed. There was faint singing and I sleepily raised my head to see if I had left the TV on. I was out again in seconds

Chapter 17

PEPE' MARCOS BARBOSA

———❦———

Pepe' sat atop the riding mower lost in thought. He had mowed this acreage so many times he was on auto pilot, only having to turn the wheel this way or that every now and then. As he navigated an area where he needed to slow down around the concrete curb, he stopped. He stared off into the trees thinking. With a sharp pain of longing and remorse, he got it. Miss Minerva reminded him of his mother. Not in their physical looks but in her open and loving personality.

His mother had been a small and kind beauty. She had stunning green eyes and long, black hair that hung almost to her waist. He hadn't been able to save her. He missed her terribly.

He had been born on a stormy night in South America. The rain beat against the tin roof of the shabby structure where the mid wife swabbed the forehead of Angelina Barbosa, his mother. She cried out as the labor broke her back and the thunder crashed overhead. Her newborn son was cleaned, swaddled in a tattered blanket and laid across her chest. Angelina just lay there with tears streaming down her cheeks, grateful that her baby boy was perfect and beautiful.

They lived in Sao Paolo, in one of Brazil's worst slums. Hardship was all they knew. As Pepe' grew, he came to understand that the frantic game of hide and seek he and his mother often played was more than a game. Without a very good hiding spot, his father would find him. Carlos was a bastard with a heavy fist and bad temper. He was a low life, always drunk and on one drug or another, and he had always blamed Angelina and Pepe' for his failed and sorry life.

It enraged the man to see this woman and child together. Their beauty and goodness drove him mad and he lashed out. The last time he had corrected them both, the pathetic boy had tried to defend his mother. They both received a beating that they barely survived.

Pepe' was fed up and wanted a better life for him and Angelina. His father came and went. Work was scarce and Pepe' did whatever odd jobs he could beg from people to keep them fed. Right now he was sixteen years old. His mother lay in the cot of a neighbor's shanty, hanging on for dear life. The monster had ravaged her while Pepe' was working and it had been too much. She was literally broken to pieces and barely breathing with a punctured lung and many broken ribs. They couldn't afford doctors or hospitals. She was receiving care from her kindly neighbor who knew what a demon the man was.

The neighbor's son had found Pepe' and brought him home, telling him it was urgent. His mother was slipping away and was asking for him. He knelt down next to her and smoothed her hair from her forehead. He kissed her cheek gently and whispered. His mother reached beneath her blanket and placed two pieces of jewelry in his hand. She told him to use these to get far away. He did not want to accept that she was dying. She assured him she loved him and they would be together again someday. She told him goodbye and was gone.

Pepe' ran and hid. He sobbed for his mother, he screamed out in rage against the evil man who had killed her. He beat his fists against the brick wall of the cemetery where he sat. When he finally could think clearly he had a plan.

He found a small shop in a dark alley and pawned the diamond and gold necklace. He'd never held this much cash before. He headed to the docks where all the freight haulers sat. There was a lot of activity with ships loading and unloading the cargo. He walked up and down the wet boards, begging captains to give him passage to the United States. Part of the money had purchased him a forged passport. He was twenty one according to the papers he held.

He was becoming desperate when finally, someone listened. The captain was tanned, unshaven and grizzled. He yanked the papers from Pepe's grasp and for a moment the kid was afraid he would be betrayed and cast aside. The captain had sized him up and offered a very small cabin below decks. It was literally a door and bed. He would have to climb three flights of stairs just to use the facilities. No one on the big ship had paid him any attention. By the second day, he felt brave enough to climb the stairs to the main deck and wander around amid the huge stacks of loaded containers.

He was bursting with hope. He had never been out on big water before and he marveled at the size of the waves crashing against the long and powerful ship. He breathed in the salt air and let it whip his hair around.

He would make a new start, in a country rich with possibilities. At least that's what he had been told. He hadn't attended school. Truant officers didn't bother with the neighborhoods where he grew up. This did not mean he wasn't smart. He knew exactly what he wanted.

Five days later the ship anchored in a port in Texas. He had a tattered map and hitched a ride in the back of an old pick up. He wandered around the strange city. He used a very small portion of the money he had left and went into a café for lunch. He shyly asked the waitress what this place was called and where he might find work. The girl had laughed loudly and told him he was in Beaumont, Texas and he had to find jobs at the employment office downtown. He thanked her and left.

The lady behind the desk in the frightening office kept staring at him making him feel obvious and paranoid. What she was doing was noticing his muscled arms. She had a job listing for a gardener at the Lancaster Estates retirement community and sent him off with a note for a Miss Pepper and a wish of good luck.

Evelyn Pepper had stared at him oddly as well. She was put off by his lack of resume or references. He was relieved when she finally decided to give him the job. Included was a small, one bedroom apartment connected to a gardener's supply building. His food was part of his wages and he worked hard every day to prove himself. He thanked God and his mother. His life was forever changed and it had been ten years since he'd arrived. Life was good, but he missed his country and longed for his mother.

He reached up and rubbed the St. Christopher medal around his neck. This was the patron Saint of travelers. He looked to the heavens and thanked the Saint again for his safe passage to America. He never took the necklace off.

Chapter 18

PROGRESS AT THE OAKS

Time was flying by. Pearl had called to find out when I was coming back to Florida. I had called Jim and he arranged for the jet to be waiting for me in Beaumont. I didn't want to drive for eight hours or stay in New Orleans, flying was quickest.

With Pepe's help, we got all my planting done and it was beautiful. I asked him to watch over my plants and the orchids while I was away. He was downcast when I informed him I'd be leaving. Maybe I'd invite him on the next trip and introduce him to the family. I reassured him I would not be gone too long.

Pearl was at the Panama City airport waiting for me. We laughed and hugged, had some lunch and headed out to the plantation. The minute we pulled into the driveway, I was surprised. The trees were beautifully trimmed and it looked wonderful. The long, crushed shell driveway was clean and white.

The small home Pearl had set off the left of the main house was adorable. It was three bedrooms and they had built a covered porch and laid a concrete path up to the front. Pearl already had flowering shrubs planted around the base of the house and beautiful flower beds. It was now fully functional and you could hear the large heating and cooling system humming out back.

She gave me a tour and showed me my bedroom. We got me situated and went into the kitchen for some coffee. Pearl reached for two envelopes lying on the bar. She handed me one and told me, "Well, it's official. Magnolia and Matilda are announcing their grand opening next week. These are out invites. Beautifully done aren't they? Let's fly in to New York together; they want us to stay at the loft. Jim and Blaine have commercial reservations and will stay there as well."

I was thrilled that it was finally a reality. The address on the invitation was on 39th Street. I asked, "Is this near Bloomingdales?" Pearl thought for a moment and said she wasn't sure. I realized I had not brought any clothing that would be suitable for such an event and told my sister. Her response was that we could shop in the city. I'd have to make sure we made time for that. I picked up the invitation and admired it while Pearl cleaned up the kitchen.

The card was thick vellum done in black with gold trim. There was a delicate, floral parchment on top with gold lettering. This was attached with a sterling silver, flat stud. Hanging from the stud was two miniature charms. One a porcelain flower and the other was a sterling silver handbag. It read,

> **WE ARE PROUD TO ANNOUNCE THE
> GRAND OPENING OF
> MAGGIE & TILLIE
> 86 PARK AVENUE ON THE CORNER OF
> 39TH STREET**

NEW YORK, NEW YORK
JOIN US SATURDAY MAY THE 12TH
FROM 7: AM TIL CLOSING
REFRESHMENTS WILL BE SERVED
"ACCESSORIZE YOUR LIFE"

It was exciting to think the big day was almost here. I would keep the two charms for my old bracelet. I'd had it since childhood and you could barely fit anything else on the links.

There was a knock at the front door. Pearl was talking and she and the contractor walked in to the kitchen.

"Jarrod, this is my sister Minnie. She's going to be here for the next week taking pictures. If you want anything documented, please let us know."

He walked toward me and we shook hands. I told him, "Nice to meet you, I've heard nothing but good things. I am amazed at the progress you've made."

He looked toward the coffee pot and I grabbed a cup for him. Pearl was right. He was definitely good looking. Pearl sat on the stool next to me and he stood sipping the hot coffee.

Pearl laughed, "Wait until you see the property. It looks so much more open now with the grounds cleared of underbrush. We have found three cemeteries so far and a pecan orchard. The Braxton's think they are in good health so I expect we will have pecans coming out of our ears."

We all chuckled and Jarrod said, "Ladies." He tipped his baseball cap to us both and went back out.

I whistled and said, "Damn Pearl, how can you concentrate with him breathing down your neck? I would be completely distracted!"

She laughed and said, "Things are moving fast now and I don't have time for those thoughts. I'm older, not dead, so believe me I am fully aware that he is gorgeous."

We both laughed and put boots on for a walk around the grounds. It looked totally different now. The breeze was better here behind the big house, without all the live oaks and their moss slowing down the air flow. The bugs weren't too bad this morning and even though it was hot and humid it wasn't overpowering yet.

There were loud sounds of construction behind us. The workers were standing in various spots on scaffolding and a couple of them were in harnesses, hanging from different parts of the roof. You could hear skill saws, table saws and hammering. Plus a rhythmic screeching of old nails being pulled from dry boards. The entire outside of the house had men working on one thing or another. The basement was poured, sealed, painted and being framed in. The house had been lowered back onto the new foundation. Besides some chill bumps, I didn't sense anything bad at the moment.

We ended up out back where a back hoe was scooping out a large area for the pool. Part of the beautiful tiles would surround this, and I knew it would be prettier than concrete. Some of the tiles would go in the new greenhouse off the kitchen and a lot of them were going into a very long and large patio off the back of the house. All the bathrooms, eight of them, would each have different tiles.

The upper widow walks had been removed and were being rebuilt. It made the house look naked in a way. The original columns were down and laying lengthwise, all being refinished and sealed with more effective, bug resistant materials. They had to use a crane to maneuver the immense columns and it just amazed me how much they had done.

One team was removing and replacing every inch of pipes and another crew was doing the same with all the electric. They had to modernize both and make major changes. When the old house had been built the only light source had been oil lamps. Years later, and probably grudgingly the owner had put in the minimal amount of electric he could get by with. There were large wooden spools full of wiring to one side of the house. They also had to run duct work throughout the entire place.

The tree service was out in the orchard now and we could hear their saws buzzing in the distance. They would tend to the pecan trees next. It really changed the mood of the place just to have all the ground litter and debris removed. It also made it safer for everyone, giving the snakes less places to hide.

I told Pearl I wanted to show her the pictures of Beaumont so we went inside. She poured us some wine and we went out back. Jarrod had built her an amazing covered back porch out here and it was screened in. There would always be one place where the bugs wouldn't eat us up. We both sat on her porch swing and chatted while she looked at my camera.

We heard her phone ringing and she ran in to get it. She was still talking and giving me a look. I knew then it was Clarissa. I was glad Pearl remained civil and she agreed that her mother-in-law would meet us in Chelsea.

We still had a few days so Pearl went back to work and I wandered around, staying out of everyone's way but capturing some excellent photographs of sweaty men in action. The best shots were those where the men hadn't noticed me.

I wondered if Magnolia and Matilda had chosen their location out west. They would need to entice people in New York with that information during the grand opening. Pearl had told me that Matilda was launching a complete new line of her flowers done in hair accessories. They were nervous about their inventory and hoped they had enough, but not too much. I had a feeling they would be placing another order before they'd planned. Everyone would want the beautiful pieces to add to their collections. We were so proud of them and looking forward to a trip to the city. I couldn't wait to see what other vendors they had brought in.

It seemed the Jarrod fellow was staying in a large camper on the back of his truck. He was too busy now to be away from the site for very long. Everything any of them needed was being delivered and unloaded at their feet. It was running smoothly. In fact, it was ahead of schedule. That is until the first accident.

We were busy cooking dinner and heard the commotion. We looked up at each other and ran outside. One of the workers was sitting on a saw horse and holding his lower leg, gritting his teeth. Pearl reached them first asking what on earth had happened.

The man was in pain and said, "I went to grab my nail gun and the damn thing shot me in the leg, twice!"

Looks were exchanged between Jarrod and us, and I asked, "Do you want an ambulance? We could probably run you in to the Seaside hospital quicker than they could get out here. Let me see that." I bent over his leg and the nails were pretty close to a main artery and it would be dangerous to try pulling them out.

I looked at Jarrod and said, "Let's carry him to the back seat of Pearl's car and we'll run him into town."

Everyone agreed and we waited while the doctor took care of the poor guy. He was fine after they removed the nails and cleaned the wounds. It helped that they had given him pain killers. We didn't talk on the way back out to the plantation. Pearl had insurance in place for anything that might happen, that wasn't the point. I wondered how it had happened. The guy was kind of spooked by the incident and drove himself home. Jarrod had gotten on the phone and reassigned the man's position immediately. He would not compromise his head count even though he felt bad about the accident.

We had all just gotten settled down and we heard another ruckus coming from the back of the house. We ran around back and gasped to see one of the men who had been up on scaffolding, now hanging from the ledge of a window. The heap of metal he'd been standing on was twisted and bent. He'd been lucky to grab the window the instant he felt the shift beneath him. Two of the other workers were already putting a tall ladder beneath him.

Jarrod looked agitated. Everything had gone without a hitch and now two accidents in one day were not cool. He apologized to Pearl and she wasn't worried about anything but everyone's welfare. My hair was standing up on my arms and I was covered in goose bumps. I walked back around front and looked up at the bedroom window upstairs on the right. There was the little black girl giggling behind one hand and pointing at something out in the oak orchard. I knew no one else could see her, there was a man pulling boards not five feet from where she was. I just gave her a stern look and didn't tell anyone.

Pearl invited Jarrod to come over for dinner and he accepted. At least I would get to know him a little better. We had fixed enough for eight people. The dinner conversation was about the big house. Jarrod was happy that in two days the electric company would be back with new poles to run lines from the main house to the back of the property. The water well was drilled and work on that was finished. They had completed the pipes and septic for the small house first. They were still working on the pipes in the big house. The lighting fixtures, wall sconces and chandeliers would be here next week. They would go in one of the storage sheds out of harm's way.

They had disassembled the old fireplace and were rebuilding that. Pearl also had the mason crew doing brickwork on some old outdoor ovens that she wanted to keep and restore. They would be off to one side of the pool. She was adding a one bedroom pool house on the other side. I couldn't wait to see it done. I just hoped no one else would get hurt.

The three of us went out to the front porch with cocktails to watch the sunset. We discussed a new wooden archway over the front entrance, it would say Live Oaks and we agreed it was a much better name for the place. That job was being done by Adam and Phillip in their Dad's shop. It was a multi-step process that had to be kept indoors until completed. They had the design that the boss lady wanted and it would go up when the fencing went up. It turns out that Mr. Braxton put Jarrod in touch with one of his people and he got a huge discount on the very large pole order. Pearl didn't want metal or anything that would make it too hard on the wildlife. A pole fence suited the place. It would be a big job and a whole lot of poles. I liked this Jarrod guy and his sons were polite and respectful too. They all took their work very seriously.

We gave Jarrod our travel schedule and he assured Pearl that he would see that any new materials arriving would be taken care of. She trusted him already and wasn't the least bit worried. He had proved himself to her the first week. They were very comfortable together. When she told me the guy's history, I felt bad for him. What a waste to be with the wrong partner for so long just because there were children involved. He seemed happy enough to me though and I watched him closely to see how he looked at Pearl when no one was looking. He was being careful and if he had any feelings for her he was hiding it.

It was getting late in the evening. The small house had two full bathrooms and Pearl had been letting Jarrod use one. I had to catch my breath when he came out onto the porch from the shower. His hair was wet and in disarray, he had a towel over one shoulder and no shirt above a nicely fitting pair of Levi's. He apologized about his partial nakedness and went to his camper. We were both trying not to swallow our tongues.

We got that loud, nervous laughter thing going and couldn't stop, like when you're a kid in church and you dare not laugh. We knew he probably had heard us but we were always laughing so we just didn't care. We sat up late chatting, mostly about the girls. I had taken my pills earlier and my headache was gone. We drank a couple bottles of good wine and made our New York City game plans. It would be so damn much fun, especially knowing everyone would be there.

I curled up under the pretty, thick comforter and slipped away.

I dreamed the little black girl was standing next to my bed. She was tapping my arm and wanted my attention. I asked her why she did not go toward the light. She nervously looked over her shoulder and pointed. I didn't want to see and just as I looked past her, I woke up gasping for air. The child was gone. I shook my head and went back to sleep.

Chapter 19

CLARISSA ANTOINETTE BISHOP-VANDECOURTE

Clarissa stood in front of the hall mirror admiring what she saw. Her cheeks were sun kissed and her skin had a slight base tan. She thought it took ten years off her looks. Having just returned from a week in the Cayman Islands, she felt positively radiant.

She was thinking about her selfish and ungrateful daughter-in-law and her precious grand-daughters. Her invitation to their grand opening lay on the entry hall table with the rest of the un-opened mail. She sifted through the envelopes and took the one to the sunroom with her coffee.

She could do nothing but bitch to her friends, looking for sympathy that they gave gladly. Pearl had called her once in three weeks. And she couldn't abide the idea of that horrid plantation and God knows what kind of money she was spending on that. Clarissa didn't want to tell her friends that she had only made one phone call herself.

Her three maids were scurrying around trying to make sure all was as it should be without being seen or heard. She had strict rules that they followed to the letter. Right now they were upstairs unpacking her vacation things and cleaning up after her. Each one of them feared her wrath in their own way.

She read the invitation and called Matilda, who invited her to stay in Chelsea at their loft during the event. She had no idea that the rest of the family would be there. That would be an unwelcome surprise for sure.

She took her cup to the kitchen and donning her designer, straw hat decided to take her morning stroll and stop by Pearl and Gregory's house. She had the spare key to her son's home in her pocket. She stopped to admire one of her rose gardens and ignored a cheerful morning greeting from the groundskeeper. She believed that servants should never forget their place and need not speak unless spoken to. She often wondered what this world was coming to.

She tapped on Pearl's front door and got no response. She slipped the key in the lock, quietly and opened the door. Leaning in the foyer, she sweetly called out to her daughter-in-law, even though she knew Pearl was most likely still in Florida. When it was obvious that no one was home, she glanced behind her and let herself in. She wandered through the large house, which had been left spotless. She didn't touch a thing, just looked in every room. She stopped in the upstairs hallway and admired a picture of her precious, late son Gregory. She missed him so and still couldn't believe he was gone. Parents were not supposed to outlive their children, it just wasn't right! After losing her husband Wilfred, it had nearly killed her to learn her son was dying of cancer.

She had never agreed that this woman was good enough for her son or family. Really, who were they and even though Gregory had told her time and again of his wife's wealth, she couldn't be convinced that he wasn't marrying some backwater hick far beneath his breeding. Her son had told her, just wait until she met her, it hadn't changed a thing.

What had softened her hard heart were those two grand-babies, the only thing left of her darling son. She adored them and blamed Pearl and her sister for keeping them from her. The truth was that she never made the effort herself; she had just expected everyone to bend to her wishes. They hadn't. She thought they were impudent and disrespectful.

She was an extremely wealthy woman and wore it like a crown. She was at the top of every A list of high society. She resided in the Hickman Hills area of Savannah, Georgia. How could she possibly lower her standards for these common people? She'd had a list of very eligible women for Gregory. He had fallen in love with that cretin from New Orleans. It really left a bad taste in her mouth.

Her husband had been Wilfred Allen VanDeCourte II. Their only son had been named after his father. His name was Gregory Allen VanDeCourte III. Then she had to face the heartbreaking news that this wife bore two female children. It was a scandal. Now the family name would stay buried with her husband and son. She felt disgraced in the company of her associates, it just wasn't fair.

She felt that whole side of the family was insufferable drunks. Looking at the delicate and tastefully done invitation she had a plan. She would take her thick address book and simply demand all her friends attend the gala event. The poor darlings deserved success and she would make sure it happened. Left to the devices of their mother and aunt she was sure they'd fail miserably. She sat staring out at her expansive English gardens with a smug look on her face. They would thank and praise her for her help and support.

Sadly what she didn't know was the combined fortune of her grand-daughters had already surpassed her own. They were billionaires. She had no idea, none. And their mother and aunt could buy and sell her many times over, she didn't know that either.

She sat most of the morning calling in favors and making sure everyone she contacted left her with a promise to attend. It would be spectacular; she would make sure of it. She would invite them all to dinner afterwards in appreciation of their attendance.

She wondered what Pearl was doing and considered calling her. When she finally reached her, it was obvious that Pearl had no intention of informing her of the rebuilding of the plantation home in Florida. So, Savannah wasn't good enough for her. Here her husband had provided her with a beautiful home and she'd gone running back to Florida and the hideous property. What could she be thinking and what did she intend to do with the house here and all of Gregory's things? It was enough to give Clarissa a slight headache. Maybe a touch of brandy would help. She made sure none of the house staff was around and went to the bar. She took the small glass of spirits out to the nearest bench in her prize winning back yard. She was alone.

Her maiden name carried a weight of its own. The Bishops had been a very influential family in the deep South and she had come into the marriage with a hefty dowry. Her union with Wilfred had been pre-arranged and she was horrified to find she was expected to disrobe and have sex with the man. It had always disgusted her and it was a wonder she'd even had one child. It was enough and had ruined her figure. She'd privately sworn never to endure any of that nastiness again. It was just so barbaric. She had wanted to adopt and her husband had been incensed when she approached the subject.

She had recently rewritten her will leaving the grandchildren sufficient funds to live on, and was giving the rest to charity. She would rather die herself before she would let their mother get her hands on another penny of the family fortune. Clarissa knew that Gregory had left his wife everything. She knew that he had also given Pearl several million dollars to go with the ugly house in Florida. She saw it as a waste. She was aware that Pearl had been going to school just about forever getting degrees for her future. She imagined her darling son had funded that as well. The woman was a commoner, and it depressed and saddened her. She had intended for his entire portfolio to be liquidated and spread amongst her favorite philanthropic recipients.

She went back inside and told the upstairs maid to lay out her newest Channel suit for her dinner engagement. She shoved a list at the timid girl and told her to have those things ready for a trip to New York City in two days. Her chauffeur was already under the portico and waiting. Slipping into her white gloves she stopped again in her favorite spot, in front of the mirror, and made sure nothing was out of place.

She raised her regal nose to the sky and stared out the limo window as they drove. She would show them, she would show them all.

Chapter 20

GRAND OPENING NEW YORK, NY

————⟹●⟸————

Pearl and I were very excited as we discussed our plans. We would fly to New York City today where I needed to do some shopping. We would see the new boutique first and help calm the girl's jitters. Tomorrow was the big day and we couldn't wait to see what would happen.

Jarrod had joined us early for coffee and was given instructions from Pearl for the freight that might arrive during the two days we'd be gone. He was confident everything would be fine and wished us well.

We laughed and talked the entire flight and the car service was waiting once we clawed our way out of the throngs of people at LaGuardia. We went straight to the loft and stowed our things then went to the new shop on Park Avenue. The girls, with Blaine's help and guidance, had found a realtor with the perfect location. It wasn't too small or too large and the floor plan was wide open. We walked in and just stared at how magnificent it all looked.

Their choice was perfect, the shop had two sides of glass and they had their name and slogan in both windows.

The lighting had been carefully placed to highlight the special pieces on sale. They were on individual stands, under glass like in a museum. There were long counters with bags and jewelry showcased and these were the ones customers could look at with assistance.

There were also scarves, hair accessories, gloves, and a stunning line of charms, a few chic hats, belts, and leg ware. They had a vendor from Europe for all the amazing stockings. They also carried a small amount of the most popular fragrances. The set up was inviting and beautiful. They had hired one woman to run the register and there were three personal assistants for the customers. Blaine had raked these poor women through the coals. He had interviewed literally hundreds of candidates. These four had made the cut. He was currently interviewing for the California location, but would join us later this evening.

We found ourselves wonderful outfits and of course we'd wear our new jewelry from Matilda. We laughed and talked with the sales clerks. When we had shared a bottle of champagne, we told everyone we'd see them very early the next morning. It would be fabulous.

I hoped there would be a great turnout. Blaine had hired a public relations specialist to handle both locations. She did her homework and had done an excellent job so far. The full page ads had run in all the major news publications. She had rented two billboards for one week and had stacks of colorful and beautiful announcement cards printed for hand out on the street or for mailing to lure in more customers.

Magnolia and Matilda told us they already had inventory for the California store and the vendors would vary to suit the location. They were coming out of their skin with nerves so we closed the shop and a guard we'd hired would stand vigil all night and trade off with two more in the morning that would stand watch all day and do crowd control if needed.

We took the kids out to dinner and they were happy that Blaine and Jim were coming in tonight around five thirty. They looked at each other and Magnolia told us, "We have sort of a surprise for everyone, but we're not sure how to tell you."

Pearl and I looked at each other and I said, "Just tell us. Honesty has always been the best policy. We can take whatever you can dish out."

Magnolia took each of our hands and said, "Gram Clarissa is coming in tonight. She won't arrive until everyone else is already here. I hope she doesn't throw a fit, but we just want her to feel welcome without any drama."

Pearl immediately sat up straighter and assured them, "You don't have a thing to worry about darling, unbeknownst to your gram; we actually do have some class and know how to conduct ourselves. A lot of the anguish in her life is of her own doing. We promise to be good. She will have to keep up, that's all I will say on the matter. You two just focus on what's ahead, it will all be perfect."

With that out of the way we had cocktails and hugs, laughing the entire way back to the loft. Tonight's sleeping arrangements would be interesting. The kids had rented rolling beds. I wondered where in the hell they had found a service for this, but there they were lined up in the central part of the loft. I figured that Jim would end up in one bedroom and Clarissa in the other. They had two sleeper sofas so that took care of Matilda and Blaine in one and Magnolia on the other. Pearl and I would get the roll a ways. It was fine and the least of our worries.

We took cocktails up to the roof terrace. You could only access this from the stairway off the kitchen. The girls had installed a key pad security system between the elevator doors and the locked chain doors at the entrance of their loft. The stairs up to the terrace was a good idea. They intentionally did not want the elevator going to the roof.

There had only been one attempted breach since they'd bought the place. Someone intent on entering had used a crowbar to pry open the elevator doors. That was as far as they had gotten. When they tried to get through the chain and front the alarm system had nearly deafened them and the police were waiting when they made their exit. I loved knowing they were this safe.

It was beautiful up here in the afternoon sun. We could hear all the chaos of the busy, bustling city below us. No one could bother us here unless by helicopter. I supposed someone in one of the taller buildings could see us, but not that well.

We sat and chatted and tried to keep the girls relaxed. We'd had to drag them away from the store. We had a good buzz going when we heard the intercom. Matilda flew down the stairs to let Jim and Blaine in. They grabbed cocktails from the bar we'd set up and joined us on the terrace.

After the greetings and hugs were out of the way, Jim stood and proposed a toast. "Here's to the two new business moguls of New York City, may you prosper and succeed."

We clapped, cheered and laughed. It was a party and Magnolia put on some music. It was a delightful evening. Time melted away and Clarissa finally arrived. The kids ran down to meet her and we stayed on the roof, contented, slightly drunk and had no intentions of leaving until the last of us couldn't stand.

Clarissa cooed and hugged the girls thinking she was an exclusive guest in the loft for the evening. Magnolia took her gram's bags to her bedroom and they gave her a tour of the loft. She had never been here but that was not mentioned. She noticed the various luggage and articles but didn't ask about that. Matilda fixed her a drink and they sat her down to give her the gifts they had.

She was tearing up when she opened the flat, leather case and saw the jewelry. Her set was done in delicate, tiny roses. Surprisingly they would match her outfit for tomorrow. The small, intricate handbag had her speechless and it was then she realized the girls truly were artists and would have no problems selling their goods. They chatted for a few minutes.

Matilda stood and said, "Gram, we have another surprise for you, bring your drink and come with us."

She followed them up the stairs and on to the terrace. She stiffened at the sound of the all too familiar voices of those seated in a group and steeled herself for the meeting. Everyone just hugged and greeted her with open arms, smiles and tried to make her feel welcome.

She sat on the edge of her chair with her drink and looked at each of us. We were too drunk by now to give two shits what she felt or thought. She was being very careful, and was civil with everyone. She was smart enough to realize she was outnumbered and this was about the kids, not her.

She noticed the gorgeous ring on Matilda's finger and asked if they had set a date. She was incredibly hurt that she was not informed of the engagement. It had slipped Matilda's mind, having been so focused on business and the new store. Had she bothered to call either of the kids she would know by now that they planned to marry. It was her own fault but she would never admit that to anyone.

She sat thinking to herself through a tight smile. I'm always the last to know. Why would this be any different? She was hoping that her own friends would show tomorrow and she was anxious to see how that would go.

Dinner was catered and we feasted like kings and queens. The champagne flowed until the last bottle was drained. We finally went to our beds and it would be an early morning for us.

Matilda was up first and had three carafes of coffee and an array of delicious pastries ready for everyone. She had hired a small, local bakery to do these and the gorgeous petit fours for today's refreshments. They each had beautifully done flowers or tiny handbags on top and we would take them with us when we headed to the store. The baker had to find a recipe for the small, delicate cakes and had made at least two thousand of them. It had cost a fortune but would be worth it. Matilda insisted on the small southern touch and we loved it.

It was five thirty in the morning and we took turns in the two bathrooms. Finally Jim told us the stretch limo was waiting so we got downstairs and situated for the drive. The girls were glowing and we looked so spiffy that I took tons of pictures, not wanting one moment to slip by without photos to remember.

When we pulled up and unloaded ourselves we got into the shop and set up the cakes. There would be two women serving champagne and desert throughout the day. This area would become a very nice stocking display tomorrow. Everyone was on cloud nine. Pearl and I each grabbed a stack of the handouts and went out front. It was ten minutes until opening time. As soon as we hit the sidewalk we saw the crowd. Laughing we walked among the lines that were already three deep handing out the beautiful cards. Everyone was happy and excited for the doors to open. Suddenly there were taxis and limos stopping traffic going in both directions. Well dressed women were pouring out of the waiting vehicles headed for the front door.

Clarissa was looking like the fox that ate the rabbit and many of these women were greeting her and whispering conspiratorially. Pearl and I looked at each other and ignored it all. We were amazed at the turn out. The activity never slowed until about five thirty in the afternoon. We were getting exhausted and went in to see how things were going. There was a steady stream of customers moving in and out. I was happy to see most of those leaving held the beautiful floral bags full of merchandise.

I hugged Pearl, happy beyond words for the excellent day. They were going to close at ten tonight and we would leave the sales staff to manage. The crowd had thinned and we convinced the girls to leave with us around dinner time. Everyone was bone tired. It had been a smashing success.

At dinner, we talked about the opening in California slated for next week. They had a spot on Rodeo Drive in Beverly Hills. Blaine had the details finalized and the kids were nervous that the inventory wouldn't be waiting for them when they flew out in a couple of days. We tried to relax them by example. I was so tired I could barely walk in the ridiculous shoes I'd worn. Comparing today's success to next week had them excited and they made sure we would be there. They thanked their Gram for inviting her friends and they had ended up being about a third of today's customers.

We went back to the loft except for Blaine who was still at the shop talking to the manager he'd hired. She had been given strict instructions on how to handle the shop bookwork and would turn everything in to him and Joshua by express delivery, fax and mail. She was to do this every two days and he finally left satisfied that the sales for the opening far exceeded their expectations. The manager was also responsible for inventory and the shelves would remain full at all times.

After the day's adrenaline rush had worn off, we were sleepy. Jim and Gram had crashed first. Pearl and I spent almost a half an hour in hysterics, so drunk that we couldn't manage the rolling beds. Matilda laughed and got us settled and tucked in. We fell asleep there in the living room giggling like two naughty children.

The next morning Jim had quietly slipped out and a few minutes later he had laid the stack of various newspapers and publications in front of us on the coffee table. He had stood by the news stand and grabbed one of each as soon as they hit the ground. Each of us grabbed one and shredded them looking for the business reviews. There was the picture I'd taken of the girls standing in front of one of the display cases. It was unanimous, they were an overnight success. Every single revue was positive and confirmed what we already knew.

Magnolia took a pastry and coffee into Gram who thanked her and she stayed there alone enjoying the quiet. She would not come out in pajamas, God forbid. She would wait until the heathens were up and dressed. She already had a ticket to return to Savannah. Pearl and I were in no hurry and lay around, enjoying everyone's company.

Blaine happily reported that before he left the shop, there were long waiting lists for the matching sets and requests for commissioned pieces. These orders would be faxed to the manufacturers then they would look at the special requests and decide which of these they would do. It was very exciting. I was hoping they wouldn't feel overwhelmed. If so, then it would be time for each of them to hire personal assistants.

We were in various, relaxed positions, sipping coffee and reading the papers when Gram came out. She was dressed and asked for the car service to be called. The girls begged her to stay, but she insisted she needed to get back. We hugged her goodbye and let her go. She congratulated the girls and Matilda offered to escort her to the waiting limo. She was actually wearing the rose jewelry and it made the kids proud. They made her promise to keep in touch and visit more often. She assured them she would be in California next week and left.

Matilda came back and lay on the couch with Blaine, finishing the article in the paper. She and Magnolia would make an unannounced appearance in the shop today then fly out to Beverly Hills and stay through the opening there.

We dragged ourselves to the shower and got ready. We decided to fly back to Florida with Jim and Blaine who would turn around and head back to New Orleans. We didn't make plans for next week yet, one day at a time, especially with our hangovers. I took my pills and Pearl had questioned me about them. I just said they were for the headaches I had been getting.

I felt horrible that I had this secret and wasn't going to tell Pearl. It was like hauling around an over packed suitcase on a weekend trip. She was becoming very suspicious of my headaches and the large pills.

After cleaning the loft for the kids we were finally ready to go. They were sad but had to get ready themselves. They were flying out in three or four hours. With tears, hugs and kisses we went downstairs and back to LaGuardia to get on our jet. It had been one of the most fun and exciting trips I had ever made to New York. I knew Pearl was antsy to get back to her house.

It was a smooth flight and once we had our bags we told Jim and Blaine goodbye and to have safe travels. We drove back to the plantation and went straight to bed for naps. We were worn out and not getting any younger. We never heard Jarrod knocking on the front door.

Chapter 21

BEVERLY HILLS, CALIFORNIA

Pearl and I woke rested. We took a pot of coffee and went looking for Jarrod, she wanted an update. The first thing we noticed was the four car garage off the left side of the old house was gone and in its place was an already framed in office. That's where we found him.

We walked around and were astonished at the progress. Pearl and Jarrod had their heads together over the blue prints. He took us inside the main house and it didn't look like the same place. The new pipes and wiring was already hidden by new sheetrock throughout the entire downstairs. There would be no wallpaper anywhere in the mansion. Pearl didn't care for it herself so this would eliminate the authenticity factor of the remodel. My sister had planned to put subtle shades of satin paint in all the rooms. Her reasoning was so that the beautiful stained glass windows would reflect light and not be absorbed by wall paper patterns and colors.

There was new subflooring throughout the entire downstairs and there were boxes of tiles stacked in the living room. These were for the greenhouse off the kitchen and the downstairs bathrooms.

We couldn't go upstairs to look; they were working on the old staircase and were accessing the top floor with ladders. They had a pulley system set up to raise and lower supplies and debris.

These guys all worked like an organized team. I commented to Jarrod, "I think that a two year deadline is a stretch. It seems to be going so fast that you will be done well ahead of schedule."

Jarrod rearranged his baseball cap saying, "You're right. I have so many good workers going full tilt, I'm very pleased. And we did have another mishap while you two were in the city."

Pearl was wringing her hands unconsciously and was afraid to ask, she just muttered, "Oh my, what happened?"

Jarrod spoke to a couple of the men then said, "Yesterday I put a guy on the graveyards. I told him to straighten all the headstones, clean out all the brush and redo the fences. Seems he stuck his hand where he shouldn't have, without looking first, and was nicked by a rattler. He's going to be ok but he went out of here screaming like a girl. We found a pretty good nest of the little bastards. It's taken care of now."

We looked at each other and were weak in the knees. Damn reptiles, we hated them. We loved animals but could not abide poisonous creatures and did not feel bad killing snakes.

Jarrod said, "Turns out you've got the remains of what looks to be a fairly large family plot back there, all Beaufords. Its' hard to imagine why they never got moved. The other two smaller plots have adult and children size graves and are a large mix of names. I'm going to guess these were slaves and in-house servants. All the graveyards are cleaned and I wondered if you would be leaving them here and if you do, I figured you'd want to plant some flowers around them. Just let me know what your plans are, and we will help you, of course."

Pearl thought about it and said, "Actually, I would like for a priest or preacher, someone, to come out and say a blessing over those poor souls, and then I'll plant something cheerful. They deserve that much respect." We agreed that would be a good plan.

The driveway had a constant stream of activity today. There were Jarrod's dump trucks going in and out, hauling the wood, and walls they had torn out. The old concrete from the basement had already been removed. It was incredible how much of it there was. The power company was almost ready to do a test on the electric. It was very exciting.

We told Jarrod we had to go to California for at least two days and I left him and Pearl going over lists, deliveries and supplies. He had mentioned there was a truckload coming in today of nothing but ceiling fans. They would have to be assembled and the ones with glass fixtures would be stained glass. Pearl reminded him they were Tiffany and to be careful. He just laughed at her. This guy had one of the most beautiful smiles I'd ever seen on a man.

We did another walk around, I photographed everything and we decided to get ready for a flight into LAX. It was another of our least favorite airports. There had been times arriving in Los Angeles where the air was literally green with a thick haze of smog. It could be extremely cloying and gross. But the closer you got to the coast and near the breezes it offered, it wasn't that bad.

I called Miss Evelyn and informed her I would not be returning as planned and asked if she would get Pepe' to continue taking care of my plants. She had assured me he would and told me to enjoy my time with my sister and nieces.

We got packed and Pearl called one of our pilots for today to let them know when we would be at the airport in Panama City. We would get in late tonight and were booked at the Beverly Hilton. We told Jarrod goodbye and headed out.

We chatted and Pearl worked on her laptop for most of the flight. I slept and read and thought about the kids. Matilda had excitedly announced the additional pieces she would launch in California. She had created a line of women's cuff links, tie clasps and broaches. This kid could not be stopped. She always had design ideas for something new. We couldn't wait to see them again even though it had only been a week.

We got to California and were dropped off at the Hilton. After getting settled in the suite we were sharing, we ordered champagne and hors d'oeuvres. We lounged around, unpacked our gear for the next morning and wondered if Gram, Jim and Blaine were in yet. The grand opening here was going to be at seven thirty tomorrow morning and it was too late to call any of them. Joshua was taking on all the work in New Orleans. Blaine hated to leave him hanging, but the stores demanded he was here.

We stayed up for a while and there was a tapping on the door around eleven thirty. I cautiously answered and there were the kids, they had a slight buzz and we welcomed them in. We served them the remaining bubbly and Magnolia had a joint. I hoped I could keep up and we laughed and talked for a couple of hours.

Matilda and Blaine had decided to surprise Pearl. They announced that they wanted to marry at Live Oaks and would have to be content with a long engagement. We reassured them that it was going to be a lot sooner than that and to start planning now. They were beside themselves with joy. Magnolia was adamant that she would choose her brides maids dress and Matilda said the three of us could wear whatever we wanted. She had found a vintage lace wedding gown from one of her designer friend's collections. She already knew that she wanted it outdoors, with nothing more than white tents; cloth covered folding chairs with flowers in back of each, and multicolored, round, paper lanterns. We thought it sounded romantic. She wanted her flowers to be calla lilies, gardenias and tiny, red rose buds to offset her ring and the different shades of white. I knew it would be beautiful.

Even as busy as they were, Matilda had been dreaming of this day her whole life and knew what she wanted. She would use the same company to print her invitations, since they'd done an immaculate job on the other materials.

They gave each of us one of the announcements for this store and it was very similar to the first ones except the background vellum was blue. The address this time was on Rodeo Drive and Blaine had hired the same amount of staff. The stores would eventually share large shipments of merchandise. Matilda was excited about how well her porcelain calla lily line had turned out. She would not release this set to the public until after her wedding.

We finally got the kids to leave and told them they needed to try to sleep so they could handle tomorrow but they wouldn't rest and we knew it. They had told us that Gram Clarissa and Uncle Jim were here in the Hilton and had gotten in earlier. We would meet for breakfast then head to the new store.

I was so tired I curled up in the huge king sized bed. Pearl was sitting in the dark on her laptop when I drifted off.

I dreamed that I was looking at Pepe' and a beautiful, blonde young woman. They were not aware of me but I could hear their conversation about me. I seemed to be floating around them and looking up, I heard singing and it felt like loving arms embracing me and I had never felt such peace.

Too early the next morning the limo whisked us through ridiculous traffic and let us out in front of the shop. This one had one large window facing the street. It was a wide and long floor plan and the interior was spectacular. The displays were backlit and all the sparkle was disorienting. Once again their ideas were perfect. We grabbed stacks of handouts and took our places out front.

We were very over dressed for this crowd. But it didn't matter; you could not judge books by their covers on this coast. The crowds were getting thick and were anticipating the doors opening. Clarissa had actually joined us and we were happily surprised that it turned out to be fun. The doors opened and not one single person left the shop empty handed. Like before, we were getting worn out toward the dinner hour.

The sales staff here was polite, professional and very excited to learn that part of their job requirements was to trade places with the New York staff. They each would eventually be cross-trained to work in either place and travel was a must. After all was said and done it had been another unbelievable success. Now the girls could get back to their studios and get more work done. Although a lot of focus for Matilda would be on her upcoming wedding. Even without a specific date, there were an awful lot of things that could be done. I took some stunning pictures and sent them with Blaine for the upcoming press releases. I hoped they would be as well received here.

We chatted and laughed and were so happy that the openings were behind us. I sat thinking that I had to go back to Texas soon. Maybe I would join Pearl at the plantation. I didn't tell her yet that I wanted to come live the remaining time I had with them, as I was just now settled and would stay for a little while, as long as I didn't get sicker or incapacitated. It was too soon to make those decisions anyway. I couldn't be sure about what new symptoms might appear and I was still in disbelief in regards to my death sentence.

The kids finally came dragging in. Clarissa and Jim were in the living room portion of the suite reading newspapers and chatting amicably. She was letting her hair down and seemed to be slightly drunk. Magnolia came over and plopped down beside me in my bed and using my lap for a pillow she stared at the ceiling and said, "Mimi, do you think I'll ever find someone to love? It just seems like such bullshit and fantasy!"

I smoothed her hair from her forehead and assured her, "Baby, you are so beautiful; you will just have to slow down and pay attention. There will be so many choices and believe me, you will know when the right one approaches you. Your heart will know."

She was drowsy and slept there curled up and snuggling me and I felt lucky to have all of them in my life. As the hours passed, we ate, drank, celebrated and laughed until our stomachs hurt. It was another perfect day that we hated to see end. The next morning we would pile onto our jet. They would drop off Pearl, the girls and I in Panama City, then the guys in New Orleans, We had talked the girls into spending the night with us at the plantation then they had reservations to fly back into LaGuardia. Clarissa had taken a commercial flight back to Savannah but had actually promised Pearl she would visit her at the plantation.

We were teary eyed to leave and got into Panama City pretty late. The girls would be astonished to see the place tomorrow morning. They loved the little house and shared the third bedroom for the night.

We woke them with the smell of hot coffee and breakfast cooking. There was a knock at the door and Jarrod wanted to use one of the showers. I crept into the girl's room and found them already awake and chatting quietly. I warned them that a man was in the house and to not come out undressed. They joined us in the kitchen.

When Jarrod came in he just stood and stared at the four of us. He sipped some coffee and said, "It's been a very long time since I've seen this many beautiful women in one spot! Pleased to meet you girls, later when you're ready I'll give you a tour of the big house. I'll leave you all now, I need to get busy." With that said he turned and went out to the crews to get everyone where they ought to be and working. He was a fair and reliable boss but did not like any down time except for small breaks to rehydrate, eat lunch or bathroom breaks.

When the girls had excitedly told him about the wedding during the tour he gave them, he pulled Adam and Phillip aside. They were so far ahead of schedule that he had an idea. They had their heads together for about a half an hour. He was going to use an old template he had and build Matilda a beautiful gazebo for her wedding.

This would be his and the boy's gift to them. They would construct this in his personal shop and it would be a surprise.

We got the bags loaded in Pearl's car and drove into Panama City to see the girls off. We grabbed lunch and after many hugs and the usual tears we got them to their gate on time. We watched them taxi away and both missed them before the plane even left the ground. They had a lot of work ahead but the hardest part was behind them. We couldn't be prouder.

I had decided to go back to Texas in a couple of days and just wandered around taking photographs and admiring the work being done. It was amazing. We had looked at the before pictures over dinner. Jarrod couldn't believe the difference himself. If he wondered about the pictures of his men, he didn't comment on it. I had forgotten about those shots. Later over drinks on the back porch, Pearl and I gut laughed about it. Jarrod probably thought we were crazy.

It was my last day and Pearl suggested we spend at least part of it in Destin at our favorite spot. I loaded a few things in her trunk and we drove to the state owned portion of the beach. We got settled and under the umbrella that Pearl never went to the beach without.

It was a picture perfect day and the surf was a little choppy. The wind was up, there was a rip current and the red flags were whipping in the wind, but we didn't care. We strolled the familiar beach looking for shells and finally came back to just bask in the sun on our towels. The sand pipers were darting in and out of the foam at the edge of the water. The day was bright without a cloud in the sky. We savored our time here and later we finally arrived at the plantation.

I was ready to go and Pearl drove me to the airport. I told her, "Well, with all of us out of your hair, you'll be able to focus on the matters at hand. Keep me posted and if you need me I'll fly back." She laughed and thanked me for being there. I wouldn't have missed it for the world. We were both crying when I boarded our jet. I would now be eight hours away from her again and it already felt too far.

The limo was waiting for me in Beaumont and before I knew it I was back at my front door in Lancaster Estates. I tipped the driver and brought my things in to my bedroom where they stayed, still packed. I was so tired, I had a lite snack and some tea then curled up on the couch.

I dreamed I was back at the mansion. It was the day of the wedding. The little black girl had grabbed my hand and smiling she pulled me closer and whispered in my ear. "They call me Elizabeth." Her hair was braided close to her head and she wore a ring of wildflowers with a small veil. Her dress was white satin with a big red bow in back. She had on white patent leather shoes. She was walking down the aisle ahead of everyone tossing flower petals that only she and I could see. She was beaming. My heart was breaking for this tiny lost soul and I wondered at the cruelty of her having been left behind. I needed to help her but I wasn't sure how to do that.

Chapter 22

DÉJÀ VU AT THE PHARMACY

———⟫●⟪———

I awoke to the sound of someone out back. I got up and put on some coffee. It was Pepe' tending to my beautiful, blooming plants. I fixed two cups of coffee and took them outside. He lit up when he saw me and I was admiring how well everything we had planted was doing. The trumpet flowers were completely covering the lattice and already spilling over the other side into my neighbor's yard. I sat and he joined me. I sipped my coffee and asked.

"So, how are you doing Pepe'? What did I miss while I was away?"

He lay the hose aside and sat next to me thinking. "Not much Miss Minerva. The older, less agile residents always hang out near Miss Evelyn and I don't see much of the others. They take no interest in a common gardener."

I sat my cup down and told him, "I don't consider you common, my friend. Who else has such a way with plants and who would put so much effort into making sure our surroundings remain beautiful?"

He appreciated my response and just sat smiling. We watched the fat, busy humming birds fighting and screeching at each other. They were methodically drinking from each bloom. We were mesmerized for the moment enjoying the tiny, fierce birds as they fed.

He asked about my trip and I tried to engage him in conversation about himself. Once he got started telling me his story he never stopped until I knew his tragic past. I could tell he wanted to have someone to confide in and he missed his late mother terribly. My heart went out to him and I assured him I would keep all this to myself. He needed to tell his story and I got the feeling no one else had heard this much. Right then I made up my mind to invite him to go with me on my next trip up the coast and would introduce him to the rest of the family. I was getting very attached to this kid.

Pearl had always said I was a magnet for wounded souls and maybe I was. What harm could come of giving him an opportunity to see some more of the South and the chance to meet others that would not judge him. He was happy when he left to resume the day's chores. I needed a few items for my bathroom and decided to check out the pharmacy and little store right here. I got dressed and headed that way.

The minute I walked into the main building I approached Evelyn. I asked her if she had a minute and she looked up at me over the glasses hanging on the tip of her nose. She was wearing a bright blue dress and I think she had on a wig, but I wasn't sure. She always dressed nice and was looking smart today.

"I'd like to ask you about the small older woman called Maddy. I wondered who was in charge of taking care of her. I'm very concerned."

Evelyn removed her glasses and looked sad. "Well, truth is she has Alzheimer's. She has one daughter and two grand-daughters. Her name is Madeleine Hornsby. They brought Maddy here a year and a half ago and deposited her like they couldn't wait to be shed of her. The daughter would not listen when I explained that this is a retirement community and not a convalescent home. I have seen the grand-daughters here several times but they don't do her much good either. I have worried about her the whole time. I took away her key card and everyone knows not to let her out the front gates. I don't want to call the state and have asked her to live here with me, but she wants to be in her own house. She's a dear, sweet soul and I'm afraid she's getting worse all the time."

I thought for a moment and said, "I have an idea. I will make a couple of phone calls and see if I can get her a live in assistant right away. If you agree to do the interviewing of the most likely candidates I will go forward. This gift will remain anonymous of course."

She sat straighter in her chair, "That's mighty generous of you Mrs. Bonet, sounds like a plan to me. I worry about her constantly and those kids leave their clothing over there. She gets confused when she's having a bad day and has come over here wearing various articles that obviously belong to them. It would truly be a Godsend if someone could help her."

I told her I'd let her know very soon, when to expect arrivals for interviews. I left her and headed for the pharmacy.

The minute I opened the doors and the bell tinkled, I stopped and just stared. The girl behind the counter was the same one I'd dreamed about with Pepe'. She looked up and then looked away, obviously shy. A gentleman walked towards us. He had come from his office behind the front counter and he introduced them both.

"Good Morning, I'm Dick Richardson, the pharmacist and this young lady is Linda Sanders. Can we help you?"

I moved forward and shook their hands and told them I just wanted to see what they had here and needed a few items. This girl had a very bright light around her and I felt a tug at my heart. The man was average height, about 5'6" with salt and pepper, short hair. He sported a handlebar mustache and wore thick, brown framed glasses. He had a belly and I would've guessed him to be somewhere around sixty five years old. He seemed friendly enough.

I wondered around with a shopping basket on one arm. They had a very nice selection of gifts and after finding the few items that I really needed I took them to the register. The girl had a very difficult time looking me directly in the face. She spoke to the ground behind the counter and gasped when her dog came around the corner to greet me.

"I'm sorry, that's Butterbean and he doesn't listen very well."

I bent down on one knee and petted the little, white poodle who was licking my hand. We were instant friends. I told her that I didn't have any pets but not to worry, I loved animals.

She said, "He really likes you; he growls at most of the people here and Miss Feltch nearly got him one day with her ugly stick. I found him wandering around my apartment complex and no one has come looking for him yet. I've become terribly attached already."

I took my items and thanked her adding, "Well stop by for tea sometime Linda and feel free to bring

Butterbean. You are both welcome and my home is pet friendly."

She smiled and her pretty face lit up at the invitation. She was a petite thing just barely 5'5" tall. She had big, blue eyes and shoulder length, sandy blonde, straight hair. She looked too thin and I would have to remember to see if I could get her over to my place for dinner. I was drawn to her like I was to Pepe' and hoped I'd get to find out more about her.

I left the store and headed out past Evelyn, going home. I heard a loud rhythmic thumping and shuffling of feet. I stopped and looked behind me when a woman shouted, "Who the hell are you? I haven't seen you around here!" She stood straight and held a tall, round walking stick. It was well worn and she used it in the place of a cane or walker. I had to look twice; it appeared she was wearing an outfit made of chenille including a ridiculous hat to match. She had silver grey short hair and thick glasses with cat's eye shaped frames. She was a tall, large woman with a scowl. I stood staring not answering.

Evelyn piped in, "Mrs. Bonet, meet Miss Gladys Feltch."

I kept quiet and she slammed that big stick on the floor again and grumping, walked back toward the kitchen. Evelyn just shook her head and went back to work. I left and went home. I could now see why they referred to her staff as an ugly stick. It suited her.

I wanted a nap and needed my medicine. I had a headache brewing and frankly was now terrified to find out what would happen without the pills I'd become dependent on. I put away the items I'd purchased and lay down waiting for relief that would come very soon. I'd noticed a slight tremor in my hands this morning and would have to remember to put that on the questionnaire to send Jim. I lay on the couch to nap and woke several hours later to a light taping on my front door.

It was Linda, she had Butterbean in tow and the minute I let them in the small poodle jumped on my couch and began to hump one of the smallest pillows. Linda was horrified and near tears while I laughed loudly and told her it wasn't a big deal. I just took the pillow to the laundry room and would clean it. The little dog looked satisfied with himself and curled up while we chatted.

This girl was so sweet and I could feel her loneliness. She didn't tell me too much about herself at first. She was terribly afraid to open up and it just made me more curious. I told her she would be welcome to visit anytime. She said she lived in a small apartment a couple of miles away and had to go home now. I encouraged her to stop by anytime and she left.

I went out to the front porch with some iced tea to swing and admire the gardenias. The perfume of the velvety blooms was delightful and even with the ceiling fan on high speed; it was just too hot and humid to stay out here long. It was different flying around on the golf cart; you could generate enough breezes to stay fairly cool.

My phone was ringing. I was thrilled to see it was Jim. He wanted to make sure I was doing ok and getting some rest after two very active weeks with the family. He asked when I might be returning to New Orleans and I said I wasn't sure. I mentioned that Pearl and the girls were coming here in about two weeks and said he should join us if at all possible. He said he'd try.

I told him about Maddy and my concerns. I also told him Evelyn agreed with me and he assured me that in a couple of days he could have the necessary documents drawn up and would find several, qualified and competent applicants. He would send them over for Evelyn's scrutiny. I was so pleased and thanked him again.

I waited for the sun to be mostly down and went for a spin on my golf cart. Today I went across the far side of the property right of the main gate. It was so peaceful and cool under the huge live oaks. The dew was falling and the breeze was ruffling my hair. I stopped and sat on one of the benches by a beautiful flower garden and admired the surroundings. I stayed there until the gnats started to bother me. Back in my house I sat at my desk and wrote in the journals I was keeping for the kids. I put that away and went back to my couch to relax for the evening.

The pills had kicked in and I dozed off. When I woke up later I was starving. I made some dinner and ate in the living room. I was thinking of activities that the kids would enjoy when they got here and would have to read the brochures I'd been given. I fell back asleep on my couch, under my favorite throw.

I dreamed of a dark and oppressive room. There was a young girl child crouched in one corner. She had her arms around her drawn up knees with her head down. She was sobbing quietly and wishing she could escape her captors. I felt a need to save her from these abusers and woke up gasping for air. I sleepily rolled over and fell back asleep, soothed by the faint sound of joyous singing.

Chapter 23

Linda Marie Sanders

———❖———

I couldn't stop thinking about the nice lady. Pepe' had told me about her and she finally came in the pharmacy. She was beautiful. I had wanted to hug her and knew if I was ever that lucky, it would be wonderful, just to feel someone's arms around me with intentions other than hate and pain.

I wasn't sure if I should tell her the truth. I wanted to but what if she hated me afterwards? My parents had always told me I was worthless and didn't even deserve what little they gave me. There were days on end when I didn't even eat. It was so hard to hide from them and I was terrified of the box.

My mother drank and did drugs. My father never worked and only came home long enough to get drunk, share drugs with mother and then he came looking for me. Most times I could hide the bruises but had given up on that and going to school. It was easier to sneak out my bedroom window and hide in one of my favorite spots. I had never known what it meant to be loved.

They often came after me together and I begged God to save me. I wasn't sure if he ever heard me and most times they laughed and enjoyed hurting me. On the real bad nights after they'd taken turns abusing me they would drag and kick me into the basement where the box was kept. It was a very large dog kennel and smelled bad. It was made of wood and had a screen door that they padlocked after kicking me into it. It still smelled of urine from the last time I'd been left there. They had forgotten about me and I couldn't hold my bladder any longer. I sat crying, covered in my own waste, hungry and scared. No one loved me and I wished I was dead. I was mostly afraid to die alone here in this box in a dark, damp basement.

No one came to save me. No one cared and everyone around us was ignorant and poor. They ignored the screams and fighting. It was a terrible part of Alabama where we lived. I didn't have anything pretty like the other girls at school. I only went for a few years. Everyone made fun of me and said I was white trash. I didn't know what that meant, but I knew I would never fit in or be a part of their world. I made it a habit to pretend I was going and then would just hide all day. I dreaded going home. Someday if I survived these two monsters, I'd run far away and try to live.

I am now twenty one years old and had figured out how to escape, by accident, five years ago. I was killing time walking near the train yard when I saw the boxcar with the open side door. Looking around there was no one to see me climb up into the rail car. I'd fallen asleep and by the time I awoke I realized the train was moving too fast for me to jump off.

I was frozen in fear and exhilaration all at the same time. I would never go back to them and where ever this train stopped is where I would stay. They'd never find me to hurt me again. I lay back down on the hard, dirty wooden floor and dreamed of a better life.

Meanwhile, life continued as usual in the Sanders home. The sad truth was that her parents never once tried to look for the missing girl. They didn't call the authorities and were relieved they no longer had the responsibility of the retched child, one less thing to worry about. She was always so needy and bothersome. Now they could drink and do drugs and not be distracted by a whining brat. Good riddance was what they would tell you.

They'd raped and nearly beat her to death the last time they got hold of her. She'd been unconscious when they'd crammed her limp body into the box. When she woke up she didn't hear them upstairs so she became furious and kicked at the screen until she freed herself. She was older and smarter now and knew to run away for the last time. She would never see either of them again.

The train continued to pick up speed and I had awakened to the sound of the train whistle. I sat near the door, the wind was blowing my hair around my head and I was awe struck at the sites that flashed by as the train clacked and swayed down the rails. I had never seen anything but the small, shabby town where I'd grown up. I would have to learn how to work and take care of myself. I would never let anyone hurt me again as long as I lived.

It was early evening the next day when the train rolled to a stop. A sign in the rail yard said Beaumont Station. I didn't know where I might be. I looked both directions and slid out of the car to the ground. I tried to brush most of the dirt off my ragged shirt and jeans. The pants were too short, something mother had gotten from a dumpster. I rolled them up so they didn't look so bad and started walking toward lights and a town.

I saw a church and headed that way. I wasn't sure why I was drawn to this old, brick building but I was so hungry and tired. I wanted a bath too and maybe these people would help me and not call my parents to tell them where I was. I went around the side of the building and knocked lightly on the door. An old woman answered and gasped when she saw me. I was terrified again and almost ran away.

"Child, what are you doing back here, can I help you?"

I had tears running down my cheeks and prayed she would not turn me away. I told her, "I've run away from home and I'm scared. I haven't eaten for days and I don't know what to do."

She looked around behind me and said, "Come in here and let's have a look at you."

I followed her down a long hallway and my mouth was watering at the smell of food before we reached the cozy, clean kitchen. She pulled out a chair and I sat down. She busied herself fixing me a plate of food and brought a large glass of milk. I know I looked younger than I was. I prayed over the food and began eating trying not to wolf it down. I was starved.

She watched me eating and said, "There's plenty more child, take your time."

I smiled and sobbed as I ate. I heard the door we'd come in close with a click and was ready to bolt. Before I could get up and flee an older gentleman came in and looked at us questioningly. His wife explained what little I'd told her and he joined us at the table.

I was crying out loud now, begging them to let me stay or show me somewhere that I could. I blurted everything in one long rush of words. The horrible and ugly truth came pouring out of me and I couldn't stop myself. The woman was sobbing and the old man was praying. I was tired, heartbroken and desperate.

The man introduced himself as Pastor Jefferson and the kind woman was his wife Mary. She told me that they would let me stay. She even had bags of donated clothing for an upcoming church rummage sale. I followed her into their small home and we dug through the bags until we found clothes for me. She showed me where the bathroom was and I waited for her to leave before I drew a nice hot bath.

I thought about these kind people while I lay soaking my sore body in the hot water. Maybe this was God's way of helping me and I was beginning to understand how he did things. I had begged them not to call the authorities and promised I'd move on if they wanted me to. They never tried to find my parents and said they had prayed about what to do.

The woman showed me a small bedroom on the back of the house and they asked me if I would like to stay. Evelyn Pepper attended this church. Giving me a job in the pharmacy had been her act of Christian kindness five years ago. I still spend some of my free time with the Jeffersons and I always attend their Sunday services. They will forever hold a piece of my heart and I thank God for them daily.

My life was blessed the day the train stopped in Beaumont, Texas. I believe God had these kind and generous people waiting to save me. Mary Jefferson was the first person in my life to show me what unconditional love was. I treasured them and all they had done for me and I will never be able to repay them as long as I live.

The pastor had promised me that I was worthy of kindness and love and he knew without question that

God loved me. I had to believe him, what else could I do? In time, I came to trust and believe the things they told me. I felt human again. Still every now and then I would look over my shoulder, worried that my safe haven had been discovered. Mostly I feel safe and loved. I'm still trying to get used to these emotions. Sixteen years with abuse, hatred and pain had left me fearful. I was trying very hard to fit in.

I tried to think about all the positive things in my life as I walked to work this morning. I had friends now and a place of my own without fear of torture. I hoped I could get to know Miss Minerva better. I felt a connection with her that I'd never felt before. Things were looking up and I smiled realizing that I deserved to be happy and was thankful.

Chapter 24

EVELYN MAE PEPPER

Today Evelyn had decided to do something she had not done in a very long time, take the entire day off and spend it with her family. It was her mother's 90th birthday and the whole crew would be there to celebrate. This included her six sisters, two brothers, their wives and husbands, 25 grandchildren and 6 great grandchildren. It had taken them a month to plan and prepare for the event. Keeping the secret from their mother had not been easy; she was elderly but not deaf or blind.

The theme of the party was "Queen For a Day." Some of the kids had raided the school's preforming arts department and they had set up the back yard of Evelyn's eldest sister, Clara to look like a queen's court. The university had gladly loaned the throne, the very large cape and wooden platform when they found out what the kid's intentions were. These would be placed under a huge white, rental tent and they had strung lights around the entire area. They would have a rented pony and his handler to entertain the children and there were a dozen tables set up for all the food, gifts and the cake.

One of the sisters had a tiara specifically designed to fit their mother's head. It was beautiful and was encrusted with crystals and semi-precious gems of every color with all of their birthstones. It had turned out perfectly and had cost a small fortune.

Evelyn had spent most of the previous night making cupcakes and butter cream frosting. There would be enough food to feed the army and there were lots of party favors and games set up in the yard for the smaller kids to keep them pacified and entertained.

The birthday cake had been made by a local baker and was gorgeous. It was shaped in 4 large tiers, like a castle and had a miniature throne in front where the greeting and age were spelled out in pearls and piping. The entire cake was covered in painted, sculpted fondant. She knew her mother would be pleased. Noella Johnson loved her babies and each and every one of the youngsters called her Nunu.

Evelyn had asked Dick to keep an eye on the place in her absence and he had agreed, telling her that there shouldn't be any problems. The only resident they ever worried about anyway was Gladys and that damn ugly stick, or maybe Barney trying to stir up trouble. Otherwise, not much could go wrong. Besides, Dick knew he could always call on Chef for help and he was built like a linebacker. They were not expecting any new arrivals and there was still a waiting list. There were two available houses on the property, but they had been retained for later arrivals and hefty deposits had been placed to hold them.

It was almost time to load her car and head over to the party, but having two hours to spare, Evelyn put on a pot of coffee and put her feet up. She'd forgotten how exhausting baking 300 cupcakes could be and had stayed up late decorating them with flowers and candy pearls.

She dozed in her chair, coffee forgotten and thought back to her beginning with the Lancaster family.

She had just gotten out of high school and was looking for a job. She'd seen an ad in the paper for a live in personal assistant. It promised generous wages and full benefits with free lodging and meals. A driver's license was required and she had gotten one, but did not have a vehicle. Being of an age where she wanted to leave the chaos of a crowded home, she called the number listed and set up an interview. She borrowed her father's car and when she finally found the address and drove up the long driveway, the site of the mansion took her breath away. She could not imagine working here much less living in a place like this. Her family was middle class and never wanted for much, but this was like something out of a fairy tale. She smoothed her hair, checked her make-up and walked up to the huge double doors.

She grabbed the large lion's head door knocker and rapped three times. Almost immediately the doors swung open where she was greeted by a woman wearing a crisp and spotless maid's uniform of black and white. She drew in her breath and held out the ad saying she was expected. The maid led her into a room off the entrance hall, asked her to be seated and said the Mrs. would join her shortly. She was suddenly stricken with fear and self-doubt and wanted to run away. What was she thinking? How could she possibly fit in here or be accepted for this job? She sat there sweating and squirming for almost ten minutes when she heard the doors open again.

A woman entered the room and walked briskly up to Evelyn with her hand extended. She was tiny, immaculately dressed and sat directly across from her. After smoothing her skirt she leaned back in her chair. In a flurry of motion, two servants swooped in leaving a silver tea service, finger sandwiches and desserts on a side table. She just laughed and thanked them; Evelyn was too dumbstruck to speak.

Raising her cup the woman said, "Now dear, I am Juliet Lancaster. My friends call me Jojo. Please tell me all about yourself and why you think you want to work for my family."

Evelyn swallowed hard and her prepared speech went out the window. She sat her tea cup down, cleared her throat and began, "Well, I've just graduated from high school and would like to find a good job to save money for college. I saw your ad and felt like I should meet you and see if I might be qualified to be your assistant. I have secretarial skills and a very large family, so I can do just about anything."

Juliet smiled and grabbed a sandwich then handed the silver platter to Evelyn; she wiped her mouth delicately and said, "I am going to be honest with you. My mother is quite ill. I need someone who can help me with my bookkeeping, shopping, organizing and of course tending to her special needs. This will include running hither and yon. You see, she is still very alert and quite in charge of her personal matters. We spoil the old dear and give her whatever she wants. It won't be an easy job and I'm afraid you won't have a lot of free time, as she is quite demanding. You're probably wondering why some of the other servants cannot do these things. Frankly, this old place is so huge, they stay entirely too busy to help me with these particular chores or mother."

Evelyn just looked at the beautiful, kind woman. She had short, silver hair and soft blue eyes. Her features made her look like a pixie. She was 5' tall and was dressed in a suit with jewelry that could have been from Tiffany's. She had a smile that melted Evelyn's heart and for some reason she fell in love with this genteel woman immediately. She finally found her voice again and asked, "If you don't mind my asking, would I be required to wear a uniform? And I need to know if I would be allowed time for my own family and mother, as we are very close?"

Juliet laughed and it reminded Evelyn of small tinkling bells. She reached over and patting her hand replied, "Oh my dear, I would expect you to bring them here from time to time and would never take you away from them completely. I would not expect you to dress like the others, that's Patrick, my husband's doing. I'm afraid he was raised with parents that have their own ideas, none of which I agree with. You would spend the majority of your time with me and mother anyway and you would have your own small house out back and free run of the place. I have an outline of the job duties, hours and your wages and already, I like what I see, so what do you think?"

Evelyn relaxed and smiled, and couldn't say no to this adorable woman. She shook her hand and said, "I can be here tomorrow and I will be happy to work for you."

Juliet reached for a small bell sitting on the table with the tea and rang it gingerly. Three servants came out of nowhere and started clearing the trays. They seemed friendly, smiling as if they were already old friends. She stood, smoothed her skirt and stepped nearer to hug Evelyn saying, "Good, then it's all settled. Welcome to my home Miss Evelyn Johnson. You begin tomorrow and

I will give you several days to get your things moved in and get a feel for the place. You will meet mother and get comfortable then we'll dig in and get you started. Wonderful, that's what this will be, just wonderful! And now I am going to excuse myself and let you get home to tell your family about your new job."

Having said that she disappeared through a side door and Evelyn was left alone in the large room. She took her purse and let herself out. She drove home not believing what had just happened. It had all seemed too easy and she wondered how many other women had even been interviewed. She found herself grinning from ear to ear. She turned on the radio and tapped her foot to the music with the window down and the warm summer breeze blowing her hair. She couldn't wait to tell her family about this. Driving away she noticed a very large construction project underway just a couple of blocks from the mansion. There was already a huge security fence up and it seemed to go on for miles. She would soon find out this was the beginnings of Lancaster Estates and would become her permanent home.

Evelyn awoke from her nap and looking at the clock realized she better get busy if she was going to make the party in time. There were all those cupcakes to load into the car and gifts. She dressed quickly and realized she'd cried in her sleep.

She missed her late husband Terrance terribly and had loved every second she had spent with him. They had moved here to Lancaster Estates when Jojo's mother, Gloria Tevis could no longer be comfortable in the mansion home. Evelyn learned the history of these people through the years and was amazed they were relatives of the founding families of this entire area dating back to the 1800's. Juliet had been a Tevis, the very first family to homestead the area, they were oil rich, being the owners of the first major oil well in the area and you would never know of their enormous wealth by the way Jojo conducted herself. She was down to earth, no nonsense and had a heart as big as a house. She was not able to have children and always welcomed the families of everyone she employed. She loved and spoiled them and their children. She never allowed bigotry in her world and made it very clear to anyone and everyone that this would not be tolerated. It had caused several rifts in her social circles and she had quite literally removed several people from her list of friends and associates for their beliefs and views. She was ahead of her time and her opinions raised many an eyebrow. She was adamant that there was no place for prejudice n her life.

Her own mother, in her younger years, had been instrumental in hiding and aiding hundreds of run-away slaves. It was a dangerous endeavor and put them at risk. Mother and daughter were of a like mind and they could not abide slavery and abuse.

Patrick Lancaster was an odd duck who was hardly ever around and when he was everyone scattered in his wake. He left all the household affairs to Jojo as he worked constantly. He was tall at 6'5", thin and sported a large neatly trimmed beard. He stayed extremely busy and had a booming laugh that could be heard several rooms away.

They had left the mansion to live at Lancaster Estates when Jojo realized what a need the area had for a place like this. Evelyn had been with them the remaining years they lived. She had inherited and banked so much money; she could never use it all and spoiled her children and grandchildren at every opportunity. She had put them through universities of their choosing and had trust funds for each one. She owned the mansion now as well. It had been repaired, put on the historical registry and was a very successful bed and breakfast, run by a co-op of some of the previous employees and their children.

The Lancaster's had included each and every family that had worked for them in their last will and testament. None would ever go hungry or want for anything the rest of their lives. When the attorney had gathered all the beneficiaries at the reading of the documents, a vial of smelling salts was passed around the room. Many would later claim to have had "the vapors" after receiving the good news. It was unanimously agreed that their employer's generosity was beyond belief.

They had spent most of a lifetime there and the business at the B & B ran like a well-oiled machine. They grew all the vegetables and herbs that were on the daily menu and the expansive gardens became extremely profitable. Everyone had duties and got along with one another. It pleased Evelyn beyond measure. Her life had changed forever the day she cut the ad from the paper and she would always have an ache in her heart for the loss of Jojo.

She finally got everything loaded and headed to her sister's house. Still feeling nostalgic, she was relieved to be greeted by several of her children and the older nieces and nephews, all laughing and cheering at her arrival. They quickly drew her out of her funk and got her car unloaded before she even got in the house. She greeted her sisters and brothers and after a million hugs from all the kids, moved to the huge back yard to see what it looked like. She couldn't believe her eyes and was pleased with the set up. Her mother would be over the moon and what a party this would turn out to be.

Her second oldest sister Melda finally arrived with their mother who after wading through all the cheering children, was taken to the back yard where she placed her hand over her heart and just stood crying silently. They led her to her throne and as everyone sang happy birthday to her, tears continued to stream down her cheeks. The smallest of the great grand babies came toddling out, with assistance, holding a satin pillow with the tiara. They carefully crawled into her lap and then gently placed it upon her head. She hugged them all and in tiny voices filled with love, they each in turn kissed her old cheek wishing her a happy birthday.

Someone put on music and the party began. The throne faced the activities and Nunu just sat there being waited on all day and evening. Hours later she was escorted in for a nap. The robe remained draped over the back of the throne and platform and became part of the backdrop for many of the pictures taken. It was a huge success and no one would soon forget the celebration. It wasn't every day someone turned 90 years old.

Evelyn helped gather up the bows and spent wrapping paper from the mountain of gifts and finally sat with her brothers and sisters, happy that they had surprised their mother, each thankful for this large, loving, and still healthy family. Evelyn raised a toast to the day and put her feet up watching all the children. It was perfect and she counted her blessings.

She would be back at her desk tomorrow and life would return to normal. She couldn't believe how fast the years had sped by. After all, she had turned 76 on her last birthday. She never told anyone her age though, and you'd never guess from her appearance. She often wondered where life would have taken her had she not met the kind and gracious woman. She would forever be grateful for Jojo and Pat Lancaster.

It was thanks to them she had met Terrance Pepper, the love of her life and father to her amazing children. She sat there missing her husband and thinking of their union. The noise around her faded as her mind drifted back to that time.

It had been a beautiful spring day. Evelyn was then 22 years old and had mailed the last of the invitations to the annual bar-b-q that the Lancaster's hosted. People came by boat, in cars and by rail to attend. Some traveled from exotic and faraway places. Many came from Europe and Asia. There was extra staff hired and not an empty guest room on the property. Evelyn was in awe of all these peculiar people milling about. The accents and different clothing had her spellbound. The amazing part was they all adored Jojo and had known her for many years. It was just as shocking to learn how many languages her employer spoke. She buzzed among her guests, conversing with each one, never skipping a beat.

Jojo had another plan this year. She had grown to love Evelyn like a daughter and worried she was devoting her life to them and missing out on love. She only dated a couple of men and had not gotten serious with either one. Each year a chef arrived to do the outdoor cooking. His name was Terrance Pepper and he was hard to get. Everyone booked him and Jojo paid him well to keep her annual party date open. She sent Evelyn to the outdoor ovens and spits where he was setting up and prepping his menu. She had been instructed to help him and it was love at first sight. He was a tall 5'8", very well-muscled, and handsome. He wore his hair short and spoke like a true gentleman. They continued to see each other every chance they got and fell head over heels in love. They were married a year later in the expansive and beautiful gardens right there on the estate. It was a small and intimate ceremony with the three families and closest friends. They had jumped the broom to the cheering of those they loved most.

They had their first child exactly nine months later and proceeded to have five more, one after the other. Evelyn's plans for college had been forgotten. They lived on the property and she only took off enough time to have her babies and heal. All the staff fought over her children and they became fast friends with the others that were constantly under foot in and around the mansion.

Jojo could often be seen with six or seven of the kids piled in her new convertible car headed for the beach or zoo. Sometimes they went for ice cream or out on the property for a picnic and games. She loved them like her own.

Evelyn still had moments of questioning how she'd been so lucky to meet these people. There had never been any barriers caused by their different skin color. She'd had a very dark time when she lost Terrance just five years ago to a heart attack. After losing Gloria, then Patrick and not wanting to live any longer without him, Jojo soon followed. It was so much loss she feared she wouldn't recover.

Her children and grandchildren reminded her often that she was loved and needed. She had finally pulled herself out of her grief and rejoined the living. There was still days, even now where a photo could bring the tears. It had been an amazing and unexpected life she'd lived.

Now her days were spent watching over the legacy left in her care. She was surrounded by colorful and interesting people and there was never a dull moment. Her own children were busy raising their families and had successful lives. She was still in good health and looked forward to each new day.

It was late when she finally got home. She got into her pajamas and went to bed, opening a book, planning to read for a bit. She was so exhausted that she passed out as her head hit the pillow. She dreamed that Terrance was lying beside her smiling and happy with how the party had turned out. She turned getting more comfortable and feeling loved and content, she smiled in her sleep.

Chapter 25

Fun Times In Beaumont

—————➤●◄—————

Part of the family was coming in this afternoon. I was excited and couldn't wait to see them. I had looked over the brochures and thought there was a couple of fun and interesting options. We could take a boat tour of the Neches River or take a swamp tour and see the Shangri La Botanical Gardens. I'd let the crowd vote and decide. It all sounded like photo opportunities to me. I wasn't concerned about them meeting any of the residents and I hoped Gladys wouldn't act too grouchy.

I'd gone to the market and was stocked up and ready. Linda and Pepe' had been spending a lot of time with me. I was growing to love them both. So far Linda had gained ten pounds and I had convinced her that she didn't need to look down or away from people. Confidence was a hard lesson. These kids were an infinitesimal part of a much larger and ugly picture. I had gotten Linda to confide in me finally. I had ended up holding and rocking her, knowing she needed to let go of the pain. Each day I saw improvement. Love was a sure and steady cure for part of what ailed these two.

I was not surprised to learn neither of them had graduated from high school. I saw that as an easy fix and had been looking into in home preparation for obtaining a diploma. I hoped I was smart enough to lead them through this process. I had ordered all the necessary supplies and depending on how fast they moved through the material, their goals were reachable in less than a year. With study and focus, we could do this. I was very alarmed when Pepe' told me he had forged documents. I would need Jim to help fix this one. I think he would have to study and get his citizenship also. I would talk to Pearl and get her advice on the matter and I would get Pepe' and Jim together to figure out a game plan.

I couldn't wait for everyone to meet these two, they were both so loveable. Why hadn't the people they were supposed to trust been able to love them? Theirs was a horror story and I knew there was much worse out there, you just rarely heard about it. If I could help them and Maddy, I intended to give it my best shot. They deserved better.

Linda and Butterbean would come over often after her shift at the pharmacy. She was fascinated with our family photos and the discs of photographs. She would sit for a couple hours on end watching my shots of the world. I had found out that she had never ridden in a car, didn't know how to swim or ride a bike and had never owned a book. It made me angry and more determined to share these simple things most kids learned growing up.

When the girls got here I planned on teaching her to swim. I would surprise her with the swimsuits and little cover-ups I had gotten for her. She had told me that she had never owned a new piece of clothing. Even working here for the last five years, she lived on a very fixed budget and could barely afford rent on a meager, studio apartment. Pearl would have a fit when I got a chance to tell her about these two in private. I had no doubts my family would smother them with love.

I would go to the airport this afternoon around one thirty. I had called the girls and asked them to clean out their closets. I asked them to bring everything in a size small or medium that they wanted to get rid of. I said it was for a new friend and they were thrilled to help.

I hired a stretch limo to go pick up the girls. I invited Pepe' and Linda to join me. The ride to the airport in this plush car was magical for them. Neither of them ever had a taxi ride so this was special. I had to pay too much but it was worth it to watch their faces. My goal was to show them as much about life as I could for as long as I could and I hoped it would continue with my family's help.

When I saw our jet taxing up to the gate, I was thrilled. The girls were dragging an enormous suitcase and after the hugging and hellos were done, we headed out. Jim, Blaine and Joshua would join us in a couple of days. I tried to convince Jim to stay with us but he opted for the Hilton. I knew we always tired him out so it was ok if he wanted a quiet place to escape to.

After hugging me they each in turn hugged Pepe' and Linda. They both were very emotional and we just laughed and hugged them some more. We took everyone to a restaurant on the beach for an outside lunch and so the kids could get acquainted. Linda had just stood at the water's edge staring out over the gulf. She had tears streaming down her face. Pearl had come up behind her, wrapping the girl in her arms and letting her cry. They were tears of joy and amazement and we knew we were doing well.

Pearl was surprised at how much Beaumont had grown. The girls had noticed the river walk area and asked if we could come back here. I had them for a whole week to love and spoil and told them we could do whatever they wanted. In fact there were beautiful beaches we could drive or fly to if everyone was interested.

As soon as we got back to Lancaster the girls couldn't stand to wait. They both chatted so fast Linda could barely keep up. Butterbean went from person to person then headed to the couch looking for his favorite pillow. Not finding it he curled up between me and Pearl and slept.

They dragged the big suitcase into the middle of the living room floor anxious to go through all the items they'd brought. A lot of them still had tags on them, a bad habit that we all had. They unzipped the case and Linda just sat staring in disbelief.

She finally said, "Oh my goodness, I couldn't possibly take brand new things."

The girls both threw their heads back in laughter and told her she was expected to do just that. They all pawed through the stacks of neatly folded clothing. They dragged Linda to the bedroom where they had sets of things for her to try on. Almost everything they brought fit her and she modeled some of the outfits for us. We were comfy on the couch chatting and having cocktails. We didn't want to get too sideways; we planned on swimming lessons tonight. Linda was terrified but excited and the girls had taken to her immediately, they swore none of us would let her drown.

We took turns with the golf cart. It was a big hit. Linda had the whole day off and I could hear them howling with laughter as they sped around the property paths. Pearl just shook her head and we retired to my patio out back. She loved the flowers and humming birds. We had a roast in the oven and went in to refresh our drinks and to baste the meat.

When it was time to go to the pool, I sent Linda to my closet and told her the large bag on the floor was for her. The girls pawed through it with her and she picked the swimsuit I figured she'd love. It was covered with hibiscus flowers and she looked adorable. She hugged me long and hard and was so grateful. We headed over to the pool.

Pearl and I slid into the water and the girls followed. We started floating Linda with our arms under her, teaching her the basics of going underwater, dog paddling and leg kicks. She took to the lessons like a fish and she was beaming. Pearl and I left them there and I gave my sister a tour of the place on the golf cart and then headquarters where we drew quite a bit of attention.

But when I introduced her to Evelyn, she got up and hugged Pearl. I was surprised and she said, "I'm happy to meet family of Miss Minerva. She does good things for people!" We laughed and told Evelyn that if she ever got to tear herself away, she was welcome to join us for a cocktail. She grinned showing her gold tooth and said, "I might do just that!"

The girls finally came dragging in and Linda said she needed to get home. We made sure everyone sat down and had a healthy dinner before they went anywhere. Magnolia asked where her car was. She hung her head and was embarrassed to admit she took public transportation or walked everywhere. I looked at Pearl and we decided to put driver licenses on our list for her and Pepe'. He drove Lancaster's truck but I wasn't sure if he had a license or not. Magnolia got my keys and they drove her home.

The girls said they had helped Linda hang up her new clothes and told us she didn't own hardly anything. We explained that she was lucky and happy just to be alive. They understood and already felt an attachment.

We decided to book tours on both the river and the swamp and of course included Pepe' and Linda. I had told Mr. Richardson that we would be stealing his girl for a few days. He had winked and said he thought that was wonderful and he was happy to hold down the fort. We were supposed to board the big river boat tomorrow morning at nine and decided to get some rest. It had been an excellent first evening and I was so tired I never changed positions in bed all night.

We ate breakfast in the cafeteria so we wouldn't have a mess to clean up and headed for the dock. It was going to be hot today but fall was almost on top of us. We took one backpack with light jackets for everyone as we'd be out on the water all day and evening. It was amazing to see all the wildlife and I couldn't take pictures fast enough. I took a lot of pictures of Linda and Pepe' and they had never been photographed before so they were astonished at the images of themselves and those of the birds and scenery. Neither of them had ever done this. Pepe' had been on the ocean but they were like little kids today and we laughed until we were exhausted.

We found a fun place in town for late snacks and drinks and then headed back to my house. The kids insisted on driving Linda home again and Pepe' rode along just for the company. Pearl and I discussed the situation and agreed that they needed an education and she had a brilliant idea.

"You know that once I open my office after the grand opening of Live Oaks, I am going to need a personal assistant. Linda might be a good fit."

We both smiled and had a thought about Pepe' at the same time. We laughed and agreed that she would need a gardener for the plantation as well. I told her Miss Evelyn would never forgive us for taking these two away from her but knew in the end she would see the beauty of it.

We finally got to bed. It was late but there just weren't enough hours in a day. Especially once they were numbered.

I dreamed Magnolia, Matilda and Linda were tiny girls again. Pearl and I grabbed their hands and we danced in a circle. The moon was high and bright and the sweet sound of children's laughter floated on the night breezes.

Today we were doing our swamp tour. I warned the kids to keep their hands inside the small boat at all times. When they asked why I told them that our fingers might look like chicken to the spoiled, old alligators that followed these tourist boats waiting for handouts. Linda had become terrified and we assured her she could sit between us and the reptiles would eat us first. Everyone got a good laugh except her.

I pulled her aside and said, "This is another one of those trust situations Linda. I promise we won't let anything happen to you, ok?"

Timidly, she had agreed and off we went. We had been the smart tourists that had the bug spray. We ended up hosing down the other people with us. It amazed me how the average person lacked common sense. I mean, we were in a swamp, after all. It was a fun day and I captured yet more amazing pictures. I had already promised to give the kids discs with our adventures on them.

There had only been one near mishap all day. The guide was holding a piece of chicken out over the side of the boat and calling an alligator by name. As a very large reptile jumped up for the meat, another one jumped across him nearly flipping the first one into our part of the boat. The huge, open jaws of the reptile were even with the girl's faces until it slid back into the dark water. Linda, Magnolia and Matilda were screaming as if they were being eaten alive. Even the guide was shaken up. Once we got the traumatized kids settled down, the captain of the small craft moved away from that spot. I hoped they wouldn't have nightmares because of it. Pearl and I had laughed loudly once we knew there were no reptiles actually on board.

Later in the evening we got comfortable in the living room. The girls were on their computers and phone with Blaine and Jim taking care of business. Both of the boutiques were doing very well and still closing well over what a day's quota needed to be. We talked with Matilda and looked at her invitation ideas and her lists for the wedding. Pearl said she would try to get with Jarrod and nail down a completion date. The invitations would have to go out in plenty of time. The rest would be easy and realistically should only take three months to organize and make reservations for the tents, chairs and caterers. The florist in New York was already informed and held a list of the needed flowers. She was only waiting for a call to place the order. She would then overnight them by refrigerated express delivery. The musicians were already scheduled and a deposit had been paid so a lot had already been done.

The next afternoon Pearl and I snuck off to town with Pepe'. We took the Lancaster truck and came back with four bicycles. We didn't spend an awful lot and they were all girls' bikes. We hoped Linda would take to this as easily as she had swimming. Later with four of us to catch her, she wobbled and fell only once, she was determined to do this. By the end of the day they were riding those bikes over every inch of Lancaster Estates. They were squealing and laughing and me and Pearl got it on video.

We spent a couple of hours walking the streets of Beaumont and ended up with bags of deli food on the river walkway. We had to use the bug spray again and it was so humid our clothing stuck to us, but finally an early evening breeze was coming up and it was perfect. Pearl was ready to go back to my place so we left the kids there.

They came in later, showered and wanted to hit a club or two. We made them take a taxi and wondered what would happen if Linda got carded. She smiled and said the Jefferson's had gotten her a picture identification card. She wore one of the new outfits and I noticed she hadn't looked down for days. This was such good therapy.

With the kids gone we could talk freely. I was worried that Pepe' didn't have a green card and he needed that to be eligible to fill out the citizenship application. I didn't know what to do and Pearl agreed we would have to wait and ask Jim. It would kill us to see him be deported. According to him there was no one in Brazil to go home to.

We chatted about the plantation and Pearl told me the greenhouse off the kitchen was amazing. The tiles she'd ordered had worked out perfectly downstairs. All the chandeliers, wall sconces and ceiling fans were hung. She still hadn't decided on window treatments and didn't need any on the stained glass windows anyway. The downstairs of the plantation was done except for a few more coats of varnish, stain or paint here and there. The electric and water was done and they were pouring the pool and then they'd lay the tile.

I was so excited. They had the pool house framed in and her office was almost done. She said the fire pit and oven had turned out nice and the long and wide downstairs patio was being poured with leftover concrete from the pool. The tile for the patio was Spanish and gorgeous. The tile around the pool was Italian but they would complement each other. She had decided to use roll up canvas awnings on the back of the down stairs. The paperwork that came with it had said it was mold and mildew proof and we had a good laugh about that.

There had been a surprise in the conversation. Clarissa was blue for everyone and she had already visited the kids in their loft and had just left the beach house in Seaside. I was very surprised but glad. She was reaching an age where she might need people around that would want to help her. I'm not sure any of her servants would want that job after these past years of rude treatment.

Pearl mentioned that they were going to lay sod in a very large portion behind the big house. I hoped it would take hold and stay nice for the wedding. Jarrod thought it would be fine and would be much nicer than sand and spurs. Only weeds had grown on those yards for many decades. They had brought in loads of rich top soil and that would ensure success.

I had asked Pearl about Jarrod and if he had asked her out yet. She had gotten a sly smile and informed me that I was the one he kept asking about. We both laughed and I would have to think about that revelation.

The guys had called and they were coming in tonight. Pearl and I went for a swim then came back to get ready to pick them up. They got into the Beaumont airport on time and with their bags loaded we headed back. We were so happy to be back together and Joshua had made it this time. I kept thinking we needed to close the gaps of distance between us. I was still thinking about what I wanted to do. I had no way of knowing how much time I had left. I seriously tried not to dwell on the inevitable.

The kids had prepared a big spread of sandwiches, crackers, cheese and dips. There were long island ice teas and virgin tea. After the noisy reunion, we all grabbed plates, drinks and a part of the living room and ate our dinner. Linda and Pepe' joined us and we proceeded to have a spectacular evening.

The kids all went for a stroll through the grounds and Pearl and I talked with Jim. We asked him what to do about all the documents for Pepe'. He said he'd need a sponsor to get a green card and he'd be able to print an application for the citizenship test. It would require arduous study and memorization. He told us he'd be happy to represent Pepe' and be his legal counsel throughout the process. He recommended we get the green card right away. He promised us he would look into all of this as soon as possible.

Jim finally left for the hotel and everyone got into their pajamas. Linda and Butterbean stayed with us and Pepe' went back to his apartment. We made a pallet on the floor for Joshua.

I decided to ask Linda to live here with me instead of paying rent. She agreed, so happy she'd had tears streaming down her face. I had noticed my leg was trembling and took my pills. I fell asleep to the comforting sounds of the kids chatting. Maybe I should take it easier tomorrow.

I dreamed we were all at the plantation. The orchard was full of paper lanterns swaying in the moonlight. Children were dancing in and out of the trees. They were laughing until one motioned to all the others. Suddenly they ran to hide and I did not want to face what was chasing them.

Chapter 26

TEA FOR TWO

⟿➤●◄⟾

I got everyone to the airport and on their way home. On the drive back to Lancaster I was feeling lonesome already and hoped it wouldn't be long before we were together again. It was so early I decided to go back to bed.

It was going to be hotter than the gates of hell today and with the 100% humidity it would be like getting trapped in a sauna. I had awakened the second time feeling like total crap. I lay in bed contemplating my splitting headache and considered just hiding here all day feeling sorry for myself. At times like this I figured what did it matter if I got up or not? Being terminally ill didn't leave much room for hope. But that wasn't my style so I dragged myself to the kitchen and the pills that I knew would relieve the unbearable pain. I took a steaming hot shower and then dealt with the nosebleed that followed. It took three bags of frozen vegetables laid across my face, with my head tipped back, before it finally quit. I ate breakfast then threw it back up, still nauseated by all the blood I had swallowed. I was glad Linda was already at work and didn't see any of this. I was thinking about how much running around I had done with the family and I wondered if that was to blame. I was thankful it hadn't happened while they were here. I felt scared and miserable and needed a diversion.

I wrote in the journal I'd been working on and if I had any way of knowing how this long and strange day would go, I might have been better served to hide in bed all day.

After dressing in long sleeves and pants I pulled on my leather boots, baseball cap and grabbed my camera. Taking pictures always calmed me and my curiosity with the woods and bayou was my focus right now. I left my golf cart at the edge of the lawn and took off down a path in the middle of the back property. I had my small walking stick from my last jaunt and used it to separate the foliage ahead of me in the places where it was too thick across the barely visible path. It looked like I might have to turn back a couple of times when I found the briars tangled in with the other thick brush blocking my way.

I cautiously pushed on and saw two birds ahead of me in a small clearing. The cranes were rubbing their long necks together and opening their wings slightly and gently. I was stunned and frozen in place. It appeared this was part of their mating ritual and I captured it on my camera. They made soft and strange noises to each other and so far were oblivious to me standing not more than ten feet from them. They eventually moved off into the underbrush and soon I heard their wings as they took flight. My spirits were lifted and smiling I walked further down the path. It was a relief to see an open area ahead of me, the light was brighter and I noticed an unexpected object out of the corner of my eye and went closer to see what it was.

Someone had taken a huge, blue tarp and covered a very large pile of something, then sloppily had tried to camouflage it with branches. I took a few pictures of this and wasn't quite brave enough to wade through all the brush and lift the tarp to see what was underneath. It struck me as being odd and out of place back here. I was very close to the bayou now and the pungent odor of dark water and rot filled my swollen nose. I would never get used to that smell, swampy places always scared me a little and I was watching my surroundings closely for reptiles.

The old fence was just ahead of me. It was pretty much useless here as it was rusted, twisted, broken and lying flat except where some of the strongest vines held it up.

I heard violent splashing and birds screeching and I couldn't move, my heart was racing and I was afraid to go see what was causing the commotion. I crept to the fence and then closer to the edge of the water. There was a very huge alligator eating one of the cranes that I had seen moments earlier. The second bird was overhead, wings spread and feet rigid, frantically trying to defend its new mate. The reptile was not fazed by the squawking and continued to gobble down the beautiful bird without much effort. The surviving crane let out a plaintiff moaning sound and careened off, up and over the treetops. I felt sad and repulsed by the spectacle. I tried very hard to think of the food chain and still didn't feel any better about it. After a few seconds, I reminded myself to breath and took pictures of the beast with the zoom feature of my camera. I froze again, terrified and knew the reptile had seen me and was headed straight toward me. I had to get away but had been told to never run from them. It slowly pulled itself out of the water and laid on the grass and brush not 20 feet from me. I feared I would pee myself and started walking backward very slowly. He watched me and for every step I took, he slithered a few feet forward. I was scared shitless and just as he opened his enormous mouth, a very loud and obnoxious car horn blared and even back here it was loud enough that the stinky dinosaur and I both jumped. He swished his tail violently and I turned and ran for dear life. The thorns were ripping at my skin and clothes and I didn't feel it. I was almost at the edge of the grass, only a few feet more and I would be safe.

I was soaked in sweat from head to toe. I got to my golf cart and spun it around toward headquarters. I was gasping and could not catch my breath. When I got around to the front of the building I saw the black Rolls Royce, brilliant in the blazing sun. I just sat there admiring the beauty of it. Finally I was able to breathe normally. I was no expert on cars but had seen one of these at a car show with Graham. It was a black, rag top Phantom.

The driver's door swung open and a bent and elderly gentleman stepped out. He did a squat and jumped back up. He wore a tweed beret, had silver white hair and even as blistering hot as it was, he had on a light sweater over a polo type shirt and what looked like corduroy pants. He shuffled his Italian leather loafers a couple of times and I couldn't stop staring.

He had a ruddy complexion and a handlebar mustache. He wasn't more than 5'5" and reaching into the car again he produced a cane. Now he bent backwards, stretching and looking around he spotted me. I figured he was well into his 80's from the looks of him.

I was flustered to see he was walking toward me, now there would be no time for an easy escape.

"I say, you there!" He slowly came forward and stood ten feet from me. He seemed to be staring at me and suddenly I was uncomfortable. "Be a dear and tell me where I might find Miss Evelyn Pepper."

He had a very heavy English accent and I was speechless for a moment. Finding my voice I pointed and said, "She's at her desk there, in the building behind you."

He smacked his lips, tapped his cane on the pavement and lifted his beret to me. Then he turned on his heel and walked toward the porch and stairs.

I waited for him to go through the doors then went to admire the car. What a magnificent machine this was. The interior was brown button and tuck leather and in the back seat were two light brown, leather steamer trunks. Both had the initials CQ burnt into the surface right above the locks. There were colorful stickers dotting the tops and sides and it reminded me of pictures of cruise ships and days gone by.

I was so fascinated; I walked around the vehicle twice. I had almost forgotten my harrowing experience on the bayou. I needed to get something to drink immediately and now that the adrenalin had subsided, I was hungry. I went into the front and the old guy was at the desk talking to Evelyn. When she saw me she gasped, got up and ran over to me.

"Minerva!! My goodness, look at you, what in the world happened?"

I had forgotten that I had just sprinted through the woods and did not think about my appearance. I glanced in a wall mirror by one of the fountains and almost shrieked. My hair was sticking straight out, there were bloody scratches on my face, neck and hands, half of my shirt was hanging out and my pants were ripped and bloody. I'd forgotten about my boots too. One was untied; the long lace was trailing behind me. My baseball cap must have been left somewhere in the briar patch.

I tried to smooth my hair down and said, "I just had a close encounter with an alligator and ran for my life. Sorry, I forgot what I must look like."

The Englishman was taking this all in and then I noticed, Gladys, William, Maddy and a strange man I had never noticed before, all gathered by one of the game tables staring at us.

Evelyn moved my hair aside and checked my face. "Well, at least it's just scratches and should heal soon, you sure you're ok?"

"Yes, thanks, I just need something to drink, I'll be fine."

She moved back into her chair and said, "Minnie, this here is Mr. Chesley Quinn. He's your new neighbor in the house behind you."

All I could muster was, "Pleased to meet you." I then headed to the cafeteria for some iced tea. I did not want the chef to see me so I hurried, then almost sprinted back to my cart.

The creepy guy, was out on the front porch and it startled me as I ran past him when he very nastily asked, "My, my and who you be?" I was at the bottom of the stairs before I turned to look at him. He was standing now and staring at me. He sounded like a French Cajun and looked gross. He had short curly hair with tufts coming out of each ear and his nose. His eyebrows were bushy and unkempt and his face was unshaven, dirty and tanned. Something about him made my hair stand on end and I felt disgusted and wary. He was wearing a dirty, thermal, long sleeve shirt with polyester pants held up too high with suspenders. This made his lower extremities bulge and that was his intent. He looked to be in his late 50's and was wiry and muscled. There was a toothpick in the corner of his mouth that he kept rolling around. He was wearing dingy white socks and worn shoes with the tongues sticking up. His pants were hiked above his ankles. Who was this despicable man and why would Evelyn consider housing someone like that? I had certainly never noticed him and he must have moved in while I was in Florida. I decided I would find out later, right now I just wanted to get away from him and go home. I gave him the look of death and turned my back on him. He laughed at me with the strangest, high pitched giggle, I had chill bumps and flew home on my golf cart and locked my doors.

I got showered and felt clean and respectable again when there was a light knock on the door and Linda came in for lunch. Butterbean was so excited to see her he stood on his hind legs and danced in circles. I had never seen him do that and we laughed at his antics.

She had been terrified when she noticed my scratches and I showed her the pictures of the reptile that almost got me. I convinced her I would be fine and asked her about the horrid man hanging out at headquarters.

"Oh, that's Barney Ladou. Evelyn wouldn't tell me much about him except to keep an eye on him and never allow myself to be alone with him. He moved in while you were with your sister. I didn't ask more because he scares me and makes me feel creepy!"

I sat two glasses of iced tea on the coffee table in front of us and agreed with her completely. "That is probably a very good idea; he made my hair stand on end and I plan to ask Miss Evelyn about him.

Linda sipped her tea and sighed, "Well, he doesn't come into headquarters too often and Gladys can't tolerate him. She has already threatened to beat him with her big stick and I don't think he is too welcome with anyone. He seems sneaky and pops up when and where you least expect him."

We sat there chatting and looking at pictures of the swamp and the cranes and Butterbean was between us with all four paws in the air, snoring without a care in the world. We laughed and talked about Chesley Quinn. His moving van was out back and they seemed to be done unloading his belongings.

Linda had to get back to the pharmacy. I felt like a nap and curled up on the couch. Hours later I woke to what sounded like someone scratching on my front door. The poodle was barking ferociously, being protective and making a lot of racket. I got up slowly and went to see what he was fussing about and saw the edge of a white envelope that someone had tried to cram under my door. The weather stripping was too tight and it had only made it inside by an inch. One corner was bent and ripped. I was still half asleep and looked out the peep hole, not seeing anyone I opened the door and grabbed the envelope. I laid it on the coffee table and feeling groggy and stiff I went to wash my face and apply some antibiotic cream to the scratches that were now stinging and itching. I ran a comb through my hair and the dog was sitting by the sliding doors, whining to go out. I grabbed a lead I kept above his bed and took him out back to pee.

I needed to water the flowers again anyway; in this heat you could spray them all day. The plants were thriving and gorgeous and they made me so happy and relaxed. The humming birds were busy and darting all around me. I let Butterbean romp around so he would burn up some of his never ending energy. I had bought the mutt a bed, leash, brush, organic treats and squeaky toys. The tiny bed kept him out of my own for the most part and he usually ended up sleeping with Linda. The toys had turned out to be an irritating and noisy mistake. He loved the high pitched sound that the rubber monkey made and it was half his size. He fought and wrestled with it when he was bored. I hadn't seen him hump it yet, he preferred the brocade couch pillow, but it was probably only a matter of time. I turned the ceiling fan on high and stretched out in my chaise lounge, just relaxing and enjoying the colorful blooms.

Across the street the new resident was spellbound. Chesley was unpacking boxes in his living room when he heard a small dog barking and playing. He moved over to the window and noticed the beautiful woman and poodle. He stepped behind the drapes where he couldn't be seen and just stared. She was stretched out with her head back, smiling at something. He admired the curve of her neck and her long, shapely legs. He had noticed her exotic, blue eyes earlier today but was taken aback by her disheveled clothing and wild looking hair. Regardless; it had aroused him and made him more curious. That was when he put his fantasies for this early evening into motion. Feeling randy, he had written a note and snuck around to her front door to deliver it. Then he was running from bush to bush attempting to hide and get back to his own house without being discovered. He knew if anyone caught him they would think he was daft, but he was excited and anxious to see if she would respond to his invitation.

Laughing to himself he continued to dust and place his belongings and get comfortable in his new home.

He thought living here would turn out to be one of his best ideas, and only Miss Pepper knew that he had been a close friend of the Lancaster's. He enjoyed roaming and traveling and had been here before. This would be his home base while he explored the Western part of the US. He owned a palatial manor in the Northern part of England where he raised sheep and horses and had no family left. He had become bored at home and left his servants to run things for a while.

Smiling Chesley stood back admiring his living room and decided to work on the bedroom next, just in case things went the way he imagined they might, once his guest arrived. He glanced back at the woman and she was heading indoors so he got busy making his bed and arranging things in the bathroom. Across the street, Minnie was unaware that anyone had been watching her and had enough of the heat.

I took the dog in when it got too suffocating outside. I was still struggling with the humidity, my breathing was labored sometimes and I wondered if it was a new symptom. I needed to let Jim know I had been doubling my meds each day, for almost a month now. He would put it on the report and the Dr.'s would mull it over. I knew that it wouldn't make a difference, but they thought differently, so I tried to mention when anything felt unusual or seemed to be getting worse.

I made myself some lunch and realized I was exhausted. It was only 1:30 in the afternoon and it felt like I had run a marathon. I grabbed the ripped envelope and sat on the couch. The dog was playing and I read the invitation twice. It was handwritten in beautifully done calligraphy and said,

Please join me for tea
Around 6 PM would be lovely

Chesley

I left it on the coffee table and went to grab ice cubes for the orchids. I was considering the invitation, and thought it might be entertaining to hear the stories he would have to tell me. It might be fun and it was just a cup of tea, there was no reason to make it more than that. Maybe I'd take him a plant as a housewarming gift; I hated to go empty handed. I went out back and potted a nice succulent from a cluster growing in a large pot. I watered the plant and cleaned the pretty ceramic container then heard my phone.

It was Pearl and even without being able to tell her how terrible I'd been feeling it was a comfort to hear her voice. I recited what had happened on the bayou and she was horrified. I told her about Chesley and then Barney. She had become alarmed and begged me to be careful and keep my gun handy. She suggested I come back to Florida as soon as possible and I told her I would.

I took a shower and wore a conservative, purple sundress and white sandals. As an afterthought, I grabbed a headband and shoved it into my hair. After feeding and watering the dog I left a note for Linda to let her know where I'd gone then headed across the street to Chesley's house.

I rapped on the door and smelled something sweet and cloying. Before I could place what it might be a voice gently raised called out, "Yes, please do come in!"

I opened the door and froze in the entryway almost dropping the plant. I was trying to let my eyes adjust and at the same time wrap my head around what I saw in front of me. The smell was from twenty or so scented candles placed here and there in the front room. Standing before me was a very naked and hairy Chesley Quinn. He was grinning from ear to ear and the most shocking and bizarre part of the spectacle were the helium filled balloons, at least half a dozen, floating and gently bobbing right above his head. My eyes traveled down the ribbons and one was carefully wrapped around his very old and flaccid penis which was bobbing up and down as the balloons moved around. I involuntarily gasped and yelled, "Jesus!"

I turned around quickly and almost leapt for the front door. I got outside, shut the door, sat the plant down and walked briskly back to my place and never looked back until I had my door locked and the blinds drawn.

I could not believe what had just happened! I should have seen through his sly smile earlier today and here I thought he was a sweet, harmless old English gentleman. He looked older than dirt but was obviously very young at heart. I felt a bit of sympathy for him that he couldn't get his penis up without help from helium. Maybe he didn't know the gas was in short supply.

Linda came in from work and asked me if I was ok. I assured her that I was fine. She headed to take a shower and then went to her room. I called Pearl and replayed what had happened. We laughed until we cried. It was hard to accept everything that had taken place today. Lancaster Estates always seemed to have another surprise waiting. Now I wondered how I was supposed to act when I ran into this guy again. I decided that I would just pretend it never took place and hoped he wouldn't say anything about it.

I got into my jammies and went to bed. I passed out quickly from sheer exhaustion. The air conditioner was working overtime and the overhead fan was turned to high. It felt like heaven in my bedroom.

I dreamed that Pearl and I were flying down the coastal highway in a shiny, black Rolls Royce with the top down. The moon was high and full and we laughed at the absurdities of life. The bundle of balloons Pearl held above her head was straining in the wind behind us.

Chapter 27

The Chef With Two Hats

I woke this morning to the crashing thunderstorm raging outside. The lightning was flashing so brightly it lit up my room and the storm was directly over us. There was a whining, trembling poodle begging to get in my bed and I heard Linda in the shower getting ready for work. I reached down and lifted him onto the comforter and he immediately got under the covers and burrowed next to me where he calmed down.

I lay there thinking about Barney, not sure why my internal alarm was going off and I had a terrible feeling about him. I was glad Linda was here with me and it was easier to keep an eye on her. The dirty bastard always showed up when you least expected him. Because of this I had put a full clip in my gun and it was always within easy reach.

Linda had been around us all so much now that she had begun calling me Mimi some time ago. I was very comfortable with her living here and happy she was saving the majority of her wages. Dick had been suspicious about the nasty man also and was keeping an extremely close eye on him whenever he wandered into the pharmacy or near Linda.

By the time I got up, showered and cooked some breakfast the storm had moved south and out over the gulf. Today I decided to go back to the trail on the left side of the back property. This might be one of the last chances I'd get to take pictures there so I put on my boots and baseball cap. After covering myself in bug spray I grabbed my camera and just in case, this time I took my gun, it made me feel better having it with me and the fence was still intact on this part of the bayou. Not far into the walk there were so many gnats and mosquitoes that I had to re-apply my bug spray. I stopped to take pictures of a very beautifully colored trumpet flower. It was so humid and hot it felt like you could cut the air with a knife.

I was almost at the old gate where I could take some great shots of the old mossy pier and fishing boat when I heard the rhythmic, chugging of a large motor. It wasn't an airboat or outboard and I had to wonder what was approaching. The heavy rains had the bayou running deeper and faster but I wasn't sure just how deep it was.

I kept clicking off pictures when things began happening very fast. Someone grabbed me from behind with their hand over my mouth and eyes and with a strong arm around my waist I was dragged down and into the thick underbrush. I was drenched in sweat and my heart was pounding out of my chest, I was terrified. I soon realized that whoever it was didn't intend to harm me and the boat was almost directly across from us now. A calm, deep voice whispered in my ear. His lips brushed close to my hot skin giving me a shiver.

"Miss Minerva, I need you to be very quiet and stay still, it's Chef."

He took his hand away and relaxed. Still whispering he told me, "You've stumbled into a mess and that boat is full of smugglers with guns."

I let him gently push my back so that I was now lying flat, next to him and he nudged my shoulder meaning for me to scoot further back behind him. He was crouched and intently focused and two things worried me. One was the possibility of what could be in these bushes with us and the other was the bad men who were now right next to us on the water. I could smell burnt oil from their engine and cigar smoke drifting over us on the humid air.

I noticed Chef's attire. He had on a black cap, shirt and pants and there was a camo backpack next to him. He smelled wonderful and I smelled like fear and sweat. I stifled a fit of hysterical laughter at the thought and feared I might be losing my mind right about now. This was certainly not the time to be thinking such things and suddenly I heard rapid Spanish being spoken by at least four men. Two were laughing and I could hear faint salsa music coming from below deck in their cabin. I just hoped they would keep going but they had come to a stop and were discussing something with one of the men sounding very stern and serious. After what seemed an eternity they continued on their way. When we could no longer hear them Chef rose slowly and bending over me he grabbed me gently under the arms and picked me up as if I weighed nothing. He looked at me and put a finger to his lips meaning for me to stay quiet. He then spoke into a radio and all he said was, "Clear."

I had no idea who he might be signaling and he looked in both directions and spoke to me calmly saying, "I need you to stay out of these woods for the next couple of days. It's for your own good and you'll have to trust me, I'll explain everything very soon."

He bent down and pulled a wallet out of his pack and took out two different business cards. One of them had an emblem on it that I couldn't quite see and the one he handed me was white and plain except for a name and phone number.

He looked me in the eye and said, "Keep this handy and call me if you need help. My name is Agent Robert Barrett."

All I could manage was, "Sure, no problem." My speech was slurred and my mouth was dry. He walked away and left me standing there holding the card and watching his back disappear into the woods next to the water.

I turned to go back down the path to my golf cart with so many questions swirling around in my head. What in the hell else could happen around here? It was surreal and I felt drugged and sluggish. Why was an agent posing as our resident chef and what the devil was going on back here on the bayou? Had smugglers been here before and had I been putting myself at risk all the times I'd been exploring? It made me faint to consider what could have happened to me. I was thankful he had been there but was extremely anxious to have him explain what was happening. And why did he think that I might need his help? That comment had me nervous.

I took a nice hot shower, had some iced tea and took my pills. My head hurt like a son of a bitch and I was drained from what had taken place. I called Pearl and she was beside herself almost threatening to come and take me away from here and back to Florida with her. I assured her that I intended to heed Robert's advice and steer clear of the woods. We finally laughed but nervously and I promised her I would keep in close touch.

I went to the kitchen and began to cook dinner, it relaxed me a bit and the pills kicked in so I finally felt human again. I would not share any of this with anyone. Who would believe me anyway? I wondered how much Miss Evelyn knew and wasn't sure if I should even mention it to her.

I was beginning to think that maybe I had lived here long enough and wasn't sure how much more I could endure. It had been a long, strange day and I would be happy to go to bed.

We had dinner and Linda could tell something was preying on my mind. I kept trying to change the subject and she accepted that I wasn't going to tell her why I was pale, drawn and worn out. I tried to blame everything on a headache and smiling I kissed her good night and crawled under my covers.

I dreamed that Chef and I were in the kitchen. He was still wearing his black outfit, only this time he had on his white chef's hat. We moved in slow motion and he turned to look at me holding a plate of food and winked. Before turning back to the grill he mouthed "no problem" without speaking. I drifted back into deep sleep with the sound of faint singing all around me.

Chapter 28

BARNEY LADOU

Barney had gone back to the house the black woman had insisted he rent. He didn't have any money and was suspicious about who was paying the bills. The county had moved him here to Lancaster Estates when they had last released him on three misdemeanor charges. He had a rap sheet as long as his nose hair. The clean house made him nervous and he snuck off to his shack at the edge of the swamp when he figured everyone was asleep. No one noticed his leaving and he was careful to return before sunup. He was more comfortable in his own place, surrounded by his belongings and treasures with no one for miles around to invade his privacy.

He thought of himself as a brilliant criminal mind. Truth was that he was despicable and evil. He had secrets that even he couldn't face at times. He was antsy and pacing today, pissed off at the ugly, giant woman named Gladys. She had threatened him with that big stick of hers again and had called him a retched swamp goblin. He was thinking of ways to hurt her. Until he could do that he decided to resort to the ritual that always calmed him. Digging through the moldy, green Army duffle in the corner of the bedroom, he found what he was looking for. It wouldn't be as satisfying here as it would have been in his home. None of them knew where he really lived and he would make sure they didn't find out.

The small pink tee shirt still held a faint reminder of the sweet young tramp he had pulled it off of. She was 15 and had crossed Barney at the wrong time. He had sweated and planned until he was able to lure her outside of the backwoods bar. Everyone inside was drunk and rowdy and no one heard her screaming for help. He'd had to knock her out quick because she was young and had fought to live.

She managed to claw his ugly face hard enough to draw blood just before the crashing blow that killed her. He had thrown her in the back of his pickup, covered her with a tarp and went back to the swamp and his cabin. He raped her cooling body and after tying weights around her feet and wrists he flung her out into the dark water off his back porch without another care in the world. The tee shirt was his prize and it would remind him over and over of his power. It wasn't the only one either. He had carefully hidden various articles he'd taken from each person. Sometimes it was nothing more than one earring. His habit was to hold and rub the item along his flesh. It made him tingle and felt like a small electrical current running through his veins. He would always cum the hardest when the objects held a scent.

At one time the cabin had been a lovely, respectable little retreat for normal people who enjoyed a brief stay in the wild environment of the swamp. Barney had discovered it by accident many years ago on a day of paddling through the swamp in his stolen boat. He had approached it from the back and had carefully checked to make sure no one was there. The brush in front of the place was thick and the long driveway was grown back in. He had removed the sign at the edge of the county road and Turtle Cove had simply ceased to exist on the county assessors records. The last person to come to make an appraisal had not found the sign or house and it slipped through the cracks. The owners were all deceased and oddly no one had made an effort to investigate further.

After a time Barney felt safe there, as most were fearful of the dark water, alligators and poisonous snakes. He hadn't repaired anything for over 20 years and it was literally rotting down around him. There was no longer running water or plumbing. He had an outside water pump and an outhouse. He never bathed anyway and hated water. He always stank and liked it that way. The house could no longer be seen through all the trees with the Spanish moss hanging low and the thick vines and brush making a perfect and complete cover.

Barney needed money and was trying to figure out where he'd get some without having to run the risk of being caught stealing. He was already on probation and couldn't risk going back to jail. One evening at the backwoods bar he frequented, he was approached by a large, intimidating man who spoke broken English. The guy had scared him at first when he had bought him a drink and had given him a business offer. The Spaniard had been watching the small, odd man all night from across the room and figured he would be the perfect patsy for the task. He hadn't seen anyone come near him or show him any attention. Barney had puffed out his chest and boasted that he could handle anything they needed him to do if the price was right.

This would be the largest amount of dope he had ever seen and his eyes were glazed with greed. He was to drive to the coast, meet a seaplane and help load the bails of pot into his truck then deposit them on the bayou in a place that would be easy for the four men to access. The man with the scarred face and large cigar knew that Barney was too stupid to be a threat and that no one would miss him if he got in their way.

Unfortunately for Barney, there was another solitary man in the bar that night whose sole purpose for being there was to keep an eye on the sickening Cajun and he had overheard their whole conversation. Information was then passed from one agent to the next and plans put in motion. The drunker he got the louder he boasted about how rich he would be and very soon. No one listened or believed him.

Barney only had to wait one more day for the men to come for their stash. He feared the wildlife would find the pot and somehow damage the goods. He had crept into the woods most nights to check on it. He had sprayed urine and sprinkled blood meal around the exterior of the pile of neatly wrapped bails. This had proved to be effective and he was able to relax a little. He had seen that woman back here taking pictures and she had made him nervous and suspicious. It had confused him but he had dismissed her for now.

He was hearing the voices in his head tonight and they were telling him how wonderful it would be to fuck up the Minerva woman and the horrid old bitch Gladys. He just wanted to kill her, but the other one could be fun and satisfy his needs. He was frustrated and didn't have time to think and make plans for this pleasure. There was the deal that had to go down and he needed that money.

He was a little afraid of the dark skinned, Spanish man who'd hired him. He didn't want to screw up or cross him. He imagined there was plenty of time for the bitches. Oh, he would fuck them up alright, as soon as he got the chance. There was the sweet, young one at the pharmacy too. He had decided to save her for last. Yes, living here might end up being very satisfying after all.

He rubbed the tee shirt across his naked body and could hear only his heart drumming in his ears and the voices. After satisfying himself, he stretched and smiled in the darkness. Now he could sleep. Soon he was going to be very busy. He had to try to stay focused; sometimes it just seemed impossible to do that. He needed the money but what he really wanted would have to wait and was more powerful than greed.

He thought he had heard the black woman and the young girl talking about her living with the fancy bitch. Maybe that would work to his advantage and he had never taken two at once. It needed careful thought and planning though and right now he just wanted to close his eyes. He would wait until the pot had been loaded onto the boat and then give it his full attention. It gave him something to look forward to and quieted the voices for now. They kept telling him to hurry up, but he knew that could get him arrested and worse. It would be wise to move slowly and carefully.

After tomorrow night he could relax and have some real fun. He wanted nothing more than to leave this place and go home. The cops had said he had to stay here for his probation period and he hated every minute. He still didn't understand why he had to be here. It was confusing and didn't make any sense. At least the food was good and he hadn't had to hunt and kill his supper for weeks.

He would get up soon and go check the blue tarp and make sure all was well. The men that hired him had already checked out the bayou and knew where he had put their pot. There were 24 bales stacked neatly waiting to be loaded on their boat, it wouldn't hold more. They had expended all the other waterways in the area and the river was too risky. Barney didn't think anything could go wrong. He had a big surprise coming and not the kind that gave him a hard on.

Chapter 29

GOBLIN IN THE NIGHT

Linda and I had breakfast and chatted about upcoming events. Pepe' had come by to deliver a notice from Miss Evelyn. They were spraying the property tomorrow and everyone was asked to stay off the grounds all day and the amenities would be closed for the entire day and evening. He had coffee with us then left to distribute the notices to all the other residents.

I didn't question this and saw it as an opportunity for Linda and me to have a wonderful outing. We decided to have a girl's day and would do some shopping, take a road trip to a beach she hadn't seen and find interesting places to eat.

The weather was very hot and sunny but the breeze off the gulf was heavenly. Butterbean was worn out from running back and forth chasing the sand pipers and his coat was stiff and stinky from the salt water, he finally lay on the blanket with us enjoying the shade of my large umbrella.

It was 8: o'clock in the evening when we finally got home. We dragged in our purchases and put the beach things away in the garage. After we had both showered and had a snack of leftovers we decided to call it a day and go to bed. It had been such fun, buying shoes and clothes and Linda couldn't get enough of the beach. We were both worn out.

I took my pills and was so tired I fell asleep right away. I was tossing and turning and dreamed that Graham was concerned, he kept telling me to wake up and to grab my gun. I rolled over thinking how strange this was and that's when I heard something outside my bedroom window. I looked at the clock and it was 2:30 in the morning. Suddenly I was wide awake. I quietly slipped from the bed but squatted beside it rather than standing up. I froze when I heard someone trying to get into my bedroom. My heart was in my mouth and I wondered if Linda's window was locked. A feeling of fear swept over me. When I no longer heard anything, I grabbed my gun from the nightstand and quietly slid the drawer open grabbing the card Chef had given me with his phone number. I wouldn't call just yet.

I tiptoed to Linda's room and looked at the latch on the window. A shadow moved by, barely visible through the blinds. One street light shone dimly on this side of the house. I moved to the bed and shook Linda with my hand gently placed over her mouth. I leaned over her and whispered, "Linda, it's Mimi, be quiet and come with me, someone is trying to break into the house!" I grabbed the throw on the foot of her bed and she sleepily followed me to the pantry.

In a whisper she asked, "What are we going to do? Mimi, I'm scared!"

I hugged her shoulder and said, "I've got my gun right here and a number to call for help."

I led her to the farthest corner of the huge pantry, covered her with the throw, then told her, "Be very quiet and no matter what happens you stay here until help comes, understand?"

She just looked up at me with huge eyes filled with terror and nodded yes. I crept to the living room and felt a cold chill when I saw that both the front porch light and the back patio lights were out. I always left them on and was now extremely glad I had lowered the large blind over the bay window. I held the gun ready and went into the kitchen. Someone was trying to get the sliding glass doors open. There was only two ways to do this, they would either have to have a glass cutter or smash the glass as I had installed steel security bars midway and at the bottom.

My skin was crawling and I was so alert I could hear every move they were making even being inside. I knew they would now move to the bay window so I moved back into the living room and knelt down by the coffee table to dig my cell phone out of my purse. I ran on tiptoes to the bathroom, closing the door and called Chef. He answered on the first ring.

"Robert Barrett here."

I tried to be calm and told him, "Robert! It's Minerva, sorry to wake you but someone is trying to break in. I've got my gun but we're pretty scared!"

He was breathing hard indicating he had sprung into action and was already on the move.

"On my way, I'm close, stay hidden!" With that said he disconnected and I peered around the corner and saw and heard the front door handle being turned left and right. I could hear metal in the lock as they attempted to get in. I thought the dead bolt would hold and figured they'd have to kick in the door and knew that was a possibility.

I took a deep breath and tiptoed to the door and even though I was terrified to do it, I looked out the peep hole. I saw that it was Barney and now I felt anger mixing with the fear. I then made a decision that could've gotten both me and Linda killed. Holding my gun gave me tremendous courage and I planted my feet, put a bullet in the chamber and flipped the dead bolt.

The door was flung open so suddenly and violently that I jumped back and got ready to fire on this horrid man. He almost fell into the house not expecting the door to open and that had given me a chance to move back and take a defensive stance. Without yelling but with a stern tone I asked,

"What do you want? Stop now or I'll shoot!" Oddly Butterbean had been quiet up til now and he stood closely behind me with his teeth barred and growling deep and low. I raised the weapon and leveled it on his head and said again, "I will kill you if you don't stop!"

He had a maniacal look about him and his eyes were red and glassy. I knew at that instant he was very crazy and perfectly dangerous. He stood still and in the most repulsive voice I'd ever heard said, "You shoot Barney and you miss all the fun I got for you."

This time I told him loudly, "Stop! I'll shoot you!" Then I noticed him raising his right hand which was holding a very large, curved and deadly looking knife. At the same instant he started to move toward me, I heard gravel crunching out front in the dark. Without hesitation I lowered my gun and shot him in the foot. He dropped to the floor, grabbed his foot and was screaming insanely but still gripping the knife. He attempted to get up and that was when Robert landed squarely on top of his back and slammed him to the floor. In one swift motion he relieved Barney of the knife and flung it behind them out into the dark and cuffed him so quickly it was a blur. He continued to scream in anguish, I had mangled his foot and as far as I was concerned he was lucky there wasn't a bullet between his eyes.

Robert looked up at me and asked, "Where is Linda? Are you two ok?"

I lowered the gun and assured him that we were both fine, then went to the pantry to let her know help was here and it would be ok.

Barney was screaming at me, "You bitch! I'll cut you in a million pieces!" No sooner had he spit those words toward me than Robert proceeded to cuff him upside the head and told him, "Shut up now or I'll let her finish you off!" Grabbing his radio Robert spoke to the officers that pulled up in my driveway. The pulsing and whirling red and blue lights lit up the entire front yard and my living room. It was all so surreal.

I had taken Linda into her bedroom and hugging and kissing her, I told her to stay there and not to worry; everything was going to be ok. She was sobbing and didn't want to let go of me. I told her to get dressed and she could come join us and I'd put on a pot of coffee.

Robert had grabbed a kitchen towel and roughly tied it around Barney's foot and was already dragging him outside and cramming him sideways into the back seat of the cruiser. He came back in and they left through the front gate where I could hear the monster screaming the whole way.

I came from the kitchen and Robert was wiping his brow and rearranging his cap. He asked again, "Are you sure you two are going to be alright? His eyes were moving from one window to the other looking for signs of forced entry. That's when I knew what his next question would be.

"How did he get in?" I laid my gun on the coffee table and Linda timidly came out and joined me.

"Really, we're fine and I'll have coffee in a second. I hate to tell you this but I saw who it was through the peep hole and opened the door so I could shoot him myself. I know it was a stupid move, but frankly I was furious. And I would have killed him to protect Linda."

I ran my hand through my hair and was beginning to feel calm again. I asked him how he liked his coffee and brought each of us a cup. He sat across from us and shook his head. He looked at the floor and said, "Well, it worked out this time Minerva, but that guy is dangerous and meant to hurt you both. He's got balls, I'll give him that."

He sat the cup down and told us, "I should get down to the station, there will be paperwork to fill out and don't worry, he won't be leaving jail for a long while, you shouldn't have to worry about him anymore." He stood and moved toward the front door.

I walked him outside and said, "Robert is he why you gave me your card? Did you suspect something like this might happen? I have so many questions for you, but I will never be able to thank you enough for getting here so quickly. I didn't want to kill him but was definitely going to do just that!"

He shook my hand and said, "I'm going to come over later this morning and bring another officer that I believe you've already met. We'll have Miss Evelyn with us and

I'll explain it all then" I moved toward him and reached up to give him a hug and then he was gone.

I was certainly not sleepy anymore and just felt numb. I was trying to figure out who the officer that I had already met could be. There wasn't a lot of blood on the floor considering I had nearly blown the man's foot off. Linda and I got busy and had it clean and sanitized in no time. She sat with me on the couch afterward, cuddling and was finally convinced we would be ok.

I felt bad that all the hard work we had done to help this girl had almost been undone in one night of terror. We talked about it and finally ended up laughing and agreed that we should have called in Gladys armed with her ugly stick. Linda was sure Barney could not possibly be any uglier. Butterbean had gone to the spot on the carpet and peed on it with a smug look of satisfaction on his tiny face. We laughed and cleaned it once again. Linda scolded him but not too badly, he was making a statement and we understood why.

It was almost sunrise and we decided to have breakfast since we were up. I called Pearl while Linda cleaned the kitchen and she freaked out. I got her calmed down and told her that pretty soon she was going to have us there with her. This had been the final straw, and she could not abide my being here any longer. I assured her that Barney was securely locked up and couldn't hurt anyone.

I sat on the couch thinking about all the strange and unusual things I'd been through while living here. At least it had brought Linda, Pepe', Maddy, the Jefferson's and Miss Evelyn into my life so it had been worth it. I felt that everything in a person's life happened for a reason and they were why I had been led here.

We realized that before long we would have company so we each took a side of the couch and decided to grab a little rest. Butterbean settled between us and lay there with one eye open, watching over us. I smiled to myself realizing that Graham had been watching out for us too, even from afar. We napped soundly.

Chapter 30

AGENT WITH A HOOK

———

Linda woke me by shaking my foot and I was momentarily disoriented as to where I was and what was happening.

"Mimi, wake up, what time were those men and Miss Evelyn coming over this morning?"

I sat up rubbing my tired eyes which felt like they were full of gravel. Yawning I saw it was 8: o'clock. I thought for a moment and said,

"Well, I'm really not sure, but let's get up and put on some coffee and put out the pastries so we have something to offer them."

She took the dog out back for a few minutes then we took turns in the bathroom freshening up and waiting for our guests. We didn't have to wait long. A half an hour later they were knocking at the front door. I went to let them in and there stood Robert, Miss Evelyn and Alex Jackson. Suddenly I had an epiphany and it was all coming together. So this was the other agent and that explained a lot. Our past encounter back on the bayou played forward in my mind and now I knew why he had acted so strangely.

After all the greetings, we gathered in the living room and Linda busied herself serving everyone. Miss Evelyn was beside herself, almost in tears and spoke first.

"Miss Minerva, I am so sorry about what happened last night. I feel terrible having slept through the whole thing. I would never have allowed that man to stay here had I known how dangerous he is!"

I got up and hugged her and assured her, "Don't you apologize for that maniac, how could you have known his plans? We are just fine and thanks to Robert, no one was killed and Linda and I are shaken up but perfectly fine. I would never blame you for any of this!"

Alex had brought his brief case and he sat it on the floor beside him. He spoke next saying, "I am told you have pictures of the blue tarp, may I have those? We will add them to the evidence and if you don't mind I'll take them now. I want to apologize as well. I wasn't at liberty to tell you my intentions or purpose for being on the bayou the day we collided."

I got up and grabbed my camera off the desk and handed it him. He reached in the briefcase and pulled out a USB cord and proceeded to download my photos onto a small and sophisticated tablet computer. He was done in minutes and told me,

"We had to make sure you had no connections or involvement with what has been going on back there or with Barney. None of us could figure out your fascination with the bayou and you have been watched since you arrived here. I hope you don't take offense at this; we were just doing our job. We have been living here and using this as our base of operation for almost two years. The smugglers are getting cleverer every day and we had wind of them using the bayou to move drugs out into the river and on to larger boats. I'll let Robert tell you the rest." He then put his tablet and cord back in the briefcase, sipped his coffee and leaned back in the chair.

I just stared at him and then exploded in laughter saying, "I am about as far from being a smuggler as you can get, and the only connection I would ever have with someone like Barney Ladou would be to attend his funeral after I filled him full of lead. Let me ask you this, do you really enjoy fishing or is that just one of your disguises?"

He sat his cup down and smiling told me, "I do enjoy fishing and thanks to Robert and I needing to be back there, we were able to add fresh fish to the menu. Lucky for all of you that Robert was actually a chef in his past work experience. It became a win, win situation."

Robert spoke up, "The reason for all of this beside what you've just heard is the arrangements that Ladou made with a group of nasty men who will stop back there tonight to load all the bails of pot under that blue tarp onto their boat. Miss Minerva, it was them when I had to put you in the bushes with me. They are supposed to be here around 7: o'clock this evening and that is the reason we had Miss Evelyn close the amenities and try to keep the residents off the grounds. We're hoping we are able to apprehend them without anyone being injured or killed and there are many agents in place to insure it goes smoothly and quickly. They've been watching your movements also."

I asked to see both their credentials and each of them reached for their wallets with the badges. They flipped them open revealing an FBI badge for Robert and Alex had one for the DEA. I asked what would happen now that Barney would not be there to meet the smugglers.

Robert sat his cup down and wiped crumbs from the corner of his mouth saying, "I don't think it will stop them. He was just an easy scapegoat for them; they only needed him to put the contraband in a spot that would be easy to access. Even though he is out of the equation, none of our own covers have been blown except to you and Linda. Miss Evelyn has known from the start what the situation is and was kind enough to house and feed us and we commend her for keeping our identities safe. It will all be over tonight and then will only be a matter of policing the bayou by boat from time to time. I am deeply sorry that you had to endure the events of last evening. We had no idea that would happen and we only had him under a partial surveillance, had we known his true, sinister nature it would have been round the clock. I'm very grateful no one was harmed."

I ran a hand through my hair and said, "I don't want to think about how it would have gone down had you not gotten here so quickly, that guy scared me senseless and I'm just glad I didn't have to kill him, I'm a very good shot and we won't worry about him any longer. I looked at Miss Evelyn and asked, "Would you like to come and wait here with me and Linda tonight?"

She refilled her coffee cup and smiled saying, "Yes I would love to, and we're as far away from it as we can be here without actually leaving the property. I don't think we'll need to, these men here have everything planned and it should be over very quickly. Now if you all will excuse me, I need to get back to my desk. Gladys is in a foul mood this morning, as usual, and I like to keep an eye on her. She does seem to be sweet on the new cook I've hired though and I don't want to miss anything." Laughing she got up and hugged me and Linda in turn and left for headquarters. Just before going out the front door she hesitated and turned back to tell me, "Miss Minerva, Robert has one more thing to tell you and you must decide if Linda needs to hear it. It is so disturbing I will have nightmares no doubt. I'll see you all later." We watched her leave and I looked at Robert waiting for this revelation.

The men looked at each other and I took the hint, Linda had been through enough. I asked her, "Honey, would you mind giving us a few moments of privacy and take Butterbean out back?"

She smiled and seemed relieved to be excused, after hugging me and Robert she whispered, "Thank You" in his ear then went out back with her dog. I looked at Robert waiting.

He cleared his throat and seemed to pale before speaking, "After what happened last night we went into the house Miss Evelyn put Barney in and made a gruesome discovery. We found a woman's earring, a girl's tee shirt and various weapons. Our detectives pressured the cretin into telling us where his cabin is, turns out Barney Ladou is responsible for the deaths of at least eight women that we know of so far. We are still gathering evidence and I cannot say more just now. He won't ever be leaving jail and our discoveries have us all sickened. None of them was as lucky as you and Linda and we have our work cut out for us."

He looked at the floor and shook his head then told me, "We should be leaving now, there are a lot of good men ready to wrap this mess up, you will be safe here and I'll have a couple of officers placed in a location to assure just that. We don't want anyone getting hurt and we ask for you to stay indoors tonight until it's all over."

Elizabeth Sabin

He stood and reached to shake my hand, and Alex did the same. Mr. Jackson was a man of few words and had been happy to let Robert do most of the talking. I walked them outside.

Alex got in the car and Robert told me, "We have suggested that Miss Evelyn hire some security to remain on the grounds and she agreed. We have very capable men who are willing to live here and do just that. It seems the wise thing to do and couldn't hurt."

I reached up and hugged him, thanking him again and promised that we'd all stay here behind locked doors until they finished the job this evening. I wished him well and asked him to be careful and stay safe, he smiled and he and Alex left.

Linda came back in and we had the same idea, sleep. We were strung out and here again there would be another evening of excitement. We decided to nap until Miss Evelyn joined us later tonight. We went to our rooms and both passed out. I'm not sure we could've handled hearing what was going on out at Barney's place. We'd had enough.

The investigators had roughed Barney up to get him to talk and even then his answers were fractured and vague. They managed to get the general location of his cabin as being Turtle Cove and they had combed maps and city records trying to locate the place. It hadn't been easy and you literally could not see a thing from the road. They had fanned out and began walking toward the swamp, hacking at the thick brush and vines until they found it almost an hour later.

There were local law officers, a hazmat team, the FBI and Alex was the only DEA agent on site. There were detectives and several men from the coroner's office, the woods were swarming with men and the going was slow and physically straining. Using machetes they eventually hacked their way to the front of the house where they began removing vines and brush in earnest so they would have room to maneuver.

The shack was falling down; the rusty nails could no longer hold the decayed boards. The front screen door was full of ragged holes and mold covered most of the damp wood. The porch was sagging and caving in. The glass in the two front windows was broken out and only large shards remained. The roof was rusted and the tin was curled and bent with the whole thing sagging inward.

The first two officers to reach the front door were hit so hard by the smell inside; they reeled covering their mouth and nose. Everyone could smell an outhouse nearby but it wasn't visible yet. One of the men turned and spoke into his radio, "Boss, this is going to be bad, get us some better gear out here."

Without hesitation the lead agent spoke into his own radio requesting the lightweight hazmat suits to protect his men. They all continued to hack away at the vines and underbrush so no evidence would be overlooked. A team of detectives in town were combing the missing person's files and opening all the old cold cases.

Once the two men were suited up they carefully entered the shack. What they found in the front two rooms made their stomachs flip. In the kitchen area there was a partially butchered nutria rat. The flies and maggots had been busy and a pile of rotting entrails was in the corner on the floor. There were stacks of dirty dishes, overflowing garbage and roaches everywhere. The other side of the room had a ripped chair with the stuffing coming out. A lamp with a torn shade was placed between that and the window and thick vines had found their way past the broken glass, attached to the frame and were trailing down the wall to the floor. It was apparent that the swamp had been busy reclaiming this place for a long while. The ceiling was bare wooden beams full of old cobwebs and all sorts of bizarre things suspended by fishing line. They saw bells of all sizes, animal bones and wind chimes. The men looked at each other shaking their heads and moved toward the large back room. There was a ripped screen door that led to a deck and beyond that was wide open swamp.

The sun was still high and some natural light shone through the door and windows, but both men switched on their powerful flashlights. The electricity had been disconnected long ago and they didn't want to miss anything.

One of the men jumped backward yelping and startling his partner. He pointed and they both backed up as a very large snake slid from underneath a pile of junk and disappeared into the debris in the front room.

This area appeared to be where Barney slept. There were large piles of dirty clothes, trash and a nasty pallet with a nearly black pillow on the floor. They couldn't have been more grateful for the suits that protected them from what they were wading through and they knew the smell would be overwhelming.

They noticed a small closet door in the corner that was slightly ajar and kicked things out of the way to open it wider. Cautiously they both peered in and then looked at each other. There were several shotguns, knives, coils of rope and a large rusty metal box with a padlock. After pulling out the guns and removing the shells, they ended up with quite an array of weapons. It was easy to break into the metal box and it contained most of Barney's most incriminating treasures. There were several drivers' licenses, bras, panties, jewelry, a hairbrush, cell phones and wallets. Each item was bagged as evidence and the last thing in the closet was a large hefty garbage bag full of women's clothing.

They carefully moved out the back screen door stepping onto the unstable decking. The cypress knees had raised one end up and off the foundation. The lichen covered boards had splintered and the railing was rotten and falling apart.

Looking into the swamp there were several alligators just a few feet away watching their every move, and acting like they were expecting something. That's when both men looked down and one spoke into his radio, "Boss, you better come see this."

Their captain made his way to the deck and looked where they pointed. Not more than five out into the water it was clear enough to see a skull, half buried in the mud.

"Son of a bitch!" he exclaimed then he hurried back through the house and got on his radio to headquarters. The officers were bagging and tagging evidence left and right and now arrangements were being made to dredge the swamp looking for remains of Barney's victims that the alligators had left intact. It was now clear he had tossed them out his back door with no fear of being discovered, assuming that nature would clean things up for him.

The men worked all day and brought in lights that evening. One by one the different crews left and the only men still working were out in the swamp. Armed officers stood guard over them so the reptiles didn't get any ideas. They would end up being there for two more days and found the remains of several people.

Barney Ladou's killing spree had come to an end and he would be lucky to not receive a death sentence himself. If so he would pay for their lives with his own.

Chapter 31

SMUGGLER'S BLUES

⟢⟢◈⟣⟣

None of the Lancaster residents had worried about the notice that Miss Evelyn had distributed. She took extremely good care of her inheritance. The grounds were sprayed once a year. It was just being done a little sooner this time. She also scheduled annual home inspections to keep an eye on maintenance needs, pest control and it also gave her a good idea of anyone who might be hoarding or slipping into unhealthy living habits. She would be heading over to Miss Minerva's house around dinner time and thought it would be an enjoyable evening regardless of the situation taking place on the bayou.

Gladys and the other residents were in their homes for now. She did not plan to re-open any of the amenities until the next morning anyway, she went to the pharmacy and told Dick she was going to take a nap at her place and asked him to hold down the fort. He was closed for the most part, catching up on his bookkeeping and would only open the doors for emergencies. He had told her to go rest and not to worry.

I heard Linda stirring and decided to get up and showered. It was near 5: o'clock and she was in the kitchen cooking dinner. Whatever she was making smelled wonderful and I joined her to help. Pepe' would join us women and we'd wait together for the all clear from Robert. We had fun chatting and doing the dishes and then ended up in the living room where the kids wanted to watch a movie. Miss Evelyn and I had some wine and we just waited. We knew we'd hear the large trucks rolling through the front gates. I told her I was mildly disturbed that I had been watched anytime I left my home and wandered the grounds. On one hand it was comforting that they could have interveined if anything happened and on the other hand it felt very invasive. We laughed and I told her I would have some tall tales to share with the family and we both agreed there was never a dull moment around here.

It was already 7: o'clock when we heard helicopters. We flew to my front porch and thought we heard a single gunshot. Miss Evelyn hugged me and we looked toward the back of the property where all hell was breaking loose. The kids joined us and then the woods were suddenly lit up by spotlights on the choppers. There were muffled voices shouting but we couldn't hear anything distinct being this far away.

Within moments the gates swung open and a very large black truck with painted windows rolled toward the back grounds. This was followed by a prison type van with bars on the windows and the last two vehicles in were an ambulance and a sheriffs car.

We decided to go back inside and wait for information. It wasn't easy after hearing gunfire.

Robert, Alex and a large group of men were hiding around and near the blue tarp and the pot. When they heard the boat approaching they took their places ready for anything. The boat was lit up and music could be heard below in the cabin. They stopped very close to the bank and two men jumped off and tied the boat to nearby trees. They counted five men now as two more jumped onto shore and the one of them in charge stood in the bow smoking a cigar. As soon as they walked up to the tarp the choppers were overhead spotlighting them. A bullhorn boomed the command to put their hands in the air, amazingly they simultaneously did just that. Not one of them had brought a weapon off the boat. Robert came from one side of the brush and Alex the other. There were three agents with weapons trained on the men and they yelled at them to hit the ground and began cuffing them. Robert came forward with his gun drawn and told the single man on the boat to put his hands behind his head and to get off the boat.

He smiled and remained where he stood. Alex saw the man raising his right hand and the light reflected off the weapon he held. That was when Robert shot the gun out of his hand wounding him and then they swarmed the boat. The large Spaniard held his wounded arm and never dropped the cigar; it was firmly clamped between his teeth. They began marching the men through the brush to the footpath and out to the waiting van where they were cuffed again to the bars on the seats. Their leader was loaded in the ambulance with two officers and the EMTs' treated his wound. He continued to smile and didn't seem fazed.

Another team of men were loading the bails of pot onto all-terrain vehicles and began transporting it to the edge of the woods and the waiting truck. They quickly loaded the evidence and left three men with guns in the back and one in front with the driver.

Robert, Alex and four other men searched the boat and radioed to the men waiting on the bayou blocking the way ahead telling them that they were done and the area was cleared and secure. Two men stayed on board to pilot the boat to an area where they could impound it and the men's weapons. The choppers turned off the spotlights and left. The woods were dark once more and the frogs and crickets picked up in earnest, filling the night with the normal sounds of the bayou.

Alex and Robert got into their vehicle and drove to Minnie's house to let them know it was safe. The large black truck, ambulance, prison van, and two trucks that had the ATV's loaded on trailers rolled out the front gates one by one.

I heard a tapping on my front door and Robert leaned inside and said, "I'm happy to say you're safe now and it played out better than we expected."

I told him and Alex to come in and Linda went to get them both coffees. Miss Evelyn hugged them both, relieved to see they hadn't been harmed. She had become attached to the two men and would be very sad to see them go. Everyone gathered in the living room and the men looked drained. I could not imagine the adrenalin rush they'd experienced.

Alex spoke telling us, "We wounded the guy in charge of the operation but not fatally, he will be fine after a while. You folks should have peace and quiet from here on out."

They were grateful for the coffee and had a full night's work ahead of them with the evidence and the paperwork they'd have to submit for the arrests. They sat their cups down and thanked us.

Robert told us, "This went more smoothly than we imagined it could. They were over confident and Barney had convinced them that no one ever goes back there, they hadn't expected us to be there and we're grateful that it's over. You never know with these guys. It's routine deportation for the hired hands. We send them home to jail; they get out and sneak back in. It's never ending. They'll do just about anything for the money the drug runners promise them. It's sad really."

I asked them if they were hungry and they graciously declined the offer to have some dinner. Miss Evelyn spoke to them both saying, "Well thank the Lord you two are alright. I want you to know that you're welcome around here anytime and I'm sure going to miss your good cooking Chef. I can't thank you enough for everything you've done and I think I'll head home and to bed. Good night everyone." She hugged us each in turn and Pepe' decided to walk her home and go to bed too. Linda announced that she was tired and went to her room. Everyone was completely exhausted.

Alex took his cup to the kitchen and told me, "It was nice meeting you Minerva; you should be able to roam freely back there now, but just keep your eyes open. Thanks for the coffee, Good night." He told Robert he'd wait for him outside and went to their car.

I walked Robert to the door and told him, "I'm sure going to miss your squash casserole."

He hugged me and laughing said, "Maybe I can cook for you some evening. I'd enjoy that a lot. Besides I admire a woman who isn't afraid to protect herself."

We walked out to the waiting car and I told him, "As good as that sounds, I am seriously thinking of joining my sister in Florida. If you're ever in the Seaside area, feel free to look me up and I'm sure anyone can direct you to the old Beauford Plantation. Robert, I can't thank you enough, I'll never forget what you did for me."

Smiling, he joined Alex and they left. I waived and watched them roll through the gates. I went inside, locked the house and went to bed.

I dreamed that I was piloting a very large boat out on open blue water. The sun was high and bright and the gulls soared above us. A large school of dolphins followed us, leaping beside and ahead of the boat. They were all there, my new friends and acquaintances from Lancaster. Linda, Pepe', Miss Evelyn, Robert, Alex, Maddy, William and Gladys were all seated around the bow and smiling, letting the breezes cool them. I wasn't sure where we might be headed except to a better tomorrow. We didn't care; we motored toward the sound of a multitude of joyous voices raised in songful praise. Thankfully I slept more soundly than I had in weeks.

Chapter 32

MANY HANDS MAKE LIGHT WORK

The months were speeding by. Nothing surprising had happened since Barney and the smugglers had been jailed. I was sticking close to home and my symptoms were getting noticeably worse. I was terrified. I had been getting dizzy spells, extremely bad headaches and tremors in my extremities. The pain in my head was so intense; I was now running to the bathroom, so nauseated I would hug the toilet for hours. I'd even awakened once on the bathroom floor. I had been getting nosebleeds and once I'd found a trace of blood on a Q-tip after swabbing my ears. I was running out of time and didn't want to face it. I tried very hard to hide all of this from Linda and it wasn't easy. I blamed it on migraines and she tried to understand.

The plantation was finally complete for the most part. There were only minor details left and Jarrod had a list he was going through. Pearl had sent announcements for the open house and I received a magnificent wedding invitation too. The events would be two weeks apart. I needed to call and offer my help, not to mention needing to shop for formal wear for the open house and a bride's maid dress. I felt like crap and hoped I could pull this off.

Pearl was moving into the big house and Jarrod was going to rent the small one. He had already sent a crew and his sons to the beach house to figure out cost and materials. He thought that project would only take five or six months. He would remain on the plantation while they worked on the cottage and only use his camper when workdays ran too long to drive back and forth. He had been completely agreeable to let anyone that needed to share the extra bedrooms while he stayed on the plantation.

I called Pearl and Jim. I arranged for the jet to be in Beaumont to take Pepe', Linda, Butterbean and myself to Florida. We had about two weeks to get ready and I was going to invite these two to make it a permanent move. They had both sailed through their studies and both had proudly obtained a diploma. Linda had been so thrilled with the books; she was now enrolled in an online program that was offered by the Junior College here. Soon she would have a degree in business management.

I had helped them with everything, had shopped for computers and they were both pros now. I told Pepe' I wanted him to meet us for dinner here at my house. I also invited Evelyn; I wanted to be honest with them all. After giving them the schedule of the upcoming events, I made the proposal of them making a move to Florida with me. Evelyn had been encouraging and both the kids agreed right away.

Linda and I had spent an afternoon with the Jefferson's and told them the exciting news. They had grown to love her like we did and tearfully wished her well and said they couldn't be prouder of her. They made her promise to keep in touch. I of course invited them to the wedding and offered to fly them and Evelyn in our jet so they wouldn't miss it. Linda wanted to show off the office she would be sharing with Pearl working as her assistant.

I called my sister and asked her if she was ready for three, permanent house guests and a poodle. She was thrilled at the prospect and told me she wished I hadn't waited so long to decide. She was fighting tears and it was because she was so happy. She assured me that there was plenty of room for all of us including the pillow humping dog.

We had managed to make Pepe' a legal and proud citizen of the United States. It had been a long and complicated journey of red tape and paperwork. Jim walked the kid through every step and had been there by his side through the entire process.

We had taught Linda how to drive and they both had valid driver's licenses. Everything had gone smoothly. I would sell my cute house here at Lancaster Estates and move to the plantation. Linda was excited for a better paying job that was a career position. Pepe' was happy to be the groundskeeper for Pearl and couldn't wait for the move. I didn't think Butterbean would mind, as long as he wasn't left behind. We sat and made plans. Our belongings would be loaded on one truck and the three of us would fly into Panama City on our jet. These two kids were so excited they were walking on air.

Miss Evelyn had pulled me aside one day in the cafeteria and asked me about my health. She said I looked pale and drawn and I told her I was having bad headaches that left me looking this way. She had accepted my explanation but knew there was more.

I felt a desperate need to be with my sister and confide in her that I was sick and in trouble. I just prayed she would not be angry and would forgive me for not telling her sooner. She had gone back to Savannah and had a long heart to heart discussion with Clarissa. It went well and they had taken a week, going through all of Gregory's belongings. Most of it went to Goodwill and Clarissa kept a few things to remember her precious son by. The house there on the VanDeCourte property would be willed to the grand-daughters along with the rest of Clarissa's estate. She had confessed that she had changed her will for the final time. The moving truck had arrived and Pearl left with a promise from her mother-in-law to attend both events that were fast approaching.

Pearl now had a peaceful feeling and a renewed love and respect for Clarissa. She had softened considerably over the past two and a half years and wanted desperately to be forgiven and included now whenever there was a family event. She was in her early eighties and only wanted to be close to the few people that loved her. She had been invited to arrive early and stay through the events and her offer for help was readily accepted. It would be wonderful.

The first challenge for Pepe' would be purchasing, loading and hauling the flowering plants and shrubs that would be placed around the grounds, all before the open house. He said it wasn't a problem and he had a list of what he'd need before we arrived. Pearl had made the task so much easier by having lists of her own and diagrams of where she wanted everything planted.

Blaine and Jim would be flying in about the same time we were arriving and Pearl would be up to her neck in company. They planned to stay through both events and Blaine was becoming a nervous wreck. We assured him that all he had to do was be dressed and show up on time for the wedding, we would take care of the rest. He had laughed nervously not realizing that it was that simple. Joshua would tie up loose ends in New Orleans and arrive last.

I checked in on Maddy and sadly she was not doing well. Her live in nurse was adorable and had fallen in love with the old dear right away. She actually remembered me the day I came to say goodbye and a tear rolled down one cheek when I bent to kiss her sweet face. I tore myself away from her and never looked back. My heart was breaking and part of my anonymous gift included the cost of a very fine funeral for the time when she expired. It was all I could do.

We found ourselves busy and excitedly packing and making our plans for leaving. Now there was something to look forward to and I tried not to dwell on having to say goodbye to everyone here. Besides, they would be with us very soon and more memories would be made. Time was short and I worried how much I actually had left.

Chapter 33

THE CAT WITH BLING

———⟶●⟵———

I was enjoying my coffee and looking at the boxes I'd packed. The moving truck would be here tomorrow for mine, Linda's and Pepe's belongings and then would drive eight hours to my sister's plantation in Seaside, Florida.

It was bittersweet leaving Lancaster Estates after such a short stay. I'd only been here two years and a few months. I had been drawn here seeking changes in my life. I had gotten just that and then some. I had captured the beauty and essence of this place with my camera and it truly was an amazing area.

If only I had more time. I thought about Pepe' and Linda and wondered if they were ultimately the reason I had ended up here. I was happy to help them and knew they were destined for great things in their lives.

I have always been of a mind that friendships are lasting creations of the heart and during my stay here, I had made some fine ones. The residents here were as diverse as the weather and I had only gotten to interact with a few. They were unique characters and some more loveable than others.

I headed over to headquarters to hug Dick and Evelyn goodbye one last time. I would make them promise to keep in touch.

The new chef was a very tall and goofy looking fellow with a heart of gold. His name was Larry Jepson and he could cook circles around all of us. He had short red hair and light green eyes. He had a comical manor and laughed and joked with everyone. I thought Gladys might be sweet on him and found that surprising and although it was comical it was a little scary. I was sorry I wouldn't get to know him better and be here to see how their relationship would end up.

I was in the kitchen getting food for tonight. Pepe' would stay with me and Linda and sleep on the couch. We didn't want to cook at home and everything was packed anyway.

I heard a lot of commotion in the lobby while Larry was preparing our take out dinners. I wandered back into the front room and Evelyn commented, "Looks like our new resident has arrived." She noticed me and said, "Except for your house Miss Minerva this lady is taking the last of the two houses on the north side of the property. They're both three bedrooms and she has quite a gang in tow."

I stood by Evelyn's desk watching Maddy, Gladys and William. Gladys wanted to be front and center for the best view and yelled at William. "Look out you old fool, find another window!"

Poor William looked downcast and moved his tall walker slowly to the opposite side of the room where he could see the spectacle outside. Maddy was terribly confused today and with her tiny hands clasped to her chest she exclaimed excitedly, "Oh how wonderful, the

Queen's come to call!" Sadly she had ignored me, not remembering who I was.

Gladys took one final look outside and grumpily slammed her big stick on the floor then turned and headed for the kitchen to flirt with Larry. William waited until she was a safe distance away and then rejoined Maddy at the best window.

Evelyn laughed and said, "Lord, help me. That's a gal named Beatrice Paplovich. She has the most beautiful and breathy voice, kind of like Marilyn Monroe sounded, if you know what I mean."

I laughed and walked over to join them and couldn't believe my eyes. Beatrice was taller than Pearl. She must have been 6'7" or so and was thin yet shapely. The sun was glinting off her diamonds. She was dressed in light tan cashmere from head to toe including her designer gloves and even her pumps were expensive tan leather. Her beret was held in place by a very large diamond hat pin. Her sweater had a V-neck and her necklace was gorgeous. I'd never seen so many rocks on someone. Her bracelet was 1 and ½ inches of solid gold and diamonds and literally blazed with reflected light in the bright sun.

Larry came to join us and give me our food. I thanked him and left but ended up sitting on one of the porch swings not wanting to miss anything. That was when I noticed the cat. At first I thought it was a weird looking dog. This feline abomination sat regally by his master, was enormous and appeared to be a Siamese of some sort. He was on a long gold leash and wearing a very large gold collar studded with diamonds.

Looking behind them I saw three vehicles parked in a row in the circular driveway. One was a silver Bentley and behind that were two black vans with dark tinted windows. An eighteen wheeler slowly pulled in behind the last van and parked. The uniformed chauffeur stood behind the woman and there were two uniformed maids standing with another driver beside one of the vans. There were two other men standing at attention and they looked like body builders. It was all so weird, I couldn't look away. The semi driver finally made his way up front and approached the woman. When he stuck out his hand to introduce himself, the hell cat stood, put himself between the guy and his master and let out a growl and bark worthy of a St. Bernard. The man jumped back cussing and shocked that it was a cat.

Beatrice bent slightly at the waist and scolded the beast in a soft, whispery voice and told him, "Sam! You must be kind to our new friends!"

Just like that the cat looked at her, flicked his very long tail back and forth and walked indifferently back to his spot behind and beside her and sat down. I thought he looked like he wanted to rip someone to shreds but he minded her completely.

She, the cat and the Semi driver then came up the steps to go in and see Miss Evelyn. The truck driver gave the cat plenty of room still scared of what it might do. As they noticed me she stopped and said, "Hello, my friends call me Bea." She extended her gloved hand and I shook it saying, "Minerva, nice to meet you."

I figured she was checking in and from the looks of her entourage, two houses would barely contain them. I'd seen enough and not wanting our dinner to get cold I walked over to my golf cart and headed home.

For the rest of my days I would think about that damn weird cat and wonder about these new residents and the comical chef and feel sad that I was missing it all. Living here had brought a little bit of magic and a whole lot of adventure to my life and I would never regret a minute of it.

The day we rolled through the big iron gates for the last time, I marveled at the two young adults with me. They had taken long and frightening journeys to reach this day. I was very proud of them. Their lives were just beginning and mine was ending.

We got loaded on the jet and strapped in for the flight. The kids took their favorite places next to the windows. They were used to the jet now and had already flown back and forth several times to New Orleans and Florida with me. It was a beautiful day and I was happy for another trip. I wouldn't get many more, I knew this. I planned to make the most of whatever days I had left.

Linda unzipped the soft crate that Butterbean was traveling in. He walked around the plane then came over to my seat. He waited for an invitation then hopped into my lap where he remained for the rest of the flight. The kids were on their computers and I fell asleep to the drone of the jets engines.

I dreamed I was sitting on a cloud, high in the heavens. Graham was with me. We were peering at our families down below us. Pearl was in anguish. She was angry and heartbroken and I assured Graham that I had plans to make it right.

Chapter 34

WELCOME TO THE NEW LIVE OAKS

———=>●<=———

We pulled into the plantation entrance and I had the driver stop and wait. I got out and was admiring the new, inlaid wood arch over the cattle guard. It was beautiful and very masterfully crafted. It would stand the test of time and I took several pictures. The pole fencing looked great; Pearl had made a wise choice. We then headed up the long manicured driveway.

I could not believe what I was seeing. The front of the old mansion was bright, shiny and new. The upstairs widow walks were bigger and beautifully done. The new front porch behind the massive columns had large, filled planters with bursts of vibrant color. The porch swings were moving slightly in the breeze and the ceiling fans were slowly whirring. The downstairs windows and two panels on either side of the massive front door were the prettiest stained glass I'd ever seen. We left our bags outside and announced ourselves as we entered. Our mouths were open in disbelief as we wandered around admiring the remodeled home. The kids ran back to look at the pool and I heard them squealing. My sister had done an amazing job on every inch of the place.

Pearl came running down the staircase and we embraced for minutes, in tears and so happy. She gave me a tour and I was surprised how gorgeous the green house off the kitchen had turned out. The old chef's quarters were now a den. Every other window in the room was stained glass and the colors reflecting around the white furniture was awesome.

The heavy, French doors had beveled glass in every pane and threw prisms of light back into the entry hall. After seeing the whole house we grabbed drinks and went to relax out on the patio facing the pool. Butterbean greeted Pearl, then disappeared investigating the place. His tiny tail was wagging furiously and he seemed instantly at home.

The kids ran to put on their swimsuits. Pearl informed me that Magnolia and Matilda were arriving tonight and she thought she'd send Pepe' and Linda to pick them up as a surprise. I told her how proud of her I was and how unbelievable the mansion had turned out. Jarrod had convinced her to remove three live oaks so there would be room for a four car garage. She had agreed and it was everything you could want or wish for, I couldn't believe it was the same place.

Jarrod had joined us and I told him what I thought. He said he was most pleased to finish it all so soon and it was in large part to Pearl's expert preparations and his capable and experienced crews of men. He was anxious to start on the beach cottage and Pearl told him to give everyone time off with pay and to just relax with us until after the wedding. He had given me an odd grin when he left. Pearl had just laughed.

I told her I needed to shop and she was already a step ahead of me. The girls were bringing the bride's maid dresses and formal wear for me from the city. I just laughed and hugged her so glad that I wouldn't have to endure fittings and alterations. She said I needed to decide which room I wanted and she had taken the largest one on the back of the house upstairs. It had been two separate rooms and was now one huge beautifully decorated living space. That left four more bedrooms upstairs to choose from and two downstairs.

I told her we needed to go to the park soon; I had something I needed to tell her. She had gotten a stricken look on her face and knew it was grave if I couldn't tell her here. We let that go for now, but I wouldn't be able to relax or feel at home until she knew the truth.

The kids came back in from the Panama City airport. We had an excellent dinner and got a call from a frantic Blaine. He was having a hard time getting away and Matilda had told him to relax and leave things to Joshua until he would have to leave. He had promised to get himself and Jim there within the next two or three days. Little did he know we would be putting them to work getting ready for both events. They were good sports though and would gladly dig in when they arrived.

Matilda informed us over dinner that there had been RSVP's on almost all four hundred of the invitations. I reminded them that the caterers would need everybody here to help set up and cover that many folding chairs. We had our work cut out for us. It was exciting and I prayed my medicine could get me through it. I wasn't feeling good and I worried that it was becoming more obvious.

There was so much noise and laughter. We were almost whole now; just a few more arrivals and everyone would be here. The girls and Pepe' got settled into upstairs bedrooms then joined us downstairs in the living room. Clarissa had called and she would arrive tomorrow morning. Pearl wrote everything down and assured her that some of us would be there to pick her up. Once all the family got here we would send the jet back for the Jefferson's and Evelyn. Then they would stop in New Orleans long enough to pick up Ima and Bo. I thought they would stay in the small house. No one was sweating the sleeping arrangements. There was also the beach cottage if anyone wanted to be there. Jarrod had mentioned he might stay there during the wedding.

I reminded Pearl we needed to go to the park. We told the kids we'd be gone for a few hours and to listen for the phone. Linda was already in charge of office duties and was excitedly getting herself organized and answering the phone. Pepe' was out scouting the grounds and making his game plan.

We got to Destin and walked down to our favorite spot. I started the conversation that I had been dreading for the past two and a half years. I just had a feeling that I was not going to get the five whole years the specialists were hoping for.

"Pearl, I have some damn rough news. Let me tell you everything and why you are just now finding out."

By the time I was done we were both in tears. She was furious that there wasn't any way to make me well again. She thought of everything that Jim and I already had. There wasn't a single thing any of us could do. She blew her nose and wiping her eyes she looked at me with the saddest look I had ever seen on my beautiful sister's face.

"What will I do without you Min? All these positively wonderful things are coming together in our lives and you're telling me that you're leaving us. How can I bear this?"

She was sobbing again. I tried to stop crying long enough to console her.

"It all goes back to faith Pearl. Any time you need me, I'll be there whether you see me or not. I swear this to you and you have to promise me that you will not waste too much time grieving. The kids need you, Clarissa needs you and Jim is getting to the point that he is about to retire and he needs you. It's a shitty situation and I would never leave any of you given the choice. You have to understand that I didn't tell you because it would have changed you and the kids. None of you would have accomplished any of this had I told you. It would have rearranged your lives. I'm telling you now because I have a feeling it won't be much longer. You have to swear one thing to me, and we'll never discuss this again. When the time comes you must not call an ambulance or take me to the hospital, no matter what. I want to have everyone I love here to say my goodbyes to, if I am even that lucky. I know it's a hard promise to make. I beg you to forgive me for keeping a single secret from you. You are my life and my heart and I love you more than you know."

Pearl looked out at the beautiful emerald green water and tried to imagine having to say goodbye to this woman next to her. She couldn't. She felt numb and her heart was broken in half. She thought to herself that if just the telling could make her hurt so badly, what about the day Min had to go? She thought it might kill her. She put her arms around her sister and cried.

Finally she said, "Are we going to tell the kids? How can I act normal knowing this horrid thing? Min I will try to be strong and courageous for you but I wish it was me and not you. I'm not sure if I want to go on without you."

I told her again that she had to be strong because everyone needed her and even though she didn't believe in my shinning, I told her I'd already seen her first grandchild. She looked up with dismay and asked, "Oh Minnie, that's wonderful news. Are you sure?" I smiled through my tears and reassured her that she needed to believe in the things she had spent her life turning her back to. I told her to wait and see. I also thought we should be getting back. She wanted to wait for the sunset.

We sat there hugging each other and watched the light sink into the gulf. The sky was red, orange and purple. There was pink around the beautiful sun. We sat there until we couldn't see it any longer and wearily made our way back to the car.

She asked what she could do to make me feel better I had said, "Just love and forgive me, it's enough." We drove back to the plantation in silence. I felt miserable for breaking Pearl's heart. I didn't want to leave any of them, especially her.

Chapter 35

Introducing VanDeCourte Designs

————⟫●⟪————

Clarissa, Jim and Blaine had finally arrived and gotten situated. Surprisingly Clarissa had asked for the pool house. She said the pool pump lulled her like the fountain outside her room at home.

The caterers had arrived and had two big tents set up with one for food and the other for drinks and some seating. These would remain here until after the wedding. The orchestra had been placed under their own tent with big fans to keep them comfortable. They would also perform at the wedding.

Pearl wandered around and made sure everything was just right. We were dressed like we were going to the opera. The first guests started to arrive. Jarrod and his sons looked extremely handsome in their suits. They had rented two seated golf carts to transport people when the parking got too far away. There were two friends of Adam directing traffic, parking people up and down the long driveway. We had decided this would be a good trial run of how we'd manage the wedding crowd. So far it was going fine. Out near the entrance to the property were two sandwich boards with beautifully done signs that said,

OPEN HOUSE
LIVE OAKS PLANTATION
COURTESY OF
VanDeCourte Designs

Inside the front door was a table with a mirror above it. There were two, very large silver trays meant to hold business cards or notes to the hostess. After the first couple of hours the first tray was overflowing and the second was nearly full. Clarissa had invited everyone who was anyone in the business world. Jarrod had done the same. Jim had invited everyone he knew in New Orleans and Magnolia and Matilda invited all the movers and shakers from the city that were into owning multiple homes.

Everything was going smoothly without a hitch. Linda came down the stairs escorted by Pepe; and you could hear the buzz in the crowd. She wore her hair up and was stunningly beautiful. Pepe' looked very sharp beside her. Next Matilda and Magnolia made their entrance. Jim got the crowd clapping and cheering. We all laughed and enjoyed ourselves.

It was the best part of late spring. The grass was like a plush carpet and Pepe' had done a tremendous job on all the flowers and flowering shrubs and vines. We used spotlighting for this event and would only use paper lanterns for the wedding.

The orchestra was superb and everyone seemed to be enjoying themselves with drinks, food and good conversation. Pearl was on cloud nine. She and Linda would be so busy after tonight it would be hard to pick and choose the jobs she wanted to tackle. I was so happy and proud of her. I was beaming. I had taken pictures all day and night and had some very beautiful shots of everyone.

The caterers had done a magnificent job with all the finger foods and drinks. No one went hungry or ever had an empty glass. We now had confidence in them and knew they could handle the wedding crowd next week.

Around nine thirty people began leaving and it was pretty much done by ten o'clock. The orchestra packed up and was paid. We helped the caterers get the tents down and stored in the empty stalls of the huge garage. The chairs were there too and inside the empty downstairs bedroom of the big house. The downstairs library was being used to put the wedding guest gifts together. No one was supposed to go in there unless they intended to work on the candles and centerpieces. A lot of that was already done.

Before Jarrod's sons left, Pearl took them aside and gave them each a hefty check. They tried to decline and she wouldn't hear of it. She also made them promise to bring their wives and children tomorrow to swim and play in the pool. She had gotten very attached to Jarrod, Phillip and Adam. It was past time to include their families around here.

We changed our clothes and showered the starch out of our hair so we could swim. Magnolia put music on and we ended up out back. Clarissa was grinning from ear to ear and mentioned the table overflowing with business contacts and proposals.

The kids told us old fogies to get off our feet and brought out snacks and cocktails for each of us. Clarissa had donned a swimsuit with a fashionable cover and was happy for the drink. I'd hoped that we hadn't turned the poor woman into an alcoholic. Pearl assured me that the only revelation there was that she had merely come out of the closet with her drinking. She was an old pro. We just wanted her to be happy and comfortable.

After a few drinks the rest of us went and changed into our swimsuits. The pool was heated and it felt like heaven on earth. As the summer progressed the heater would be turned off. Pearl believed in getting every day's use possible out of the horribly expensive pool. We loved it. It was getting late and the music was getting louder. Jarrod had come back in swim trunks and I couldn't take my eyes off his rock hard body. Pearl and I giggled like two horny high school kids, it was too funny.

Before long we were dancing around that pool, singing and laughing and just blowing off steam after a night of success for Pearl. It was a beautiful celebration and we got a bit too drunk. We heard squeals and splashes and saw Jim and Clarissa splashing each other in the shallow end. We howled with laughter. Pepe' and Blaine were tossing the girls into the water and then diving in behind them. Jarrod was talking to Jim and Clarissa. Butterbean wanted to be in on the action and kept jumping in the pool. He was so tiny that Jarrod finally placed him atop a pool float and he stayed there for hours.

I had laughed and told Pearl I hoped the Beaufords had a sense of humor. We were making enough noise to wake the dead. We were finally exhausted and gathered for a toast. Jim was ready for this and banged the table with a spoon for everyone's attention.

"I'd like to propose a toast!" He seemed just the slightest bit wobbly on his feet. He raised his big snifter of brandy up to the sky and said, "Here's to Pearl, the most beautiful architect I've ever known. Good luck and good business!"

With that said we raised our glasses and yelled, "Hear, Hear!"

Everyone was clapping, chattering and laughing but so tired we were literally draped over the pool furniture. The open house had been everything we'd hoped for and it would be fun to see what the two news representatives would print. The press had been discretely moving through the crowds getting quotes from guests and snapping pictures. We were relieved when they had left and we could act ourselves again.

Matilda and Blaine were the only ones left standing and they were hugging and dancing slow near the back of the pool. Theirs would be the next party and we were excited to see the big day arrive. We still had a lot to do though. Like finishing the gift candles and preparing the small bouquets for the back of each chair. We wouldn't handle the flowers until the night before. Guests would be welcome to take these if they wanted them. There would be flower petals floating on the pool and large bouquets placed here and there under all four tents and throughout the house and property. I couldn't wait to see the decorations. One more week and Pearl would give her baby to Blaine. She was silently praying that they would use her wedding gift to build a home here on the plantation. Jarrod hoped so too. He would get the contract.

I had to go to bed; I couldn't hold my head up any longer. I was in the upstairs corner bedroom off the back of the house. So I fell asleep to the sound of laughter, music and splashing water. These were the voices of the people I loved most in this world.

I dreamed Graham was here in bed with me. He just lay next to me smiling with an arm around me. I smiled and asked him why he was so happy. He had just whispered, "You'll see."

Chapter 36

MR. AND MRS. BLAINE THOMPSON

Everyone was busy with one thing or another. Blaine was the only one among us that was nervous. In two days' time he would marry Matilda.

Our dresses and the men's suits were hanging in Pearl's walk in closet upstairs. There had been one change in plans. Last night Matilda had gotten an urgent phone call from the secretary of the priest that would be performing the service. He had gotten into an automobile wreck and was in the hospital. Magnolia was on her toes and reminded everyone that a pastor was being flown in from Beaumont. Pearl called the Jefferson's and just like that, the problem was solved. Mr. Jefferson had agreed to marry them and he mentioned his wife had a lovely voice. Matilda asked Linda if she'd heard her sing. Linda told them she sang every Sunday and did it solo. She promised them the woman had a beautiful voice. Matilda called them back and asked Mrs. Jefferson if she would consider singing at the wedding.

There would be a pause in the ceremony when Blaine and Matilda would kneel on pillows with heads bowed while Mrs. Jefferson sang "How Great Thou Art." Once these new details were in place, Matilda was humming and buzzing around happy again with no worries in the world.

This morning I was down in the library finishing the gift candles that would be at each guest's place setting. Matilda had gotten two different scented candles. One was gardenia and one was magnolia. They were short pillar candles. I was tying silk ribbons around each one. The colors of the thin, silk ribbons matched the paper lanterns that would be everywhere. She had made pendant size, porcelain flowers that got tied into each bow. The flower charms had turned out beautifully and were gardenias and magnolias and they dangled prettily on each and every candle. I told Magnolia and Linda that we would make sure none were left behind when the big day was done.

Last night we hovered over a diagram of the seating and our game plan for setting up the chairs. There would be rows of ten with two hundred per side and the red carpet in the middle. We would rely on the caterers to come up with a clever plan for seating here and there all over the back of the property for the reception. For the dancing there was collapsible flooring that would be placed in the lawn in front of the orchestra. It was so heavy; it sunk into the grass and would not move. We'd given it a trial run yesterday with Jarrod's help.

Now we just tried to stay busy and were anxiously awaiting the arrival of the massive truck load of flowers that would be arriving tomorrow morning. The caterer had designed chair covers just for this wedding and her idea was ingenious. The extra fabric behind the top of each chair was folded and secured with a two inch tab that had Velcro on the fabric. After we put together the flowers for the chairs, we would pull back the tab and close it again just beneath the silk ribbon securing each small bouquet. They were beautiful. I told Pearl the woman should trademark the idea, it was brilliant and simple. She said Matilda was going for a shabby chic look and that's what she had come up with. There would be fans outside the tents blowing over large blocks of ice to cool everyone. We had done a trial run on these also. I was afraid it would make it too humid but it actually made it feel like we had air conditioning running. We would work from sun up until around ten O'clock; giving us two hours to get dressed. The hairdresser would arrive around eight. We were doing each other's make-up. The wedding would start at twelve noon on the dot on Saturday.

I finished the last candle and went in search of coffee. I made a pot and took a big mug out to the back patio. Jarrod joined me and said, "Minerva, I wanted to ask you something."

I was caught off guard and just stared at him with a goofy smile on my face. I didn't say a word.

"I was wondering if you would be interested in going out to dinner with me some evening."

I was so surprised that when I raised my mug to drink, it was still an inch from my mouth and coffee poured down the front of me. We both reacted at the same time and grabbing a napkin he stood up. We both stooped over at the same time and bumped our heads together. Now we were holding our heads and howling with laughter. We sat back down and I told him, "I don't know Jarrod. I am not sure I know how to date or any of that anymore, it's been a very long time."

He got that sly, sexy smile of his and asked, "You know how to eat dinner though right?"

We both laughed because I was being ridiculous so I said, "Sure, why not?"

And just like that he disappeared around the corner of the house leaving me to sit staring out over the pool and wondering about this upcoming date. Why had I said yes? What if I died in his car or something horrid happened? That would certainly be my luck. Most days now I felt like I was hanging by a thread and the three horrible pills were my lifeline. They weren't so hot on the days when the headaches were trying to kill me. So I needed to stop being silly, it was just dinner. I would have to share this with Pearl and I noticed that whenever I ran into Jarrod now he was whistling while he worked. I would just play it by ear and decide which part of the evening I would drop my bomb on him. I hoped I wouldn't need to but in reality what if he was witness to the big bang? It wouldn't be fair not to warn him in advance. We still would not tell any of the kids what was inevitable.

I heard women talking then the excited laughter of children. Pearl came out to the pool with two women followed by four children of various ages. She introduced the adults as Janice and Lanette, wives of Adam and Phillip. I stood and shook their hands and said I was happy to meet them. The kids were ignoring us, shedding their clothing right there, anxious to dive into the big pool. We just sat chatting and watching them swim and horse around. Pearl noticed my blouse was soaked in coffee and looked at me questioningly. I just shook my head and whispered, "I'll tell you later."

We insisted the new friends stay for lunch and I went to the kitchen to help. We brought out piles of different kinds of small sandwiches, chips, dips, potato and fruit salad and three pitchers of iced tea to the back patio. We set everything up buffet style and let the kids fix plates first. Clarissa was fussing over the children and looked so happy. We managed to coral everyone and it was a wonderful lunch.

Linda and Pepe' acted comfortable and at home like they'd been with our family their whole lives. It was perfect. The younger kids got cranky when they were not allowed in the pool again and had to go home. We quieted them with the promise that they were welcome anytime and could come back. I helped Magnolia clean up after everyone and decided I needed to take a walk. I asked Pearl to join me. She said it was getting too hot; why not take a spin while the golf carts were here. So we took off down the long driveway headed out toward the county road. I told her about Jarrod's invitation and she said it was wonderful. I didn't show the same enthusiasm and she knew why. While we were out here we decided where we would place all the sandwich boards with neatly printed signs for parking. There was also one ready to go in the entrance hall directing people where to place gifts.

I was antsy and couldn't have said why. I decided to try and nap and went up to my room. I pulled out some photo albums of Graham and found our wedding pictures. I was trying to relax as I lay staring out the window. I hoped he wouldn't mind my dinner date, I knew that was silly. I felt sure that he could see me and everything I did, but knew that earthly matters were no concern to those who had left before us. I fell asleep with an album open and my arm was draped over the color photos of the happiest day I had ever lived so far. Hours later I was awakened by my sister gently moving my hair off my face, telling me dinner was ready.

She smiled and picked up the album. She sighed and said, "That was certainly a party to remember, wasn't it?"

I propped up on one elbow and smiled remembering the day. "Yes, yes it was. Hard to believe we were ever that young isn't it?"

She hugged me and said to hurry down after I freshened up. Neither of us wanted to believe my future. Sometimes Mother Nature just dealt us the losing hand. I had faith, so I didn't question it anymore and I couldn't change my fate anyway.

Everyone was there, gathered around the long, dining table. This room had come out nicely and we told Pearl how lovely it was as we stuffed ourselves. We chatted and decided on our game plan that would begin at four thirty the next morning. The florist had called and asked if we could greet the freight driver later this evening. Pearl told the frantic woman not to worry, it would be fine. So, we would be able to get started on the flowers tonight. I thought it would be fun as long as we didn't get carried away, staying up all night. There would be at least eight of us to work on the chair bouquets, all the other sprays and arrangements were prepared, wired together and would arrive standing in buckets of water.

The doorbell rang and Magnolia went to see who had arrived. It was Julie, one of the caterers. She was dressed in a white shirt, black tie and black pants. She asked where we wanted her to put the chair covers. Pearl showed them a corner of the entrance hall where they could stack everything. They were ironed, folded and shrink wrapped in stacks of twenty. The men wouldn't let Julie lift a finger and it only took a few minutes to empty her truck and send her on her way. We were pleased that they were here this evening instead of tomorrow. The tents were going up at five O'clock in the morning and we felt like we were ahead of the game at this point.

We were out back gathered around the pool when the doorbell rang once more. Jim glanced at his watch and mentioned it was nine forty five. We laughed to think someone thought that was late evening, we were just getting started. Three delivery men began bringing the flowers into the entrance hall. The boxes with the sprays were almost six feet tall. Pearl said to not open those; we would only peek to make sure they were in good condition. She had warned everyone to pile on the quilts tonight as she would have the air conditioning set to frigid to keep the beautiful blooms perky for tomorrow. We finally got them stacked and after tipping the drivers we got to work.

We had five card tables lined up with the boxes of delicate calla lilies, gardenias and rose buds. The magnolias were also fragile and Pearl warned everyone not to touch the petals if possible as they would bruise easily. These would be the centerpieces on each table along with hurricane lamps filled with white sand, sea shells and votive candles for the reception dinner. We had Pepe' and Linda serve everyone a cocktail and before we knew it we had almost two hundred small bouquets of flowers gathered with ribbons. Pearl had a huge walk in cooler in the kitchen. She had planned ahead and had baker's racks ready. As soon as we filled the shelves of a rack, they were rolled into the walk in refrigerator. By midnight we were done, including hair pieces, boutonnieres and Matilda's bridal bouquet. The doorbell rang again as we were cleaning up and we let out a huge sigh of relief to see a very exhausted but excited Joshua had finally arrived.

We were tired but satisfied and decided to turn in. Jarrod had Pearl off to one side of the hall. They were discussing the gift he and his son's would bring before sunup and once the exact spot was decided he left. I told everyone good night and headed upstairs. I lay there for some time thinking about tomorrow, thankful that I would see at least one of the girls married. I finally drifted off.

I dreamed all the kids were on the shores of the Mediterranean Sea. The sun was glinting off the beautiful blue water as dolphins leaped and chased fish. Small colorful boats bobbed in the calm waters and the city was alive with activity. At least two of them had never witnessed such beauty and they looked out at the view. I felt as ease and drifted deeper into sleep.

Very early the next morning there was a tapping on my bedroom door and all three girls piled into my bed, kissing and hugging me awake. They were dressed and ready to get busy. I showered and met everyone downstairs. Pepe', Blaine and Joshua were already moving folding chairs into the back yard. The tents were going up and pretty soon we could hear rapid clacking as each chair was opened and placed in rows. All of us girls would go with armfuls of covers and it was easy really, they slid over the chairs and fit perfectly. Next we went back inside to make coffee and set up pastries and other sweet breads, yogurts and the left over fruit salad for a quick breakfast for everyone. We had decided to do our hair and make-up and then place the bouquets before we got dressed. We didn't want a single bloom to wilt. It was chilly in the tent. The canvas walls would be rolled up and tied for the actual ceremony.

We ushered Matilda inside and told her from here on out she was to focus on getting dressed and was not allowed back outside. She pretended to protest and ran upstairs giggling. The truck backed into place and it took all the men to guide the gazebo down the ramps and positioned in just the right spot. All us women except Matilda proceeded to cover the front entrance of the beautifully hand carved gazebo in flowers. There would be a single paper lantern hanging from the ceiling here, with very soft lighting.

We got the bouquets placed and I took tons of pictures of everything. Our hair was done and could stand up to hurricane force winds if needed. We laughed and went to get dressed. The orchestra was here and setting up, tuning their instruments. The sun was up now and it was going to be a perfect weather day for this wedding.

Jim was in charge of the men getting dressed and Clarissa had them in the pool house making sure everything was straight and perfect.

The caterers were frantically unloading their supplies and had taken over the kitchen and placed a chef at the outdoor ovens to tend the pig he began slow roasting yesterday. It smelled like flowers and pork out back.

I peeked out my upstairs window and they were laying the red carpet for the bride and groom. There were two red satin pillows on the first step of the gazebo. Pastor Jefferson looked very handsome and his wife Mary had been upstairs with us girls. She and Linda were having fun getting ready. They both looked beautiful and she was drinking warm honey and lemon water for her voice. Ima and Bo were being assisted by Magnolia and the house was full of family and love.

I went to Pearl's bedroom and tapped on the door then slipped in. The sight of Matilda standing there in that antique lace wedding gown took my breath away. We were trying not to tear up and ruin our makeup. Her veil was held in place by a comb covered in porcelain and real flower buds. I came over to her and kissing her cheek told her she was the most beautiful bride I'd ever seen. I photographed all of this and finally, it was time.

The guests had been pouring in since around eleven thirty. Almost all the seats were filled and the caterers finally began rolling up the tent walls. Blaine looked extremely handsome standing in front of the gazebo waiting for his bride. Joshua looked calm and cool next him. We left Jim with Matilda and all of us in the wedding party lined up with our escorts waiting for the cue. The orchestra began the wedding march and we followed Linda who was tossing handfuls of flower petals in front of us on the red carpet. She would stand behind and beside us brides maids, and Pepe' as the ring bearer would stand with the groom and best man. Finally it was time for the entrance of the bride. Every head was turned in anticipation; you could hear the gasps and people sniffling tears as Jim escorted her forward. Our dresses were very faint pastel colored lace that matched the paper lanterns and silk ribbons. Mine was pale blue, Pearl was in a light shade of pink, Magnolia was in a shade of green and Linda wore an ivory colored tea length lace dress with matching ribbons forming a sweet bow in back.

Matilda drew in her breath at two things, her fiance' and the surprise gazebo. When they finally got to the part of the ceremony where a hidden Mary Jefferson sang "How Great Thou Art" there wasn't a dry eye in the house. This woman had a beautiful voice and sang with feeling. Pepe' had never been more handsome and after handing over the rings, it was official. The married couple kissed to shouts, clapping and cheers that could be heard two counties away. I grabbed my camera and took pictures the rest of the day and evening. We invited the guests to make themselves at home, tour the house if they wished, use the facilities and assured them the seating arrangements would be done very soon. The orchestra played and everyone danced, laughed and made merry.

It was absolutely perfect. Matilda would disappear and change into a shorter designer dress so that she could dance and visit comfortably. She was positively radiant and they were so in love they just glowed. Later in the early evening when the last guest was departing and the orchestra was packing up we noticed Clarissa fussing over Ima and Bo like a mother hen. She had taken them over to the small house and had gotten them settled in for the evening. They were elderly and frail and couldn't take anymore. Pearl had passed out envelopes to each and every server and orchestra member. Soon she had everyone paid and there were generous tips for each one.

We had gotten changed into comfy clothes and gathered around the patio. Pearl wanted everyone's attention. She handed Matilda and Blaine a large parchment scroll tied with red ribbon. They unrolled the stiff paper together and Matilda, in tears, flew out of her seat to hug her mother. It was a deed to several hundred acres of the plantation property and blueprints of Matilda's childhood dream home. She had sketched this out in college and talked about it from time to time. Blaine and she were ecstatic with joy and we all clapped and cheered.

The room of gifts was stacked to the ceiling. They decided to open them tomorrow morning and Magnolia and Linda would assist with lists and notes for the thank you cards that would go out as soon as they returned from their honeymoon. Matilda whispered to Blaine and ran in the house for a minute. She came back with gift bags hanging up and down both arms. She and Blaine passed them out. When Magnolia, Linda and Pepe' opened theirs they were howling and dancing around jumping and screaming with delight. Pearl insisted they not keep us in suspense. Magnolia held up the airline ticket and check saying, "Oh my God, Mother, look at this."

They each had first class seats on the same flight to Greece for a week with the newlyweds. The checks for each were for five thousand dollars. We couldn't believe the kids generosity and marveled at them including these three on their trip. Linda was close to fainting. Pearl and I got porcelain hair combs and Jim and Jarrod had received beautiful cufflinks with matching tie pins. Clarissa opened her gift last and gasped. It was a handwritten invitation to come live on the plantation with the rest of the family and we had all signed it. She had gotten porcelain jewelry also but the letter was most important. Pearl was in tears knowing the kids would build and live here with us. We didn't think of the law firm or how that would go. Pearl intended to convince Jim he needed to be here too. Her dreams were coming true.

We noticed Magnolia and Linda wrestling a wheel barrow overflowing with flowers. When I mentioned it to Jarrod he just smiled and said, "They thought this up on their own, wait until you see what they're up to." We sipped our drinks with our feet up and laughed as they almost tipped the load several times. They began with the largest graveyard and worked until all three areas of graves were covered in delicate and sweet smelling blossoms. I looked at Pearl and winked. We had face cramps from smiling and laughing all day. She was so proud of them.

We older folks agreed we needed a nap. All the youngsters donned swimsuits and swam, listened to music and chatted. I hugged Pearl and commented on how wonderful the day had been. She kissed my cheek saying, "I'm thankful you're here Min. It could never have been this perfect without you." We both took naps and slept soundly for a couple of hours.

Jarrod was running the first load of departing guests to Panama City for evening flights. Our jet would take Ima and Bo to New Orleans and then the Jefferson's and Evelyn back to Beaumont. Evelyn was so beautiful and thanked us for a special day. She had spent some quality time with Pepe' and Linda and everyone was ready to go. We got them loaded and with hugs and tearful goodbyes we waved as they headed out. No one else was in a hurry to leave so we relaxed.

We had a late dinner of leftovers. We had the trays stacked neatly in the walk in fridge and would take them to the local food pantry first thing in the morning. We couldn't use all that food and there were a lot of hungry people that could.

I turned in earlier than anyone else and was in complete agony. My head was hurting and I had tremors that were shaking my bed. I was curled up in a ball when Pearl came in to check on me. She left the room and returned with my pills, water and a warm, damp cloth that she gently cleaned my face with. We never discussed the bloody tears that she had wiped from my cheeks. She was mustering all the courage she was capable of to help me. She was in fact horrified and scared to death. She finally felt my body relax with the medication and gently lay beside me on the bed. We fell asleep and I was grateful for her arms around me. I didn't dream, my head was fuzzy and I was scared. I prayed that I could have at least two more weeks and would survive all the kids returning from Greece. Someone had peeked in on us then quietly turned off the lights and closed the door. It had been Jim; he had gone to his room and sobbed himself to sleep.

Chapter 37

THE SERVICE

———————⟫●⟪———————

We were up early and had eaten breakfast. After moving the massive piles of wedding gifts into the living room we got Clarissa and Jim comfortable with hot tea and placed Matilda and Blaine on a couch by themselves. The rest of us had coffee and got situated. Linda would bring the gifts to the newlyweds and Magnolia would record the giver and the item. She filled two spiral notebooks by the time they got through the presents. They told us they wanted to give the checks and paper money to St. Jude's research center.

There were so many beautiful items they could fill three new homes. We got the paper and bows put away and the youngsters ran to pack. They would fly out of Panama City early this evening on the first leg of their adventure. We had helped Linda and Pepe' find cameras in town and they were on cloud nine. Jim gave each one travel advice, a hundred dollar bill and words of wisdom. Magnolia promised to keep an eye on the two least experienced travelers. At the last minute Pearl yelled,

"Stop!" She asked if anyone had gathered their passports from the safe. We laughed but that was a close call and would have been a disaster. She made each one secure their documents where they wouldn't lose them.

I was in and out of bed now. Clarissa kept drilling Pearl and Jim to see if they didn't agree that I needed to see a doctor. The days dragged on and I was slipping away. Pearl would help me get up most mornings and take a shower. Daily, we got me downstairs by the pool and into the fresh air. Jarrod looked mournful and I supposed Pearl had told him what was happening. Jim decided he and Clarissa needed private time and went into town for dinner the evening before the kids were returning. He told her the whole, sad truth and she sobbed quietly into her dinner napkin. He'd had to give her support to walk her back to their car. She had retired to her room and stayed there the whole next day. Pearl tried to keep the mood light and cheerful. My tremors could not be hidden any longer and those around me just watched and waited.

The morning the kids got home I felt pretty good and we listened to their excited chatter, shared the photos they'd taken and couldn't help but be happy with their excitement. They asked why I felt so bad and I told them I'd gotten sick while they were gone. They ran around the place, unpacking, chatting and ended up in their favorite place, the pool.

Later that day I told Pearl I wanted to take a walk with her. She helped me up and we walked slowly toward the cemetery behind the old ovens. We were chatting about how pretty the landscaping had turned out when it hit me.

I screamed out in pain and slipped from Pearl's grasp and was in a heap at her feet. I had both hands on my temples. I was groaning loudly and I never imagined this kind of pain existed. Pearl dropped down beside me and cradled me in her arms. She threw her head back to the heavens and screamed, "God, No! Min, my precious Min, don't leave me! Hold on, just hold on!"

She desperately looked toward the house and yelled at the top of her lungs, "Jarrod, Blaine, Jim, help me, it's Minnie, hurry!"

I forced my eyes open and looked at my darling sister; I managed a whisper, "Remember, no doctors. Pearl, I love you."

What she saw when I had opened my eyes for those few seconds caused her to scream in anguish, "Hurry, help us!" Jarrod reached us first and scooped me up like I weighed nothing. Pearl instructed him to bring me to the downstairs bedroom. Pearl was crying hysterically and told Jim, "My dear God, her eyes were literally full of blood, oh Jim, we're going to lose her!"

Jim held Pearl tightly while Jarrod got me under the covers and a pillow under my head. Everyone was crying. I was too weak to move. Soon everyone was there. The kids were terrified and crying. Clarissa took them to the living room and shut the door. She calmly explained that I was gravely ill and might not recover and they all needed to be brave for me. The poor babies, they were full of questions and sure they could help. The mood was grim and now it was a matter of time and telling each of these people goodbye and how much I loved them. Pearl wiped my face gently with a wet, warm cloth.

The sight she had witnessed would end up haunting her dreams for the rest of her days. It would bring the worst nightmares she'd ever had. She tried to calm herself and sat with me on the side of the bed. I was in and out.

Pearl never left my side. I woke up hours later and told her, "They're singing me home Pearl, I have to go. Bring the kids so I can say goodbye."

One by one my darlings sat with me and I told each one something special just for their ears. I had never felt such love for these beautiful young souls. Clarissa came in and I told her to take advantage of all the love she was being offered. Jim came in and hugged me gently, rocking me as he said his goodbyes through the tears. Jarrod came in and placed a rose on my pillow and whispered he'd take a rain check for the dinner I had promised him. I tried to smile and he kissed my head and left. Pearl stayed with me cradled in her arms. She softly sang our favorite lullaby that had always calmed her babies when they were tiny. Tears streamed down her cheeks. I used the last of my strength to hold her and in a whisper I told her, "When it's time, I'll come back for you Pearl, I promise. Be ready; live every minute like it's your last. I have had a beautiful life thanks to you, Jim and the kids."

I looked up and there was Graham. He had his hand out to me and said, "It's time to go my darling, don't be afraid." I smiled and kissed my precious sister for the last time. I told Pearl that Graham was waiting and I left with my husband.

Everyone in the house came running at the wail of pain from Pearl. She continued to hold and rock me and covered me in her tears. Jim stood behind her holding her shoulders until he bent and whispered, "She's with the angels now love, time to let her go." She turned to face Jim then held him for dear life, crying the tears of the broken hearted. Magnolia gently kissed my cheek. Every one of them gave me a final kiss and Jim pulled the sheet over my head. My time on earth was done.

Clarissa and Jim took all five of the youngsters into the living room. Magnolia and Matilda curled up with their grandmother and she held them close, letting them cry. Jim held Linda and Pepe' doing the same. Jarrod tried to console Blaine and Joshua. Butterbean sat in the middle of the floor with his head thrown back and howled. Clarissa patted her lap and the small dog jumped into her lap and continued to whine inconsolably.

Sometime later Jim excused himself to the library where he called the morgue. Everything was arranged and he would be very busy for the next week. They would fly to New Orleans with Minnie's remains where she would be laid to rest in the large family plot. There would be a funeral service in three days. They would all stay in the apartment.

Jim sat with Pearl and told her, "I'd very much like to retire and live here with all of you for the time I have left dear, if you'll have me."

Pearl was in tears again and smiling she hugged this sweet man who had been a father to her and Minnie longer than their biological father had been. She assured him, "I would love nothing better Jim, time to let the youngsters run the firm, they're capable now and I don't want to be too far from you and Clarissa."

She was exhausted and numb. She asked, "Minnie told me you would know what to do; did she leave you with all her last wishes?"

Jim smiled and said, "Yes, right down to the music she wants at her viewing." He didn't mention the gruesome facts regarding the research team who were on stand-by waiting for a call from the morgue. They would be taking her brain and major organs back to their research facility hoping to discover anything that might help the next victim.

Clarissa was wearily preparing dinner for everyone, keeping herself busy. They had to eat and this was better than the alternative. The kids were in their rooms each one trying to come to terms with the loss of their Mimi.

Pearl had walked aimlessly toward the woods behind the big house. She was out of tears for the moment and despondent. Jarrod followed quietly at a distance. She ended up by the old creek that cut through the back of the property. She sat on a rock and watched the water. She looked around and you would think it was any ordinary day, except now she was the only one left. She sat thinking of all the things Minnie had told her and wondered if it was true about the baby. She sighed and knew time would tell. She wondered how it was that a broken heart didn't kill you, it just made you wish you were dead.

She jerked around at the sound of a branch snapping behind her. Jarrod quietly came up and put his arms around her not saying anything. She reached up finally and holding his hand she told him, "I miss her so much already; I really don't know what to do with myself Jarrod. I just don't."

He held her tighter and said, "It takes time Pearl, at some point it will be less painful. It's the circle of life. We are each given a beginning and an end. We that are left behind cannot understand why it ends too soon for some. I believe that when we join your beautiful sister, we'll be given all the answers. Let's head back. Clarissa is making dinner for everyone."

Pearl and Jarrod walked hand in hand and gathered everyone to eat. No one had an appetite and the kids played with their food. They thanked Clarissa for cooking and all of them lined up at the bar, took their drinks out by the pool and toasted the most precious person any of them had known. They dreaded what was ahead but knew they'd get through it together.

The day had come for the service. The viewing the night before had the biggest crowd the place had ever seen. It was no different at the cemetery. The cars were lined up on both sides of the street. They spilled out onto the main road as far as we could see.

Pearl wore a black designer suit and a hat with a veil. She couldn't bear to face anyone. She felt ugly with grief. Her girls were on either side of her. Linda and Pepe' stood by Jim and Clarissa had her arm through his. Blaine stood beside Matilda and Joshua. The Jefferson's and Evelyn had a place next to the immediate family.

The pastor read over Minnie and prayed for the living. He told everyone gathered there that hot, humid day that we should rejoice knowing that our beloved sister, aunt and friend was with all the others that had gone before her. He begged us not to be sad but to rejoice and prepare for out reunion with her and our heavenly father. It brought little comfort to these people gathered here.

There were so many sprays of flowers that after the service Blaine, Jarrod, his sons and their families would take the time to distribute them among the headstones. Minnie's was five feet tall and made of white marble. It read,

**HERE LIES MINERVA ANN
LAFORTUNE-BONET
LOVING SISTER, AUNT AND FRIEND
SHE FLYS AMONG THE ANGELS
1944-2012**

There was a beautiful angel with spread wings on top of the large stone. After the service Jim finally motioned for everyone to return to the limo. Pearl was on her knees and tossed the last rose into the grave. Everyone gave her the time she wanted to be with Minnie. After a while she slowly got up and headed for the car.

We gathered our bags from the apartment and flew back to Panama City and drove to the plantation. Each one of us would discover one last surprise from Minnie. Jim had been busy and this had been the hardest part of her wishes to pull off.

On each of Magnolia's and Matilda's beds was a colorful gift bag. There were four helium filled balloons attached. They bobbed to and fro under the ceiling fan. Pepe' and Linda found beautifully wrapped boxes with a thick envelope taped to the top and these also had balloons attached.

Pearl heard the exclamations from each of them but she wearily went out to her office to be alone. There was a beautiful gift bag with an envelope taped to the front on her desk. There were four balloons waving madly when she walked in. She looked to see where the draft was coming from and no windows were open to cause this. She sobbed quietly and looked in the bag. There was a framed photograph of her and Minnie. It was identical to the one on her desk except this one was taken recently at their favorite spot on the beach. The older picture was them as toddlers. There was a note that said,

Pearl,

Don't open the card taped to this bag until you are sure it's time. With all my love in this life and the next, your sister,

Minnie.

She sat the framed picture next to the other one and leaned the card against them both. She sat crying and felt empty and sad.

Linda was so grief stricken; she had never loved anyone like she did Mimi. She was angry that God had taken her away so soon and she didn't understand any of it. She put the envelope to one side and opened the box. It was full of discs of photos. She began to cry all over again. She opened the envelope and a check fluttered to the floor. She picked it up and saw it was a cashier's check for one million dollars. She read the letter.

> *Dearest Linda,*
>
> *I am sorry that I had to leave you so soon. This check is for your future. I want you to know that if I could have chosen any child on earth to be my daughter I would have picked you.*
> *I ask you to be brave and strong for my sister and your new family. You will help each other through this. Pay special attention to Pastor Jefferson, he speaks the truth.*
> *Have a good and happy life and I will make sure to come for you when your beautiful life is done. Be well sweet child.*
> *All my love from this life through the next.*
>
> *Minerva Ann*

Linda buried her head in her pillow so no one could hear her sobs of pain. She was so heartbroken she couldn't breathe. She lay there and cried herself to sleep and the balloons bobbed merrily in the soft breeze of the fan.

Pepe' had opened his envelope first. He sat holding the cashier's check for the same amount as Linda's. He just stared at it in disbelief. He slowly unfolded the letter.

Dearest Pepe'

I want you to know that I loved you from the moment I met you. If I could have chosen my children I would have picked you to be my son. This check is for your future. Please look after Linda, my sister and the rest of your new family. Do not spend too much time grieving. Live every moment to the fullest and when it's time I will come for you so you won't be afraid. I will find your mother and we will be there together.
I love you with all my heart and am sorry I left so soon. Be well.

Minerva Ann

He opened the box and immediately began looking at the photographs on the discs. It was their whole time together and everything they had done. He fell asleep crying and had never felt such pain or loss except for watching his own mother die.

Pearl quietly went from room to room. She covered Linda, then Pepe' with light throws and shut their bedroom doors. She found both her daughters asleep in Matilda's bed, using each other for pillows like they'd done as little girls. They hadn't opened their gifts. She laid a throw over them and quietly left them to sleep.

All the men were out back with Clarissa. They were cheering themselves with stories about Minnie. Jarrod was sorry he didn't get to know her better. He didn't tell any of them that he had fallen completely in love with her the moment their eyes had met.

Pearl had put on some sweat pants and a hoodie and joined them. Blaine went and fixed her a drink. They sat there talking until the moon was high. Pearl could swear she could hear a small child crying. She asked the other's if they heard it, they didn't.

Pearl looked at Jim. She laughed tiredly and said, "I never got to remind my sister that now my daughter is hyphenated like the rest of us." They laughed and drank until they were stumbling. It was nice to numb the pain before it consumed them completely. Their lives would be changed forever and there would always be an unwelcome and empty chair now whenever they gathered.

Chapter 38

A LOFTY VIEW

———⊰●⊱———

I felt light as a feather as I reached for Graham's hand. We floated above everyone in the room. They were gathered around me in the bed. For a moment their intense grief held me.

The pull of the singing was stronger. It seemed we were on a beam and I wondered how the magnificent light didn't blind me. I felt no pain, or sorrow. Only joy and excitement and when I looked behind us there was a dark void. I turned back the way we were moving and there were all my loved ones. They beckoned me with outstretched arms. Everyone lifted their voices in songs of praise.

There was no darkness anywhere here. We were young and whole again. I knew at once that no issues of mortal life mattered in this place. I understood instantly that I would be given free will here, like I had been while living.

Oh if I could only tell Pearl what to expect. I wanted her to see and feel this. There were no words to describe it. None I'd ever known anyway. And time was different. All my questions had been answered. I had been shown sights that caused me to fall to my knees, humble and afraid.

I'd been lifted up and joined in the singing. It was the most beautiful experience I'd ever known.

I only had one concern. I told Graham about the children left behind at the plantation. We had gone back together. We were careful to stay on the beam of light; there was the dark, grotesque presence over the oak orchard.

I knew now they had been held here against their will. As we got closer I could hear inhuman growling and screams of anguish. It was loud and formidable. Graham held me close and said not to fear, we had the Lord with us. I leaned forward and called, "Elizabeth, where are you? We're here to take you home and your family is waiting. Come, bring the others. Do not be afraid."

Just like that, there she was, running for my open arms. She leaped into my embrace, soon the other smaller children ran toward us. I picked up a second boy child and Graham held three in his strong arms. There were at least five older children who held hands and followed us away from the dark and into the light and the open arms of their waiting families.

The demon hissed a jealous and hateful last breath, rattling the heavens with its rage. It was no match for the light.

Everyone was together now. I had one more task and it would be on the beach with my sister.

I had given her a push this morning. I told her to meet me at the park. She was grief stricken and I wiped away her tears. At just the right moment, the two angels with me were smiling and nodded.

They shimmered and their brilliance was pure joy and love. They allowed me to paint the sunset for my sister that night. It was the last matter here on Earth that I would concern myself with for now.

I had learned much already but had a long way to go. I returned with them pleased that I had been able to do this thing for Pearl.

We would all be together again. Now I understood. Now it was clear.

Chapter 39

Two Peas In A Pod

———⇒►●◄⇐———

Time marched forward. It was hard to believe it had been a year since Minnie left us. The remodel on the beach cottage was done. We didn't remove any of the original furniture except for the beds. Our old backs suffered too much otherwise and I didn't feel ready to change the feel of the place. The memories were still too fresh for me.

Jarrod and his son's along with several crews of loyal men worked diligently on Matilda's and Blaine's new home. It would be beautiful and we were putting in a few roads through the property. They would only be about a mile and a half away from us.

Blaine was working mostly with Joshua now. He was still learning the ropes with Blaine's guidance and conference calls with the man who always had the answers, Jim.

I was pleased that he had made the largest downstairs bedroom of the mansion his own. He needed the assistance of a cane now and with Clarissa being confined to a wheel chair, I often found them together. I would hear their pleasant banter and light laughter as Jim slowly walked behind her chair pushing forward and getting their daily dose of fresh air and exercise for him.

Linda's little white poodle was often hitching a ride and snuggled in her lap. Clarissa had become a different woman. She was open, kind and loving. And probably the biggest surprise for me was her gratitude. She still lavished all the children and spoiled them at every turn. We'd all been guilty of that. We still hadn't read Minnie's will. That kept getting pushed back and none of us was ready to accept the finality of her passing.

I was pretty sure the checks she had left Pepe' and Linda were just the tip of the financial iceberg. I didn't worry that the money would change them. Jim would make sure they made wise financial decisions and investments and they would be fine.

Magnolia had taken the room across from mine upstairs. She told me she couldn't bear to be alone for too long in the loft. They only used it for business now when they absolutely had to be in the city and the family stayed there when we attended events together. I would never complain to have her here. A mother can be selfish to a fault and not let go when she should. This was different. I had wanted them all here but they had returned of their own free will.

Matilda was always in and out, working and life went on. I missed my sister terribly and the envelope she had left me now had smudges, a coffee cup ring, and a tattered corner. I wasn't ready to be happy with the God that took her from us. I knew in my heart I was being stubborn and spiteful. None of this angst would bring her back or help me here. I needed a miracle but still did not feel I was worthy.

Jarrod spent more time here now in the small house than his own. We had become inseparable friends. I didn't want to admit that I had always loved him and would not be able to handle it if he were to leave. We had a common bond, the love of Minnie. We had taken things too far, but only once. It was during those first darkest days after my sister left us. No one was home. He had invited me over for some wine. I hadn't expected what happened.

He had sat close to me on the couch and as we drank the wine, the sun went down and we never turned on any lights. He moved closer and I did not protest. We both had an urgency that needed no voice. We made love that night and held each other until morning. It was enough and we never discussed it or let it weigh on our friendship. It had brought us closer together and I couldn't have healed emotionally without his support and strong arms to hold me all the times I've felt deep depression. He had told me that he'd fallen in love with Minnie. I assured him that I'd always known that. I have not told him that I felt that way for him.

I found myself feeling angry at times. I'd handle the card my sister had left for me and feel frustrated and alone and pouting, I'd leave it there on my desk. I was still blaming Minnie's God. Linda had been upset with me and never let up inviting me to attend Sunday services with her. She didn't push. She had blossomed into a drop dead gorgeous woman. She had suitors hounding her at all hours of the day and night. She had become so proficient that I placed a crazy amount of work on her shoulders. She was back in school now, at night. She had a talent for architecture. She didn't have time to devote to a relationship. It was all about the project and client and her next degree in design.

Pepe' was happy and stayed busy. He had met a darling woman named Melissa Chapman. They were crazy for each other and I figured if need be, there was plenty of property left when he wanted a home of his own. For now he was content to be here with us and it made me happy. We all loved him and Linda and they belonged to us now. He had turned the grounds into a beautiful landscape of tropical flowering plants and vines. He put his heart into his work and it showed.

The strangest weather anomaly that I have ever experienced happened two days ago. I was alone here and had wrapped up my work in the office. I noticed the air felt different as I walked back to the house. It felt heavy, thick and oppressive. The hair was up on my arms and I was covered in goose bumps. As I opened the front door, the first ear splitting crack of thunder rattled the house. I could have sworn the whole place had bounced beneath my feet and I felt fearful and uneasy. Thinking it was about to rain, I ran to the patio out back to grab the book I'd left there. I stopped in my tracks when I saw that back here it was sunny and bright. I ran to the front door and walked out onto the porch in disbelief. I was overcome with a sense of dark energy, anger and danger and it left me feeling shaky and confused.

Out here and seemingly only over the live oak orchard there was an immense, low, black cloud. The wind became so strong I put an arm around the column I stood next to and peered around it. There was lightning snaking here and there. It seemed to travel along the limbs and up and down the massive trunks of the old trees. Every now and then these tendrils would meet with a resounding explosion of color and deafening crashes. My heart was racing and I was afraid of the darkness. With several more teeth rattling booms of thunder, it was gone. I could have sworn I heard a loud zzttt sound like when a bug zapper catches a large moth. I had an unpleasant taste of copper in my mouth and could swear I had smelled sulfur.

I went back to the kitchen and made a cup of tea thinking that it would calm my nerves. My heart rate was finally slowing and I felt dizzy and weak. I stood staring out the kitchen window wondering what the hell had just happened. It had felt like it had gone on for an eternity but from start to finish the spectacle lasted only a few minutes and in slow motion like in your worst nightmares.

Magnolia came in to the kitchen and went to the fridge. She turned and saw me and in alarm asked, "Mother, what in the world is wrong?" She came over and felt my forehead.

Most of the sweat was dry now. I just said, "Must have been that thunderstorm, it didn't last long, but I was afraid we'd lose some windows."

Magnolia snorted and told me, "Mother, it has been sunny, hot and humid all day. What thunderstorm?"

"Nothing I guess." I tried to laugh it off and she just looked at me like I was crazy then went back to the library and her work.

I took my tea out to the front porch and got comfortable in one of the swings. I was amazed at what I was seeing all through the oak orchard. It was full of bright sunshine where before it was always dark and unwelcoming. Now there was a lovely breeze riffling the Spanish moss and amazingly the trees were full of busy, chattering squirrels and all kinds of birds. I seriously had never noticed them before today. Smiling to myself I had a feeling that somehow Minnie had been involved in this transformation. I rocked and imagined putting a few seating areas and birdbaths out there. I didn't understand what had happened but I was very grateful for the change.

It would be winter again before we knew it. I hoped we'd get another sunny week at the beach cottage. I was so tired lately, sometimes I was embarrassed to realize I'd been shuffling my feet. Tonight I was antsy and angry. Mostly in one of the depressions that had consumed me.

I got comfortable in my soft bed and drifted off. I never woke until the next morning. I could have sworn Minnie was there speaking in my ear. I know I had felt her hand on my cheek and a kiss on my forehead. I was groggy like I'd taken sleeping pills and had a hangover. I tried to remember what she'd said while I was brushing my teeth. Suddenly and with clarity I heard her voice again saying, "Meet me at the park!"

I dressed, ate breakfast and went to my office to begin my day. I sat my coffee down. I had a feeling suddenly so overwhelming, I had to sit. I knew what I had to do. Without letting anyone know, I went to the pool house and gathered my always full beach bag. I went into my office and grabbed the envelope on my desk, stuffing it into the bag I nearly ran for the garage. I loaded the beach umbrella into the trunk, angrily slinging it sideways and slammed it shut. I opened the garage door, backing out too fast and later would be grateful no one had been behind me. I drove the whole way with tears streaming down my cheeks. Why was I being summoned to our special place to agonize alone? I was angrier with each mile. I was sitting in my low chair under my umbrella waiting for the sunset. I was sad and felt empty. I reached for the envelope.

It came open easily, most of the glue no longer holding the flap in place. I slid the card out and gasped. I held the picture to my chest and sobbed out loud with my head raised to the heavens. I feared I would die here, on this beach, from the ache in my heart.

The card was instantly recognizable. It had been one of the first drawings that a gleeful Magnolia had proudly given me for the front of our fridge. It had been cut and folded forming this card. It was done in colored felt tip pens. It was a crudely drawn picture of a long, green peapod with two round, goofy eyed peas. They had stick arms around each other and exaggerated hands waiving gaily at the observer. The childlike scrawl beneath the picture read "Two Peas in a Pod." It was a few seconds before I could bear to look at Minnie's handwriting inside. I wiped my eyes on my sleeves and read my sister's last letter to me.

My Dearest Pearl,

If you are finally reading this, I'm pleased. I know you're angry. I want you to know that leaving you was the hardest thing I ever did in my life. I love you still and now even more if that is possible.
It's time for you to let go of the anger and say yes to all the glory that awaits you. Ask the Pastor, he will know what to do.
I have a special last gift for you. Watch the sunset this evening. I'm with you and I've been given special help to convince you that everything G-ma ever told me is true.
If I could have stayed once Graham had taken me into the light, I would have told you that heaven is truly everything you've

ever imagined and so much more. If you hear
singing, it's all of us; we will be there to sing
you home, just like they did for me.
I will keep my promise Pearl. I will be there
when your amazing life is done. I won't let
you be afraid. Gregory is here with us and
patiently awaiting your reunion.
I'm yours forever my precious sister, joy
beyond measure awaits you, have faith. I pray
you will do this for me. Have faith.
All my love forever and ever,

Minerva.

I lay the card back in my beach bag and cried for all the days we'd been apart. I cried for all the guilt I felt for being unbelieving and stubborn. I cried because I couldn't imagine being worthy. The sun was setting. Suddenly I heard them! I heard the joyous voices lifted in praise. I stood and walked a few feet toward the setting orb. The sandpipers were gathering around me and running frantically, chirping and hopping about. The wind came up, strong and sudden. My hair was blown behind me and I felt a loving caress wipe the tears form my face. As I raised my own hand, I knew it was her. The sky had never been so beautiful. The sunset was ringed with colors I'd only imagined in dreams. There were oranges, reds, purples, pinks and shimmers. It was so beautiful it took my breath. I wondered if anyone else was witness to this spectacle.

As the sun slid below the water I whispered, "Thank you Minnie, I love you so."

It seemed to take me an hour to get all my things back up to the car and stowed away. I drove home in the dark thinking. I felt light and content. I was no longer angry. I would tell Linda that I would join her this Sunday. I would speak to the Pastor and try to understand and make things right. I knew now it was the only way I could join those waiting on me.

Up and down the Gulf coast people were stopping what they had been doing and were awe struck at the spectacle in the sky. Cars pulled over and cameras were clicking. People would ask, "Did you see that sunset?" It would be a topic for weeks on end.

Matilda was beside herself when I came in the house. "Mother, where on earth have you been and why have you been crying? I've been looking for you everywhere!"

"I'm perfectly fine my darling, now what is so urgent that your mother can't go watch the sunset in peace?"

She had a smile from ear to ear. She was glowing and held one hand behind her back. She took my hand and led me into the living room. It reminded me of when she was small and would drag me into her bedroom for a tea party.

She sat me down and showing me a small stick, she excitedly told me, "Look Mother, I'm pregnant!"

———❖———